One-Eyed Jacks

One-Eyed Jacks

To Bob,

Best Wishes

Brad Smith

Brad Smith

Doubleday Canada

Canadian Cataloguing in Publication Data

    Smith, B. J.
       One-eyed jacks

    ISBN 0-385-25920-4

    I. Title.

    PS8587.M5233O53 2000   C813'.54   C99-932211-7
    PR9199.3.S64 2000

Jacket design by Gordon Robertson
Text design by Janine Laporte
Printed and bound in Canada

Published in Canada by
Doubleday Canada, a division of
Random House of Canada Limited
105 Bond Street
Toronto, Ontario
M5B 1Y3

FRI 10 9 8 7 6 5 4 3 2 1

For Bob and Jean,
those Canfield kids

Acknowledgements

Thanks to Doubleday's Editor-in-Chief, John Pearce, my agent, Pamela Paul, and special thanks to my editor, Lesley Grant.

ONE

That night the old DeSoto finally gave up the ghost, cashing her chips noisily on a nameless gravel road in the dark starless night. She coughed a little, began to hammer and clang, spit some blue smoke and then packed it in, rolling to a halt alongside a deep ditch where bulrushes grew and frogs burped in contentment. The two men deserted her there, just gathered their gear from the back and left her to the ages. They set out on foot and never looked back.

They walked maybe five miles in the dark, setting a good pace, not saying much. After six months on the road, there wasn't a lot that hadn't been discussed. Usually that fact didn't discourage T-Bone Pike from conversation, but tonight he was quiet. This was new territory to him and he was taking it in, not so much the sight of it — not in the pitch dark — but the sounds and the smells of this place, this backwoods Ontario. And his Missouri nose told him this country wasn't so different from his home. There was fresh-cut hay nearby, he knew, and there was ragweed in the hay and there was something else on the air, maybe leeks or wild onions. When they passed a barn T-Bone could smell fresh manure and hear the morning coming in the cackle of the hens and the low moaning of the cattle.

Beside Pike, Tommy Cochrane was thinking of none of this, noticing nothing as he walked. This was just home and you didn't notice home when you were there, you just remembered it when you weren't. Tommy Cochrane had been gone a long while this time, but that didn't change things. Home was home and it had nothing to do with time.

Near daybreak they hitched a ride into Kitchener with a grey old farmer in a rusty pickup truck, the pickup loaded down with ducks and geese in crates and hampers of vegetables going to market. There was early corn and tomatoes and string beans and lettuce. The two men squeezed onto the narrow front seat with the farmer, who crunched the gears getting the old Ford into low and then humped the truck back onto the highway without a word. T-Bone Pike mooched a field tomato from a basket at his feet and sat happily eating in the outer seat, juice on his lips and cheeks, teeth flashing in his smooth ebony face.

They hit Kitchener with the light of day, with the sun breaking red behind them and the sounds of doomed fowl in their ears. They left the farmer at the corner of Maple and Main, two blocks from the famous old market. Tommy Cochrane had spent a few early mornings there himself, as a kid with his grandfather, arriving sleepy-eyed and tangle-haired in a truck like the one he'd just stepped down from. But that was going back some.

T-Bone stayed behind to talk the farmer out of a couple more tomatoes and then he hurried to catch up with Tommy, who was striding away without a word, heading for the railyards in the center of town.

"Breakfast, Thomas," T-Bone said, drawing even. He tossed over the largest tomato. "Where we goin' now?"

In the truck, T-Bone had talked the farmer's ear off, asking all about the geese and the ducks and the worth of each, about the difference between sweet potatoes and yams, and about the price of hens' eggs compared to ducks'.

Now he asked again after their destination, but Tommy Cochrane wasn't saying much today. They skirted the red brick railway station and made their way along the fence at the north end of the yard. Tommy was moving faster now, his eyes on an idling freight a hundred yards away. After a moment he stopped to slide his canvas bag through the fence, then pulled the strands of wire apart to allow T-Bone to crawl through. T-Bone's belongings, wrapped in an oilcloth and slung with a cord over his shoulder, caught in the wire and Tommy freed the bundle and then followed man and bag through the fence.

"Thank you, Thomas," T-Bone said in all seriousness.

But Tommy was walking already, watching the train in the yard. It was a short train, a half-dozen flatbeds and a couple of Wabash boxcars in front of a caboose. It began to move as they approached, and Tommy broke into a trot to catch up, crouching low to avoid detection as he ran. T-Bone, behind him, high-stepped in the faint morning light, taking the rails and switches like a hurdler, grinning widely as he ran.

"Jumpin' a freight," he sang out loud.

The cars were clicking along as Tommy caught up and pulled himself onto the rearmost flatbed. He hadn't run a step since the Catskills six months ago, and he was out of breath and blowing like a fat man as he moved to the front of the car to lean against the railing there. He took a moment to catch his breath. Running was one thing he wouldn't miss. Ten, fifteen years ago he hadn't minded the roadwork, even looked forward to it as a way to get away from the bullshit that sometimes followed him around. Now he was thirty-five though and that was behind him. This morning he'd run fifty yards only to save himself a ten-mile walk.

In a moment T-Bone Pike joined him on the flatbed, smiling yet, his breath as easy as a baby's sleeping. Five years older than Tommy, he had the natural conditioning of a thoroughbred, could run like a goddamn Peruvian Indian, all day and all night.

"Jumpin' a freight," he laughed. "The rail cops see us, they bust our heads for sure."

Tommy took the tomato from his pocket, picked some lint from the skin and began to eat. There were no railroad cops to worry about anymore. It was 1959 and the only people riding the rails these days were a few hobos who figured the Depression never ended. Them and maybe a finished-up boxer and his coloured friend just trying to make it home after six years away.

"Last time I ride a train like this was back in the '30's, I reckon," T-Bone was saying. "I was 'bout fifteen maybe, and my daddy and me took the rails all the way from Missouri to Deetroit, Michigan, fixing to work in the automobile factory there. Problem was, there's no jobs when we get there. So we stole a couple red hens outside of town and headed back for old Mo. Cooked them birds over a fire two nights running, figured the country owed us something for travellin' all that way for no job. My daddy took it badly and he never voted for Mr. Roosevelt after that."

The sun was clear of the horizon now, showing a blood red sky to the east. There would be rain before the day was out, Tommy knew. That cut no ice with them, though, they'd be home and dry before it broke. Bouncing on the rough deck, he finished the juicy tomato and tossed the stem over the side, then took his handkerchief from his pocket and wiped his hands. T-Bone unslung his bundle and slid it beneath his head for a pillow. The wheels below clacked over the joints faster and faster.

"Thomas," T-Bone asked presently, "how many times you fight Carmen Mazzili?"

Tommy rubbed the backs of his fingers across his jaw; he was in need of a bath and a shave.

"You fought him once, Thomas," T-Bone answered his own question. "I was there — you remember? He throw the towel after eight. But I fought that 'talian twice. The first time he get a tetnickle knockout in the tenth, the second fight I go all the way with him. One more fight and I believe I'd of maybe had him, Thomas."

T-Bone nodded happily at the notion and eased back on his bundle. Tommy sat with his knees up, watching the farmland beyond the fences.

"'Course, he was a tough wop," T-Bone admitted beside him.

Tommy nodded slightly. Carmen Mazzili was a real tough wop and he — Tommy Cochrane — had put him on his stool for keeps in eight. But that was going back a ways. It didn't mean a thing now, you couldn't get a cup of coffee with it. Things were different then, legs weren't that important. Funny, legs didn't matter when you had them, and nothing else mattered when you didn't.

Thirty minutes later they were pulling into the village of Marlow. Tommy got to his feet and knelt by the flatbed's railing as they arrived, watching the single main street anxiously. Because it was his main street. And it was his school he could see above the houses at the far end of town. His church there by the cemetery. His gas station and his old broken wooden backstop at the ball diamond.

The train moved on without stopping, and he sat down again. Maybe he was wrong. It had been six long years this time, and he couldn't know if any of it was his anymore.

The freight had to slow to take a switch outside the village and it was still chugging, making maybe twenty miles an hour when they reached the sideroad. Tommy tapped T-Bone Pike on the shoulder and then stood up as they approached. Tommy jumped first, making for a patch of plush grass along the ditch beside the gravel road at the crossing. He landed and rolled, then felt T-Bone roll over him, arms and legs flying. T-Bone was laughing as he got up and adjusted the bundle around his neck.

"Where we goin' now?" he wanted to know.

Tommy got to his feet and indicated a farmhouse a quarter mile to the east. Then he began to walk.

"How your head today, Thomas?" T-Bone asked as he fell in step. "It been hurtin' any?"

"My head's okay, Bones," Tommy said. "I don't want you to ask me about that anymore."

"Only natural for a body to be concerned."

"I know," Tommy said. "But let's just leave it alone, okay?"

TWO

The farmhouse was white stucco, with green shutters and a sloping front porch and a split-shingled roof of cedar. The barn behind the house was in good repair, painted the green of the shutters of the house, a little bit of Ireland here and there. The henhouse alongside and the shed for the tractor and machinery were covered with the same paint, cracked and faded a little but still looking good enough, for outbuildings anyway.

The place was too damned quiet though, as Tommy Cochrane and T-Bone Pike approached along the gravel road on foot. The henhouse cooped no hens and a small yet sustained silence called from the barn, announcing its emptiness too. The house was dark and the windows dirty, and the grass in the yard was long and tangled and laid flat in places by the summer rains. And there was something else. A pane was broken from a kitchen window, the window above the sink, the window that had been for years to Tommy Cochrane a picture frame for his grandmother's head as she washed dishes or made supper or simply watched her husband at work somewhere in the yard. There was a pane of glass broken from that window, and by that single incident of disrepair Tommy knew that James Andrew Cochrane was dead.

"Whose house is this?" T-Bone asked. He was stepping cautiously through the gate, eyes sharp, like a man expecting to be chased off.

"My grandfather's," Tommy told him.

The house was locked and they went in through the broken window, into the stale interior. The electricity was off so Tommy walked around opening doors and windows, flooding the rooms in morning light and fresh summer air. The house was sour and musty, but somehow it held the smell of James Cochrane, tobacco and honest sweat, maybe some Bushmills — maybe it was nothing more than memory. Tommy climbed the back stairs and went into his old room, the one with the dormer over the side porch, the room where he'd slept a few thousand nights. But the years had dwarfed the place; the old feather bed that had once hugged him like a bear was some kid's toy now, barely five feet long.

The gas was still on in the house — the farm had its own well — and when Tommy climbed down he found T-Bone in the kitchen, putting water on for coffee. Tommy went into the cupboards and came up with canned beans and stew, and they heated these and had a proper morning meal. Tommy took a rag and wiped the dust from the kitchen table and chairs and they ate there, the two of them, looking out over the orchard where the Macs were beginning to show. After breakfast they carried water from the outside pump into the square washtub in the bathroom and they each had a bath and a shave in turn. Then they washed their dirty clothes in the kitchen sink and hung them on the line out back, where Tommy figured they would dry quick enough, if the wind stayed in front of the rain.

They sat in their underwear in the front room while they waited for their clothes, T-Bone Pike on the overstuffed red chesterfield and Tommy in his grandfather's armchair — the old man's favourite resting place — a green velvet chair with oak trim and down-filled cushions, a chair bought with money won on Emerald Lady, a bay mare, sixteen hands, out of Lucky Jim from over the pond. The arms of the chair were worn bare now, and enough down had escaped over the years to leave the cushions a little lean.

"Maybe he just move away," T-Bone was suggesting. "Go live with somebody else, like old folks do."

"Maybe," Tommy said. But he knew.

"This the house where you live with your momma and daddy, Thomas?"

"They died when I was seven," Tommy said. "My sister Margaret and I lived here with my grandparents. Grandma died — I don't know — maybe fifteen years ago."

T-Bone nodded and took time to digest the bit of history. He committed every word from Tommy Cochrane to memory; he could recall conversations from years past almost to the word — meaningless bits of talk that nobody but T-Bone Pike would ever give two hoots about.

"Maybe he on vacation," T-Bone suggested then. "Gone off to Florida or some such place."

Tommy got to his feet and walked into his grandfather's bedroom. He found a pair of overalls there and put them on. Then he walked out onto the front porch. The grass was too long for the mower — have to run the hay-cutter over it, rake it up and start again. It wasn't right to let the place go like this; somebody should be looking after things, cut the damn grass at least.

What was Peg doing, her and that tight-fisted husband of hers? All he ever cared about was a dollar. No money in cutting a dead man's grass, Tommy knew.

He heard a familiar (even after all these years) chug and he turned to see a faded Case tractor clearing the railroad tracks. The tractor was pulling a full wagonload of hay bales. Driving the Case was Clarence Morris, these days as faded as the machine he was steering.

Tommy stepped out into the road. Clarence hit the clutch, then the brake, took maybe ten seconds before he chuckled in recognition.

"Well," he said.

"How are you today, Clarence?"

"Not bad at all. Ain't you the stranger."

"I guess I am." Tommy looked at the bales stacked on the wagon. "How's the hay looking?"

"Not worth a tinker's damn," Clarence said. "We had a dry April and nothing but rain in May. Second cutting might be better."

Tommy glanced back at his grandfather's house. "Awful quiet around here."

Clarence was making a cigarette. He looked quickly over the paper at Tommy.

"I guess Peg never got hold of you."

Tommy was still looking at the house. "No, I been out of touch."

Clarence took a wooden match from the bib of his overalls.

"When did he die?" Tommy asked him.

"Just after the new year, I guess." Clarence lit the roll'em and blew smoke in the air. "Took a heart attack shovelling snow. Man delivering co-op flyers found him."

Clarence sat looking evenly at Tommy Cochrane. There was a bit of tobacco on the old man's lower lip.

"Never suffered any, so the Doc said. That's something anyway."

"Well, yeah." Tommy looked at the man on the tractor. He figured Clarence to be pushing seventy, but to Tommy he hadn't really changed in thirty years. Funny how that could be.

"How was he, Clarence? These past few years, how was he?"

"Well, his health was real good right up to the end." Clarence spit the tobacco strand from his lip finally. It landed on the steering wheel and clung there, a new refuge. "I don't suppose that's what you're asking."

"No."

Clarence removed his hat and ran his hand over his bald head. The skin there was lily white against the weathered brown hand.

"The last couple years it seemed to me he was —" Clarence shook his head and put his hat back on. "It seemed to me he was just pissed off about being old."

After a moment Tommy nodded his head. "I could see him being that way."

That was all he said. He didn't want to ask if Clarence felt the same way. He didn't want to know the answer to that one. He would wait.

"Well, I'd better get this hay in the mow," Clarence said. "Rain on its way."

"I'll give you a hand," Tommy said. "And I got a pal inside."

"No, I got the grandsons working," Clarence said. "We'll get it done. Thanks just the same." He put the Case in gear.

"I'll be seeing you, Clarence."

Tommy watched as the tractor and wagon pulled away. A minute later a blue station wagon came down the concession from the east. Tommy turned and walked back to the porch where T-Bone Pike had emerged from the house. The wagon slowed to a crawl: inside a women in a flowered hat stared out at the pair of them before hitting the gas and driving away.

Tommy stepped inside and went into a small room off the living room. The chairs were there and the picture of his grandfather's half-Belgians, Bob and Nellie. That was all there was.

"The desk is gone," Tommy said.

"How's that?" T-Bone said from behind him.

"The desk," Tommy said, returning.

When their clothes were dry they wore what they needed and packed the rest in their bags. Outside the sky was blacker than Toby's ass and the wind was whipping down from the west. Tommy found tools and a piece of plywood in the shed and nailed the wood over the broken window. T-Bone had fallen asleep on the couch. Tommy walked out to the barn and went inside. The box stalls were empty but hadn't been shovelled, the calf pen was three feet deep in manure. Above, the mow door was flung open to the weather and the hay there was black from rain. Tommy shut the door and latched it and went back to the house where T-Bone had opened another can of beans from the pantry.

"Fat city, Thomas," he grinned.

Tommy had a mouthful of beans, but he couldn't get interested. "What we going to do, Thomas?"

Tommy was standing by the window, watching. "Storm's about here," he said. "We'll wait it out and then we'll go see my sister."

"Where she?"

"About two miles east," Tommy said. "Her and her dykehopper got a dairy farm, two hundred acres."

"What's he hoppin'?"

"Dykehopper — a Dutchman," Tommy said. "That's all there is around here — dykehoppers and square heads." He looked up as the first drop hit the window. "And one Irish mick in the middle of 'em all. Only had ninety acres, but he done all right."

The storm came on then, pelting the windows and the cedar roof with rain the size of gum drops. Tommy stood and looked at the gale a while. The car pulled into the drive while he was watching the ditches fill.

Thompson came in first, moving nervously through the front door, his holster flap open and his right hand on the butt of his gun. He was a twenty-one-year-old with six months' service on the force and the only time he'd had his gun out was to clean it and to practise looking steely-eyed in front of a mirror.

"You fellas just hold it right there," he said coming in. He looked like a cat about to scoot.

His partner, Langkamp, was standing in the back door then. He was a veteran and he took a couple minutes to look the situation over.

What he saw was a coloured man eating beans at the kitchen counter and another man, this one white, standing looking out the window. The coloured was tall and wiry, his hair cropped short. He was wearing old dress pants, hitched high, and an undershirt. The other man was not so tall, but heavier — big through the chest and the upper arms. His sandy hair was curled above his ears, in need of cutting. He had an open face when he turned; his nose was bent slightly to the left. He was wearing faded brown pants and a t-shirt. The white man spoke first.

"What do you want?" he asked.

"We got a report from somebody driving by," Langkamp said, stepping easily into the room. He'd been on the force enough years to know how to handle himself. "Said a couple of bums were breaking in here." He paused to look at T-Bone Pike. "Said one of 'em was a coloured man."

"Did he say what colour?" Tommy asked.

T-Bone was easing toward the door. Tommy put out a hand to stop him.

"You guys maybe out doing a little stealing?" young Thompson asked.

"Yeah," Tommy said. "We were thinking 'bout maybe stealing your brains. Looks like somebody beat us to it."

"You goddamn smart mouth," Thompson said and he stepped closer.

"This his grandfather's house!" T-Bone exclaimed.

Langkamp stepped behind and threw a rough hammerlock on T-Bone, pushing his face against the wall. "Keep your mouth shut, darky," he said.

"Let him go, for Christ's sake," Tommy said.

Young Thompson decided to get some practical use out of his police training. He grabbed Tommy's arm from behind and twisted upward. And then the constable was on the floor, both hands behind him and his nose mashed into the linoleum. Langkamp had no choice but to put his gun on Tommy. Thompson had a spot of blood on his lip as he got up.

"You guys are going to jail," he pouted.

"I don't think so," Tommy said. "This is my house. I'm Tommy Cochrane."

Langkamp lowered his revolver. "You're Tommy Cochrane the boxer?"

"No. But I am Tommy Cochrane."

THREE

eter Vedder was a dairy farmer — and a good one, he'd be the first to tell you. He would also tell you, with little urging, that he was his own man, a man with sixty-five milking Friesian Holsteins that were the envy of his neighbours, a man who was tight with a dollar, a man who was proud of his active role in the Dutch Reform church, a man who — at age forty — was branching out some, raising fallow pigs and doing a little cash cropping on land rented from neighbours who maybe weren't doing quite so well as Pete Vedder.

Of course, Pete had been left the farm when his father died and that had helped. Without a mortgage around his neck, success had come pretty easily to Pete and, as was usually the case, he didn't have to work quite as hard as his father before him, who in turn probably had it marginally easier than Pete's grandfather, who had arrived in the area from Holland at the turn of the century with little more than a few dollars in his pocket and a stubborn set in his mind.

The only time Pete ever went against his father's grain was when he chose a wife. Eighteen years ago Pete had gone out of the Dutch community and married Margaret Cochrane — Peg to everyone. Pete had no idea what prompted this minor rebellion in himself, but he knew that the marriage was strong and his wife was obedient and that was enough for him. The fact that there were no children bothered him and he blamed his wife, of course. After all, everything else he'd ever owned — cattle, pigs, chickens and dogs — had managed to reproduce.

Pete Vedder was strong as an ox, narrow-minded and sometimes mean-spirited, and he was happy as hell with his lot in life. There were things he would not tolerate — a man who drank too much, for example, or a man who didn't give himself over at least in part to his God and his church.

A man like his brother-in-law, for instance, who was standing across the living room from Pete this wet July afternoon. Tommy Cochrane had shown up in typical fashion, with a yellow-eyed nigger in tow, the two of them escorted by a pair of cops, one of whom — Dirk Langkamp — was a friend of Pete's and a fellow member at the Lions Club in Marlow.

"What else are we supposed to do?" Langkamp was asking. "We got a tip that a couple of bums are breaking into the house. What are we supposed to think?"

"Nothing else for you to think," Pete agreed.

"Especially when thinking isn't something you do a lot," Tommy said.

Langkamp looked at Pete. "You hear the mouth on him? I guess they figure that's smart down in the city."

"Why don't you take your pup somewhere and train him?" Tommy asked Langkamp cheerfully.

Young Thompson, sullen-eyed by the door, decided to let the insult pass. He'd had enough of Tommy Cochrane for one day. He was going to have to work on his hammerlock a little; he'd been damn good at it in training.

Now Pete was shaking his head to show Langkamp that he was disgusted with his brother-in-law. And Langkamp was nodding at Pete in sympathy. And Tommy was about to puke watching the two of them and their dog and pony show. After a moment the cops decided that justice had been sufficiently served for one day and they left. When they were gone Tommy asked after his sister.

"She's in town," Pete told him. He shook his head again. "I thought maybe we'd seen the last of you."

"Well, you've always been wrong more than you've been right, Pete," Tommy told him. "I'm surprised you haven't got used to it by now."

Pete gave him one of his you're-going-to-hell-Tommy-Cochrane looks and then said he had chores to do. He took a denim jacket from a hook and stomped off to the barn in calf-high rubber boots.

"Some bad feelings between that man and you, Thomas," T-Bone said when Pete was gone.

"Aw, I suppose I'd push him in the creek if he was on fire," Tommy said. "Other than that . . ."

They sat on the porch and waited for Peg Cochrane — she would never be Peg Vedder to Tommy — to come home. T-Bone sat in a wicker rocker and stretched his long legs across the porch floor.

"Maybe we should help that man Pete at the barn."

"Naw, he don't want us," Tommy said. "He'd tell us no if we asked, then complain that we didn't offer."

They stayed for supper at the farm. Peg cooked a meal that had T-Bone Pike in his glory. Prime roast and potatoes and creamed corn and fresh baked rolls. Apple pie for dessert. T-Bone took seconds, then thirds of everything, praising Peg to the skies as he tucked it away.

"The finest cooking I had since my mama, Miss Peg," he said.

"You're eating enough of it," Pete Vedder said.

"Why, thank you, sir."

Peg was smiling at the talk but she was watching Tommy. It seemed every time her little brother came home, he wore a different disguise. Cocky teenager, triumphant warrior, flushed 'over. This time he was none of these. This time he was a little older, a little sadder. There were flecks of grey in his temples and hard scar tissue on his chin and above one eye. Scraped elbows and brown freckles had been replaced by these.

But his grey eyes were the same, and when he looked at her, they sparked and lit up and made her feel like she hadn't felt since she was a teenager. Her kid brother.

"We talked to Gus Washbone on the long distance," she said. "He said you just disappeared."

"That's true," Tommy said and he put down his fork. "We've been moving around a bit, me and Bones."

Peg reached out as if to touch the mark on his chin, but she held back. "Are you going to fight again?"

"No. That was my last shot. I'm not going to hang around, getting my brains beat out for nickels and dimes."

"I'm glad," she said.

Tommy shrugged. "So am I."

T-Bone used his boarding house reach to snare another piece of pie from under the scowl of Pete Vedder.

"No mo' pie for you, sir?" T-Bone smiled.

"I guess I'll have another slice if I want," Pete snapped. "It's from my larder, isn't it?"

"Help yourself," T-Bone smiled.

Tommy smiled. "That's it, keep your strength up, Bones."

"Have you thought about what you're going to do?" Peg asked.

"Well," Tommy said and he took a drink of coffee, "I came home to help Granddad. I guess he's beyond that. But the farm sure as hell needs attention and I guess nobody alive knows that place better than me."

Peg was suddenly looking at her food.

"That's what I want to do," Tommy said but he knew something was sour at the table.

"Tender a bid," Pete Vedder told him.

Tommy looked over at his sister. "What's this?" he asked.

"The farm's going on real estate this week," Pete said.

"Who the hell told you that you could sell my grandfather's farm?" Tommy asked quietly.

"It's my farm," Pete said. He looked over at Peg. "Our farm, I mean."

"Granddad was failing these last couple of years," Peg said then. "There were some people hanging around, men he knew from the racetrack. Pete was afraid — we were afraid that someone might talk Granddad into signing the farm away. So we talked to the lawyer and we had Granddad turn the farm over to us."

Tommy was staring at his brother-in-law. "How'd you ever get that old man to agree to that?"

"He was boozing all the time," Pete said. "The doctor agreed and the lawyer agreed and that was about all we needed."

"All you needed to steal his farm?" Tommy asked. He turned to Peg. "There was no will?"

She nodded. "There was a will. He left everything to you and me. But there wasn't much, Tommy. Not enough money to cover the funeral. Other than that, what was in the house and barns. Some equipment. Of course, half the farm is yours."

"The hell it is," Pete said angrily. "He's not going to walk in here after all these years and lay claim to the place. He gave that up a long time ago. I didn't get where I am today by being a fool. I'll not turn that farm over to have him drink it away or gamble it away or run the place into the ground."

"Half the farm is Tommy's," Peg told him.

"No," he said emphatically. "Six years he's been away. Fifteen since he lived here. He turned his back on the family to go off chasing the devil and now he'll have to live with it. Do you think he cares about family? Ask him when he last set foot inside a church."

"That's it," Tommy said. "Let's drag God into this."

"Listen to the blasphemy," Pete said to his wife. He looked back to Tommy. "The deed is in my name," he said. "If you're interested in the property the asking price is ten thousand dollars. I had it appraised. Now you can sit here and whine to your sister 'til you're blue in the face, but the place is in my name and you won't get it for a nickel cheaper. Now, I've got a meeting in town and I'm going to be late."

He got up from the table and took his coat from a hook by the door and walked outside. Five seconds later he pushed his head through the doorway.

"I want a word with you out here a minute, Tom."

On the porch Pete stood spread-legged tough, hands in his back pockets. Tommy stepped close, his eyes on a spot on the farmer's jawline where he'd love to land a right hand. Pete stepped back a little but kept his hard look.

"I won't have that coloured sleeping in this house," he said.

"You're a fine Christian man, Pete," Tommy said softly.

"I don't want you here either," Pete went on, "but you're Peg's brother, and there's nothing I can do to change that. But I won't have that coloured here at night. I don't trust those people, I never have."

"One of these days, Pete, you're going to rise straight up into heaven," Tommy said and he went back into the house.

He and T-Bone spent the night in the old farmhouse. Peg drove them in a new Studebaker, supplied them with blankets and a pair of coal oil lamps. After she'd gone, Tommy, on a hunch, went into the cellar and found a pint bottle of Bushmills stashed in the floor joists there. James Cochrane had had a habit of hiding booze and then forgetting where he'd left it.

They sat in the front room and drank the whiskey straight, the lamps showing light enough, Tommy in his granddad's chair and T-Bone stretched out on the couch, reminiscing about the meal they'd just taken.

"Never had pie so good, Thomas."

Tommy capped the bottle and tossed it over. T-Bone drank and made a face.

"And that roast of beef. Wasn't that some nice meat, Thomas?"

"It was lovely, Bones. A regular banquet."

"I reckon that man Pete don't have much use for you, Thomas. Or for T-Bone either, I expect. He surely don't want you on this here farm. Hard to figure a man like that, and married to your sister yet."

"Did you see her, Bones? Hair cut as short as mine. Her beautiful red hair." He took a drink. "I'll bet she's gained twenty pounds since I seen her last. That's his doing, that and the hair."

"Don't know if you could blame that on the man, Thomas."

Tommy was working the Bushmills pretty good now. "Cochranes have worked this ground for eighty years, Bones. I can't see turning it over to some Bible-thumper to sell off."

"He got the deed though, Thomas. Jedge always side with the man with the piece of paper, it seem."

Tommy took more of the Irish. "He pulled a fast one, Bones, that son of a bitch. The old man must have been slipping bad to let Pete Vedder get the best of him."

"Maybe we best be movin' on in the morning, Thomas," T-Bone said. "We been doin' all right movin' around. Nothing but trouble here."

Tommy finished the bottle. "I don't want to lose the farm," he said softly. "It's all that's left of the family. Now I may be just a dumb mick, but that much I know."

She made another pot of tea and carried it out on the porch to drink while she waited. ("Drinkin' tea like a Chinaman," her grandfather would say.)

It had thunderstormed noisily for an hour late in the afternoon, and the rain had cooled things off. The night was still now, the thunder had come and gone. But Peg found that her mind was not still. The thunder that was her brother had come and it had *not* gone.

Somehow she had lost herself. When it had happened, she had no idea. Maybe she had just eroded away under the force of her husband's will, little by little slipping into his shadow until she was finally just a small piece of him. A silent accessory, like the seed drill or the baler.

But a shadow in a shadow is not even that.

It took her brother's return to remind her who she was. She realized that she was beginning to despise her husband for the very things she had once admired. His cock-sure confidence, his single-minded way of handling matters, his habit of taking charge.

She had given up a lot for him, out of love or infatuation or whatever you would label it. She'd abandoned even her religion for him, to the great despair of her grandfather (he himself was a lapsed Catholic, but that didn't matter). But the Lord was the Lord, she'd told James Cochrane, and when it came down to cases it really didn't matter which road you took into town, as long as you got there.

Yes, she'd given up a lot for Pete Vedder. The one thing she hadn't counted on giving up was herself.

He came home around midnight, smelling of the cheap rye she knew was passed around the Lions Club meetings. Gold-plated hypocrite, she thought as she followed him inside the house. He was smiling as he took off his coat, from the rye and from the realization she was indeed alone in the house. His will be done.

"We have to talk," she said to him.

"You can talk to yourself. I'm going to bed."

"Half the farm is Tommy's."

"I said no. You don't listen too good, woman."

He was moving away from her.

"Goddamn it," she said. "Right is right."

He turned at the profanity. "Did your brother bring out the mick in you? Don't you know that's always been your worse side, Margaret?" He pointed. "Now get upstairs, I've had enough of it."

When she made no move to obey, he dismissed her obstinance — her existence even — with a flip of his hand and started up the stairs himself. Her voice stopped him.

"Now you listen to me," she said evenly. "You spoiled, self-centred, tit-sucking son of a bitch. Half the farm is Tommy's or I'm leaving, and I mean tonight. Come morning you'll be without a wife. Now what do you think those self-righteous, whiskey-drinking jackasses down at the Lions Hall will say about that?"

On the stairs Pete Vedder knew his life was changing.

And he wondered why he was relieved that it was so.

FOUR

In the morning they had a full breakfast — eggs and side bacon and potatoes and a home-baked loaf, all provided by Peg the night before. Afterward T-Bone washed the dishes in the sink and then dried them and put them away in all the wrong cupboards. He'd found a faded checkered apron somewhere in the kitchen and he wore this while he cooked and cleaned. Wiping his hands on the apron front, he put Tommy in mind of his grandmother, whose apron it had been. He told T-Bone this.

"You never tole me your grandmother was an ugly coloured man, Thomas Cochrane," T-Bone smiled.

"It's not something you brag about."

After breakfast Tommy took a walk back the lane, which split the farm in half. Using a broken shovel handle for a staff, he walked the entire ninety acres, land that he'd known so well for so many years that he couldn't believe he'd ever been away. But then land didn't change the way people and buildings did, the land remained the same because it couldn't be changed — if it could, then some dumb son of a bitch would change it, and for the worse, you could bet a week's meal money on that one.

Still, there were things that needed attending on the farm. The wooden bridge over the creek had begun to fall in — after eighty years it could be excused. The timbers were white oak, strong as steel in their day, but after eighty springs of high water, dry rot had taken its toll. But there was plenty of oak yet in the bush lot at the back of the farm, the same lot that had built the original bridge. Tommy would build it again, and it would last another eighty years.

At least, that's what he'd like to do.

The creek was high now from the rain, flooding the bank into the pasture field between the stream and the bush. The field where James Cochrane had summered his cattle; the creek was spring fed and had water all year round. The same field where Tommy had broken his arm trying to ride a yearling steer. The steer had had other ideas and ran Tommy into a hickory along the fence row, fracturing the big bone below the elbow and rubbing Tommy raw on the rough bark. James Cochrane had laughed and said that that was why God invented horses — so chowderheads like Tommy wouldn't be tempted to ride cattle.

The field behind the barn — the twelve-acre field — had been plowed; last fall, Tommy guessed, and walking the headlands he found an Indian arrowhead in a furrow near the lane. He slipped the flint into his pocket and walked back to the barn, where he took a shovel and pitchfork and spent the rest of the morning cleaning out the calf pen and the horse stalls.

The barn was in good shape yet. The roof had been been kept up, and the eavestroughs, too. Those were the essentials for keeping a barn in trim, James Cochrane had always said. And Tommy remembered most of what his grandfather told him. It was strange, but if someone you loved told you something at age eight, you regarded it as gospel the rest of your life.

The barn had once been purgatory to Tommy, though, representing nothing but work and more of the same. Nothing personal against the building, it was just that shovelling shit out of a calf pen ranked pretty far down a teenager's list of preferred activities.

The top boards on the horse stalls needed replacing, worn down by wind-sucking and gnawing. How many horses had occupied these stalls in James Cochrane's day? In Tommy's day even? In his mind he listed the names he could remember. Dancer, Big Elmer, Sure-Shot, Candy, Angel, BillyBob, Apache (Tommy's paint), Thunder, Little Elmer (the mule), Fast Eddie.

Tommy was staring into the stalls when T-Bone came in behind him. T-Bone followed the look but missed the horses.

"What you starin' at, Thomas?"

Tommy turned with a start. "Nothing," he said. "Ghosts."

"Don' be sayin' that." T-Bone glanced about the barn. "I looking for a corn broom to sweep that house out. See one out here, Thomas?"

Tommy shook his head and leaned his arms against the closest stall.

"Your granddaddy a horse man, Thomas?"

"He loved horses," Tommy agreed. "Had 'em all his life, wouldn't be without one, no matter how hard the times." He laughed softly. "You know what galled him though?"

"No, sir."

"He never once saw a foal born. A mare won't foal if anyone's around, as a rule."

"That private business for a horse," T-Bone said. "That much I know."

Tommy smiled again. "Granddad had a dapple grey mare — I forget her name now. When she was in foal he was bound and bent he was going to see that colt born. It was winter, I remember, and he had her in that big stall there. When she went into labour, Granddad went to the house and brought back a bottle of Bushmills, sat on that railing and waited. All night he waited, and so did that mare. Colder than a witch's tit, too, it was. Damn near dawn, Grandma came out and found Granddad almost frozen, the Bushmills all gone. She finally talked him into the house for a cup of coffee and a sit by the stove. After fifteen minutes, he headed right back for the barn. And that grey mare and her foal were standing there side by side, waiting for him."

T-Bone smiled. "That was a stubborn mare, Thomas."

"A stubborn old man, too. He wouldn't talk to my grandmother for a week afterwards."

"That's a fine horse story, Thomas." T-Bone turned for the door. "But I got to find a broom, get that house swept out. Getting on suppertime."

"Molly," Tommy said suddenly.

"How's that?"

"The mare's name was Molly."

Tommy went back to his pitchfork. He heard a car as he was finishing up and he walked to the house and found Pete Vedder inside, standing nervous and impatient under the smiling scrutiny of T-Bone Pike.

"Mr. Pete like to talk to you," T-Bone said.

"Well, let him talk."

"I've been thinking this thing over, Tom," Pete said. "And it seems to me that half this place is rightfully yours."

"That's how it seems to you?" Tommy asked. "Seems to me it didn't seem to you like that yesterday. You coming apart at the seams, Pete?"

"You might try to understand why I did what I did," Pete said. "The old man wasn't himself. Who knows what he might have done? I was real worried about him, Tommy."

"Well, that's the kind of man you are, Pete."

"You can save your wisecracks," Pete said evenly. "I'm not one of your pals from the gym. If you want to listen, I'll tell you how it is. I own half this farm. And farming is my business, it's how I support myself and how I support your sister, you understand?"

"Sure, I understand."

Pete nodded and then stole a quick, uncomfortable look at T-Bone.

"We understand," T-Bone assured him.

"What I'm saying is — if you want this place, you'll have to come up with five thousand dollars," Pete said.

"Five thousand," Tommy repeated.

"Five," T-Bone said.

"You got the money?" Pete wanted to know.

"Sure," Tommy said. "I'll have to go into Toronto to get it. I've got money there. I'll take my grandfather's truck, I see it sitting down at your place."

Pete Vedder had been using the pickup to haul grain. His own truck was just a few months old and he didn't like to get it dirty.

"The licence is run out on that truck," he said.

"You let us worry about that," Tommy said. "We'll be driving the truck to Toronto."

"I wouldn't dally if I was you," Pete said. "I got a solid offer on this place not an hour ago. Ten thousand dollars. I put him off for thirty days, but when the time's up, I'll let him have it. You'll get your half of the money and then you can be on your way."

"Wouldn't that bring a tear to your eye," Tommy said.

Pete turned to the door. "No, it wouldn't," he said. "I've had enough of you to last six more years, Tom. You got thirty days."

Tommy was following him across the room. He stopped his brother-in-law by the front door.

"Where's the desk, Pete?" he asked, gesturing into the den.

"What?"

"My grandfather's rolltop desk. Where is it?"

For a moment Pete had a notion to lie. He decided against.

"It's in my office," he said. "I'm using it."

"Bring it back."

Pete wouldn't learn. "Seems to me that half that desk belongs to me," he said. "Maybe I'll have my hired man cut it in half."

"Whatever you do to that desk, I'll do to you," Tommy told him. "Bring it back, Pete. And while you're at it, get that famous hired hand to bring a mower down and cut the grass around here."

"He's got other work to do," Pete said.

"The desk and the grass, Pete," Tommy repeated. "Or should I talk to Peg about it?"

And he saw Pete's eyes go funny and his face change and Tommy saw how it was now and he damned near laughed out loud. Pete managed to nod unhappily.

"See you later, Pete," Tommy said in dismissal.

Pete shook his head. "You're a long ways from God, Tom. A long ways."

"I don't know if either one of us has lived so good that we should be measuring our distance from God, Pete," Tommy told him.

He followed Pete outside and watched as he drove away. T-Bone was standing inside, head cocked.

"You awful hard on that man today, Thomas."

"I think," Tommy said, "he'd better get used to it."

"He don't like a coloured man, I can tell that," T-Bone said. "T-Bone make him nervous as a long-tailed cat in a room full of rocking chairs."

"He say something to you, Bones?"

"He didn't say nothing. He don't have to, he show his thinking like a bad right hand. T-Bone Pike been around enough men like that to pick him out right off." He crossed to the couch and sat down to rub his hand across his stomach. "Why you telling him you got five thousand dollars, Thomas? You only draw two thousand for the Rinaldi fight and I 'spect most of that gone. Where you getting any five thousand dollars?"

Tommy stood in the doorway and pulled a wad of American bills from his pocket. T-Bone, on the couch, was beginning to think about lunch. Been a while since they'd eaten regular meals.

"A hundred eighty," Tommy said when he'd finished counting.

"You 'bout forty-eight hundred short, Thomas."

"We got thirty days, Bones. This one-eighty will bankroll that. We're going to Toronto."

"I been there one time," T-Bone said. "Fought down at the hockey gardens there. Fought a man who work on the railroad, a coloured man big as a house, and I knocked him colder than a well-digger's belt buckle in the third round. Bust my knuckle on his hard head."

"Well, there'll be none of that this time," Tommy Cochrane said and he closed the door.

FIVE

Herm Bell was stepping smartly through the failing daylight along Parliament Street. He was wearing his dark green suit with the pegged pants — Sinatra all the way — with a pink shirt and his lucky Atlantic City tie. He'd stopped in the drug store in front of Toot's pool room and bought a new rat-tail comb and a tube of Brylcreem and he'd gone into the bathroom and worked his hair until it was just right, ducktailed in the back and in front curled across his forehead with enough grease to hold its own in a typhoon. On the way out he'd bought two packs of Player's filters and a new Zippo lighter and a deck of Bicycle cards, just in case.

Herm had had a hell of a day and he wasn't about to let it end. He'd got up that morning in a bad way, with the devil's own hangover and a cut beneath his eye from a fight last night over on Shuter. His mother had ragged him from the time he rolled out of bed until she left for work at the five and dime. When did he plan to get a job? Why did he drink? His father drank, where did it get him? Why was he fighting, couldn't he get along?

Herm wasn't exactly flush with answers to those kind of questions on a good day. This morning, he'd kept his mouth shut tight, searched the house for cigarettes and waited for his mother to leave.

But then luck — rumoured to be a lady — came to call. And she stayed all day, bless her fickle heart. Her calling card was the change purse Herm found on the sidewalk as he trudged foggily to Lem's Diner for breakfast. The purse held three dimes, a penny, and a crisp ten-dollar bill. There was no identification in the wallet, sparing Herm any potential moral dilemma. True, he could run an ad — but the thoroughbreds were running at Greenwood and this perfumed lady was blowing in his ear. The change provided streetcar fare to the track and half the sawbuck went on the nose of a steel-grey three-year-old — like his father, Herm was a sucker for a grey horse — named Early Hour, a winless gelding who beat the field going away and returned fifty-eight dollars on the five.

Herm then risked twenty to show on another grey, this one Kenny Boy, who went off at thirty to one and finished second to pay Herm eighty bucks on the show ticket.

It was house money then, and Herm laid fifty to win on a third grey, this one the favourite, Village Square, a two-to-one shot who lost by a nose, but then won the race on an inquiry. Herm collected a C-note the hard way. He took the inquiry as a sign though and he folded his winnings ($213, he counted) and walked out into the gorgeous summer sun. Life was good again, at last. Outside the track he lent a fin to Daytona Dave Burns who had a hot horse and nothing to bet.

Herm then had passed the afternoon shooting Russian billiards in the rear of the Stafford Hotel. He drank a half-dozen bottles of lager and added another twelve bucks to his roll. Yeah, life was good, and the lady on his arm was acting like she had no place to go.

And now he was on Parliament, checking the bars and the pool halls, the alleys and the flats, the restaurants and hotels. He was looking for a game and he didn't particularly care what kind. Cards, dice, midget wrestling — he'd bet anything today. Herm Bell was hot after a cold, cold season and he would enjoy the heat while it lasted.

Darkness on the street fell like soft velvet over happy Herm, and he went into the beverage room of the Boston Hotel where he gathered a pair of draught at the bar and went to sit with Stan Jones (the elder) and Chalk Johnson, who'd come out of Millhaven a week earlier and had been drunk as a failed preacher every day since. Herm sat down and kept his good fortune to himself. You didn't brag on holding money in these parts.

"Good day, gents," he said. "Or good evening, I guess. Night has fallen."

"Who fell?" Chalk asked.

"You don't buy a beer for your friends, Herm?" Stan the elder asked. Stan was flat busted and had been nursing the same lager for half an hour. "I hope Frank Bell raised his boy better than that," he said, figuring to shame Herm into standing for a round.

Herm's wad was in his left pants pocket. He'd slid three singles in his right coming in and he showed these now.

"Three bucks to my name, Stash," he said. "But a man looks after his friends." He called to the waiter, told him to bring a pair over.

"You're in a hell of a fine mood," Stan said, waiting happily for his free beer.

"Why shouldn't I be, Stash?" Herm laughed. "I'm young, good-looking and out of work. I got it made in the shade."

Chalk Johnson blinked in surprise at the full beer in front of him. "Wha' sis?" he asked.

"Nice to be out — eh, Chalk?" Herm asked. Then he looked at Stan the elder. "They playing any cards over at Gino's tonight, Stash? I feel like a little game."

Stan narrowed his pig eyes. "You gonna play poker with three bucks in your pocket?"

"I got a pal up the street owes me half a hundred," Herm told him. "Maybe I can get him to spring, if I can find a game."

"Well, Gino's in Italy," Stan the elder said. "He took his mother over. Some cousin or something died, Gino told the old lady he'd take her over if they went sixty-forty on anything she got out of the will."

"She went for that?"

"I heard they cut cards on the percentage."

Herm drank off the first of his beers and set the empty glass aside. He took a Player's from his pack and offered one to Stan the elder, who declined.

"Not good for my physical conditioning," said Stan, who had the body of an ailing aardvark. "But I might know where there's a game. Close by, but I'd like to play myself, you know."

"I ain't the Bank of Montreal, Stash," Herm told him. "I bought you a beer."

"Montreal?" Chalk Johnson asked and he fell asleep in his chair.

"Okay," Stan agreed. "There's a running game every Wednesday night over at Fat Ollie's on Queen Street. Half a yard to sit down and it's straight poker, no wild cards. The game starts at midnight."

"I've had my problems with those Queen Street boys in the past," Herm said. "Maybe I better give it a pass. They might not appreciate me walking in and taking their money."

"What makes you think you're gonna win?" Stan asked. "Awful damn cocky, ain't you?"

"I'm dancing with this lady, Stanley," Herm said. "Who plays at this game?"

"The fat man, for sure. Danny Bonner from River Street. Maybe the Callahans, maybe the Swede from the island. They come and go, you know." Stan the elder nodded seriously. "You're all right if you're with me."

"I ain't going to back you, Stash."

"Buy me a couple beers and I'll watch."

They left Chalk Johnson sleeping in his chair — better there than the alley — and walked out into the heavy summer night. Stan Jones the elder was a short, beer-bellied man and he had to hustle to keep up with Herm, who was lean and long-legged and who liked to fashion his pace after Jimmy Stewart in *The Philadelphia Story*. They walked south on Parliament, past Gerrard, by the old school where Herm had copped his first feel and gotten his first fat lip. Stan the elder was soon blowing hard with the effort of the walk; occasionally he reached out to touch Herm's jacket sleeve in hopes of slowing the younger man down. They finally pulled up in front of Fred and June's Diner, where Herm turned and placed his palm against Stan the elder's dirty shirt front.

"I'd better go this alone," he cautioned. "This guy's a little funny about paying his debts. I wouldn't want him to think I'm bringing in muscle."

Stan was still puffing from the walk, but he pulled in his gut and drew himself up at the compliment. "I'll be right here," he assured Herm. "You know, just in case."

Herm gave him a knowing wink and then strolled into the diner. The supper crowd had cleared out by now and the place was empty except for a couple bums sipping coffee at the counter. June was washing dishes in the back; Herm could see her peroxided head through the serving window. He waved to her without stopping and then went into the gents'. There, he pissed and washed his hands and then took several minutes to re-sculpt his hair. Before leaving he transferred two twenties and a ten from his left pocket to his right. He hit the street whistling an up-beat version of "The Streets of Laredo."

"How'd you do?" Stan asked excitedly.

Herm showed the fifty from his pocket.

"Like a burglar, Stash," he said. "My pal had a lucky day at the track. Picked three greys in a row, the stiff, and he's rolling in dough like a baker's fingers."

Stan the elder was happy as a clam, showing his bad teeth all over the place. He was broke, true enough — and had been for years — but never mind, tonight he'd be playing in a big game. He'd be standing behind Herm, watching every card laid, every bet made, making note of the players and their expressions, winner and losers, too. As the two walked down Parliament, Stan began to practise his own stern poker face, rescued finally from these years in mothballs.

Herm sprang for beans and wieners for both of them at a grease joint on Jarvis, and then they took the streetcar down to Fat Ollie's, arriving at eleven thirty. Stan the elder took the lead with authority then, walking round to a rear door and giving it a conspiratorial rap.

"Secret knock, Stash?" Herm asked gravely.

Stan thought it over and then said that it was. Inside the room he drew himself up — his full five foot three — and introduced Herm to five card players seated at a table in a room that might have been a warehouse at one time. The ceilings were high, with exposed rafters and bare lightbulbs. The walls were boarded and unpainted, the windows covered with paper.

It was Stan the elder's moment — such was his life — and he made the most of it. Red-haired Billy Callahan, the younger of the brothers, was looking Herm over pretty good.

"I've heard of you," he decided.

"What have you heard?" Herm asked.

Billy Callahan glanced at the others a moment. "Well, I hear you get a lot of mouth from booze and you're a son of a bitch in a fist fight."

Herm looked at the punk and tried to decide whether to walk out now or wait to be asked to leave. The big man, Fat Ollie, slipped his hands beneath his suspenders and puffed noisily on his Havana. He put his eyes on Callahan.

"And do you hear that he cheats at cards?" he asked.

"No, I never heard that," Callahan admitted.

Fat Ollie laughed at some private joke and then turned to Herm. "Show us fifty dollars, Mr. Bell, and take a chair," he said. "We play straight poker here — five card stud, jacks or better, straight seven. You wanna play wild cards, you got the wrong game."

Herm tossed the fifty on the table and took off his jacket.

"Wild cards are for old women and pansies," he said, sitting down. "Straight suits me fine."

He shook hands with Fat Ollie, then with the punk Billy Callahan and his freckle-faced brother Martin, and with Danny Bonner, who Herm knew a little from Lem's Diner, and with the fifth man, a slick, dark-eyed stranger named Tony Broad.

The Callahans and Danny Bonner were drinking beer, Tony Broad had a bottle of bourbon, and Fat Ollie, Herm learned, was on the wagon for a month.

"Wife bet me a hundred I couldn't keep off the sauce for thirty days," Ollie said.

"You gonna make it?" Danny Bonner asked.

"Sure."

"What'cha gonna do with the hundred?"

"Get drunk."

Herm asked after the beer.

"Two bits a bottle," Ollie told him. "Same for a shot of whiskey."

Herm bought a bottle of beer for himself and another for Stan the elder and they began to play. First hand Herm drew to a pair of fours and caught the third, but got beat by Danny Bonner's spade flush. Herm didn't mind — you win early and you lose late.

Fat Ollie gathered the cards and began to deal. "Saw Dave Burns at the track today," he said, shuffling. "Caught himself a twenty-five to one. Old Daytona had him five on the nose."

Across the table Herm smiled. His money was winning and he wasn't even holding it. Now that's hot, you better believe.

They played straight seven. Herm bet a pair of nickels until the sixth card, then folded when Tony Broad bumped on what looked to be a high straight. It wasn't and Danny Bonner won again, kings over sixes.

"Same guy wins 'em all," Billy Callahan complained.

"Go on, cry me a river," Danny laughed.

Stan the elder was standing so close Herm could feel his sour breath on his neck. Herm turned to hand Stan a cigarette and motioned him away from his chair. Stan the elder moved back, but continued to hover, a rank mother hen in whiskers.

"Went to see that movie last night," Danny said, waiting for the deal. "Where those two guys dress up like broads, what's it called — *They Like It Hot*? You should see those guys, with the lipstick and everything."

"I don't go in for that queer stuff," Billy Callahan said.

"I saw that," Herm said to Danny. "*Some Like It Hot*, it's called. Pretty funny movie."

"You go in for that queer stuff?" Callahan asked.

"How about the dame?" Danny asked of Herm. "Built like a brick shithouse."

"Marilyn Monroe," Herm agreed. "Great set of knockers."

Herm won the next hand. Jacks or better, he drew to a pair of kings and caught a third, raised the bet to five bucks, had two callers and pulled in twenty-seven dollars. Stan the elder was pissing his pants at *their* good fortune. He'd have stories to tell tomorrow down at the park.

"You guys want to talk about the movies, talk to Tony here," Fat Ollie said then. "He makes 'em."

Tony Broad smiled from behind his thick mustache. With everybody watching he decided to stand and remove his pin-stripe jacket. He wore scarlet suspenders and matching garters at his elbows.

"You're the guy who makes the movies?" Danny Bonner asked.

"Not the movies you see down at the Bijou," Ollie laughed. "These movies are for men only, you know what I mean? You don't advertise in the newspapers for these movies."

"Beaver movies," Danny said excitedly. "A friend of my brother-in-law knew somebody who had one."

"We call them stag films," Tony Broad advised.

"I thought they made them movies out in California," Callahan said.

"I make 'em all over," Tony Broad told him. "I've made a few out there."

"Got to keep moving in that business," Ollie said. He was having a hell of a time with Danny Bonner; he liked to get the kid going.

And it was working — Danny wasn't thinking about poker anymore; his hand lay scattered on the table. Fat Ollie was putting a match to his Havana and chuckling.

"You get to fuck all those broads or what?" Danny wanted to know.

"Sure he gets to fuck 'em, you jerk," Callahan said to Danny. "That's part of the deal, right?" And he looked at Tony Broad.

But Tony just showed his oily smile again. "Hey, let's play some poker, boys," he said. "I don't want you guys pulling your rope, you'll get the cards all sticky."

"Who's got openers?" Herm asked. Danny Bonner's cards were still on the table.

"What about this Marion Monroe?" Danny wanted to know. "You meet her out in Hollywood?"

"Marilyn Monroe?" Tony Broad asked. "Yeah, I might've met her. That's right, I did meet her, at a party one time. I remember now, she stripped her clothes off and jumped into the swimming pool."

"Sweet Jesus," Danny said.

"Open for a deuce," Fat Ollie said. "Look at your cards, Danny boy."

Herm won again, queens over tens. Danny Bonner was thinking about the actress Marilyn Monroe swimming naked in a pool and he folded a pat straight.

And the game went on.

Stan was closing in again, so Herm bought him another beer, and a shot this time, and by two o'clock Stan was down for the count, sleeping on a couch in the corner. Herm had the old man off his back and it had only cost him six bits to do it.

By three in the morning Herm was up $150. Only Billy Callahan was losing heavily; he was getting lousy cards and he was a bad player to boot. His brother Martin, the freckle-face, said not a word all night, not even to bet. When he won, he pulled his money in and neatly stacked and counted it each time.

At some point Tony Broad began to win more than he lost and Herm decided to watch him, and to let him know he was being watched.

"Straight seven," Fat Ollie called. "And somebody pull the blind over that broken window. Be light in an hour and I don't want to know when it is."

"Amen," said Martin, and Herm knew the freckle-face wasn't a mute anyway.

Ollie dealt. Herm rode a pair of tens through the sixth card. Billy Callahan had a pair of sevens showing and he was betting them. Fat Ollie declined to chase a three flush, and Bonner and Tony Broad got out early. Callahan bet ten dollars, and his brother tossed his hand. Herm called the bet and waited for his hole card.

"Down and dirty," the fat man said and he delivered.

Herm let the card lie while Callahan checked his and threw another sawbuck into the pot. Herm flipped the corner to see his third ten and doubled the bet.

"That two pair's gonna shit on you this time," Callahan said and he bumped back.

Herm came back with the final raise — three bump limit at the fat man's — and it was a hundred-dollar pot. Callahan produced his third seven and leaned forward to stick it under Herm's nose.

"Lucky sevens," he laughed. "My kind of cigarette."

Herm rolled his hole cards. "Thirty days," he said.

Callahan stared at the cards. "You cocksucker," he breathed. "I'm bust."

Herm shrugged to show that he didn't give a shit and pulled in the pot.

"You're hotter than a three-dollar pistol, kid," Fat Ollie said.

"Been that way all day, Ollie," Herm admitted. "I hit three in a row at Greenwood this afternoon. Three greys — boom, boom, boom."

"Always liked a grey horse myself," Ollie said.

"I always liked 'em, too," Herm said. "Lately, they haven't liked me much. I been in a slump now, maybe six months. Ever since I dropped a couple yards on the Cochrane fight. Got so I wouldn't bet on the sun coming up in the morning. Never had a dry spell like this."

Ollie saluted with his cigar. "Well, I believe you're over it now," he laughed. "How 'bout letting the rest of us in a little?"

"Not if I can help it," Herm said grinning. "Not if I can help it."

"I saw him today," Danny Bonner said suddenly.

"Who'd you see?" Ollie asked.

"Tommy Cochrane."

"Bullshit." This from Billy Callahan, still sulking.

"Over at Lem's," Danny insisted. He looked at Herm. "You go to Lem's, right? I was there having the chili special they have on Wednesdays. I tell you, for four bits you can't beat it — a big bowl of chili and four pieces of toast. And that chili is a meal by itself, it stays with you all day."

"So does the clap," Tony Broad said.

"Never mind the restaurant review, kid," Ollie said to Danny. "What makes you think you saw Tommy Cochrane?"

"Well, I'm sitting at the counter waiting for my chili, shooting the breeze with Bucky, the cook," Danny said. "And I sees this nigger sitting in a booth in the corner. So I says to Bucky, 'What's a nigger doin' in here?' Right? I mean, you never see any niggers in Lem's."

"Get to the point, kid," Ollie said. "Before your chili gets cold."

"All right, all right," Danny said. "Now Bucky says, 'You better watch what you say 'bout this particular nigger, 'cause he happens to be sitting with Tommy Cochrane.' So I can't see Cochrane because of the booth, so I gets up and takes a walk to the can and when I come out I get a good look at him and, sure as hell, it's Tommy Cochrane in the flesh."

"Did you talk to him?" Ollie asked.

"I don't know the man," Danny said.

"But you talked to him," Ollie insisted. "You'd talk to the devil himself if you could hold him down long enough."

Danny shrugged. "I told him the chili was always good on Wednesdays."

Fat Ollie laughed and banged his hand on the table. "You son of a bitch, Danny boy! You're a piece of work, by God. Recommended the chili to Tommy Cochrane, did you?"

"Did you ask the cocksucker why he went down in the Rinaldi fight?" Billy Callahan demanded. He was broke and out of the game. Pissed off. He'd tried to borrow money from his brother and hadn't gotten as much as a word in reply.

"I was at that fight," Tony Broad announced. He cupped his hand and made a diving motion. "Johnny Weismuller, know what I mean?"

"I don't know about that," Herm said.

"I do," Tony Broad said. "I was there, my friend."

Herm wasn't sure he wanted to be Tony Broad's friend.

"Why would he take a dive?" Danny Bonner asked. "If he beats Rinaldi, he gets a title shot. Why would he throw that away?"

"Money, you idiot," Callahan said. "Why do you think?"

"They paid him enough to give up a title shot?" Danny wondered.

"Why not?" Tony Broad said. "What's Cochrane gonna do with a title shot? Patterson would kill him. I know — the champ happens to be a friend of mine."

Danny, of course, was impressed. "You know Floyd Patterson?"

"Sure I know him," Tony said. "I've had the gloves on with him a half a dozen times. I'll admit that he can hit. He's good. He'd take this fucking Cochrane's head off."

"Maybe he would," Herm said. "And maybe he wouldn't. Tommy Cochrane is no stiff. He's got heart."

"Yeah, and you know what else he's got," Callahan laughed. "A pocket full of money 'cause dopes like you bet the farm on him."

"He didn't look like he had a pocket full of money today," Danny said thoughtfully. He looked at the fat man. "What do you think, Ollie? You think he went in the tank?"

"I don't know, Danny boy," Ollie said. "That's a hard thing to answer. It's not easy to say what a man might do. Sometimes a man doesn't know what he's going to do until he does it."

"Let's play cards," Herm said then. "I got this lady friend who's getting impatient."

"Where is she?" Danny asked.

"She's right here, boys. She's right here."

SIX

She spent the afternoon looking for a room, walking to save bus fare, the *Telly* tucked beneath her arm, soft lead pencil handy behind her ear as she went down the list of rooms to let. The day was a scorcher and she wore a yellow cotton dress and flats and no stockings. After checking out a half-dozen places that barely qualified as rat traps, the heat grew worse and she pulled her dark red hair into a pony-tail and fastened it with an elastic.

She finally found a third-storey room on Baldwin — the joint was far from perfect, but then her standards had dropped some since morning. She was sick of the heat and sick of looking and she was ready to rationalize that she didn't really need much anyway.

The room was clean, with a double bed and a large dresser and small closet. The bathroom was down the hall and she was to share with two other girls. No drinking, no smoking, no men. Sort of what Lee had always imagined hell to be like. But it would suit her for now — it was a ten-minute walk to the Blue Parrot and above all it was cheap — twenty a week. The market on Kensington was a block away, and she could shop there, maybe even sneak a hot plate into her room, although Mrs. Royce, the landlady who looked like an over-the-hill fullback, had advised her that cooking was not allowed.

She paid for a week in advance and then walked to the old Canfield Hotel to pick up her bags. She'd been in town a couple

days and she'd decided to stay at the Canfield — not for any sentimental reasons (hell, no) but to avoid any contact with her dear
mother. Showing up broke and out of work on the old girl's
doorstep would just lay herself open to a lot of grief that she could
live without right now. As of today she had a place and a job. In a
couple of weeks she'd give her mother a call and announce that she
was home — not that Toronto felt like home anymore, but you had
to fix the name to something, she guessed.

She'd auditioned at the Blue Parrot that morning, after hearing
about the job from her ex-manager, whose continuing expertise in
the business was such that he was now selling suits on garment row.
The Parrot's manager, Mel Dunston, was looking for somebody to
cover for his regular headliner, a girl named Tempest Torrence.

"Tempest Torrence?" Lee had asked. "Didn't she do the weather
at the CBC?"

"I'm not sure about that," Mel had replied.

It seemed that Miss Torrence was winging her way to
Hollywood to screen test for some musical. The story was familiar
enough to Lee — she'd run basically the same gauntlet a couple
years earlier. Now she'd come full circle — what goes around
comes around.

She and another girl — a blonde named Lorraine something or
other — had in turn sung along to a phonograph for Dunston and
some runny-eyed flunky called Bix or maybe Blix, who was there, as
near as Lee could figure, to jump up and down at Dunston's request
to try to make the manager look like a bigger wheel than he would
ever be.

Lee had sung "Moonlight in Vermont" and "My Blue Heaven"
while Dunston sat fatly in a chair chewing a toothpick, and Bix/Blix
hovered behind. The girl Lorraine had a great set of pipes, but Lee
got the job and they both knew that the difference had been Lee's
appearance. Maybe she should have been bothered by that, but she
wasn't. She'd come to believe that her looks had brought her as much

grief as they had good fortune over the years and that things eventually evened out anyway. Yeah, what goes around comes around.

"Maybe next time I'll wear some padding," blonde Lorraine had sniffed as she packed up her records and aspirations to go.

"This is just me, kid," Lee had told her. "You think what you want."

"You're probably sleeping with him," Lorraine decided then.

"Dunston?" Lee had laughed. "I'd fuck the Riverdale Zoo first."

The job was a hundred a week, and it was good for a month at least, long enough for Lee to get on her feet and decide what she was going to do with what was left of her screwed-up life.

"We'll have a sign made up," Dunston said as she was leaving. He was short and fat and he combed his hair straight forward from the back of his head to conceal impending baldness. "It *is* Lee Charles? Spelled as it sounds?"

"Well, I was thinking 'bout maybe using Hurricane Hazel," Lee told him. "But I hear it's been taken."

Dunston nodded uncertainly. "Yes, I've heard of her."

Dunston's sign painter was no Matisse, but he worked fast. That afternoon — out looking for a room — Lee had walked by the Parrot and seen the new billboard in the window: Lee Charles, Recording Artist. Appearing nightly, the sign had advised. Recording artist, for sure. If you count two singles cut seven years ago. And don't bother asking for them in your local record stores, folks.

She took a cab back to her new home on Baldwin. She'd been on her feet all day and she'd be goddamned if she was going to lug her bags fifteen blocks in the heat. After unpacking she washed some stockings and underwear in the sink down the hall and hung them in her room to dry. Then she walked to the market and bought some fruit to eat for dinner.

She didn't start at the Parrot until the next night, the Friday, so she had the evening to herself. Another familiar feeling. She went down the hall and had a long bath before the other tenants, who were working girls, came home. She shaved her legs and washed her hair and then went back to her room and fell asleep. For the first time in months, she dreamed of Tommy.

Her dream life was as fucked up as the real article. In it she was singing on an outdoor stage — it seemed to Lee that she was at a county fair or carnival, which surprised the hell out of her since she had never been to either. But she was onstage singing, and her microphone wasn't working, and the crowd, mostly rural types, was ignoring her completely.

Worse yet, Tommy was in the front row and he was talking and laughing with two farm girls — buxom lasses in gingham dresses, brightly coloured ribbons in their cornsilk hair. And there was Lee onstage, fighting with the unco-operative mike and watching Tommy Cochrane, who never favoured her with as much as a glance.

"Son of a bitch," she said when she woke up.

It was dark outside and in the room. She flicked on a light and sat up in bed and ate an apple from the market. She got up to toss the core in the garbage pail and stopped briefly to examine herself naked in front of the mirror. But her body didn't interest her as much as it did everybody else, and she crawled back into bed and tried to read a magazine she'd bought a couple weeks earlier on the coast. But she gave up on it again and decided in a snap to go out.

The dresses she'd carried across the country would only encourage pursuit (oh yeah, those Hollywood rags drive men wild, don't you know?). She ignored them and pulled on houndstooth slacks and a white blouse. Then she fastened her hair behind her neck again and put on the brown leather jacket Tommy had given her ten years earlier. She checked the results in the mirror, hoping that the woman she saw there would discourage any pointy-shoed Romeos who might be prowling the dark Toronto night. But she had little faith in the notion; it had never worked before.

She gathered her purse and her cigarettes and went down the two flights and into the street, heading south toward Queen. For all the heat of the afternoon, the night had grown cool and she was glad as she walked that she had worn the old jacket, although that's not what she had in mind when she put it on. She had a cigarette as she walked, puffing guiltily, knowing it was lousy for her voice, which wasn't in the best of shape these days anyway. She hadn't sung much these last months and she would find out in a hurry tomorrow what she had to work with. She would cut out the cigarettes if she had to. She'd begun to smoke years ago to irritate her mother, now she only used the weed when she was bored. She'd been smoking a lot lately.

She went to the Rooster without thinking; when you lack the energy to run your life, just turn it over to old habits. The place was maybe half full. There was a folkie on stage singing Woody Guthrie songs and strumming a twelve-string. Lee walked in the front door and ran directly into her old pal Patty Simmons. They'd sung the Colgate jingle together all those years ago.

Patty squealed and gave Lee a crushing hug.

"How you doing, kid?" Lee said, pulling away. "You're squeezing the life out of me, I hope you know."

"My God, look at you," Patty said. "It's not even fair. Don't you get any older?"

"Every day. Take my word for it."

"Like hell," Patty said. "You could pass for twenty-one, woman. You make me sick, you know that?"

Lee laughed. "Yeah, well God gave me good genes and poor judgment," she said. "I'd trade 'em one for the other if I could."

Patty had put on a few pounds, Lee could see, but she looked good. Her black hair was in a bouffant and she was fairly poured into a blue dress. She was a wild one, part Mohawk Indian and part Scottish; she loved to sing and she loved to drink. And she loved to sing while she was drinking. They'd done some commercial work together years earlier; Lee could never keep up with her though.

"You still got half of Toronto after your ass?" Lee asked.

"Me?" Patty shouted in indignation. "Men were jumping off the goddamn viaduct when you left town. They were hauling 'em away by the truckful. Broken-hearted loverboys, squashed like bugs on the parkway."

"Wasn't that a country song?" Lee asked.

"Hank Williams, I believe," Patty said. "Come on, I'll buy you a drink. You still like gin?"

"I wouldn't turn Tom Collins down," Lee said. "But I have to tell you, Patty, my serious drinking days are behind me."

"Say it ain't so."

"I guess I just got sick and tired of being sick and tired."

"I'm gonna cut back too," Patty said. "Bobby and I are trying for a kid. Once I get a bun in the oven, then that's it for the booze, I have to take care of myself."

She went to the bar and got a Tom Collins for each of them, and then they walked to a table away from the stage and sat down. Howard Coulter was working the lights for the folkie. When he spotted Lee he waved his arm like a man flagging a cab. He would be over directly, she knew.

"So who is this Bobby?" she asked as they sat. "Don't tell me you got yourself domesticated?"

Patty showed the gold band on her finger. "You remember Bobby Saleski, the horn player? We've been married two years."

"He was Robert when I knew him."

"He's Bobby now. He's a DJ over at CHIK, and it's a better image. Bobby is hip — Robert is kinda like your old granddad or something."

"For sure," Lee smiled. "So this hip Bobby cat is trying to knock you up, is he?"

"Well, we're working on it. Bobby's hot to have a couple of kids, right quick."

"How about you, Injun?" Lee asked. "You looking forward to a papoose?"

"Yeah, I think I'm gonna like it. I can tell you one thing — I'm sure getting laid a lot. One of the fringe benefits of motherhood no one ever told me about."

Lee smiled again and tasted the gin. They made a decent Collins at the Rooster; some things did stay the same.

"So what's up with you?" Patty asked. "You home for a visit?"

"Yeah," Lee said. "Maybe a long visit. I kinda left that scene out there. It wasn't going anywhere I wanted to be."

"Christ, you were in a movie!"

"Actually, I was in three movies, kid," Lee told her. "And if you went for a bag of popcorn or blinked your eyes, you would have missed me." She shook her head. "It was just horseshit out there, Patty, don't let anybody tell you different. Sitting around in a bungalow all day, painting my goddamn nails and reading magazines. I wasn't singing, I wasn't acting — except maybe acting happy for a bunch of jerks who claimed to have my best interests at heart. And living with these dense broads, all bleached blondes, sitting around doing bust-enlargement exercises and talking about going to the Academy Awards some day. Every couple weeks my agent would show up and tell me that they were still looking for something special for me. A property, he'd say. Well, I'll tell ya, if I want to wade in shit every day, I'll get a job with the sewer department. Me and Ed Norton, right?"

The folkie onstage broke into a spirited version of Guthrie's "This Land Is Your Land." A going-into-break song if she'd ever heard one, Lee thought.

"So you just left," Patty said in disbelief. "You walked away from Hollywood, the movies."

"No, I ran away from Hollywood and the movies."

Patty was looking at her like she had two heads.

"A couple weeks ago," Lee told her, "there was a casting call for this new Elvis Presley movie. And this auditorium is unbelievable — wall-to-wall bimbos, all squeezed into girdles, tits pushed up, lipstick smeared all over their faces. And there's nothing these girls wouldn't do to get a part in this movie. Nothing — you hear me? So I decided I either had to be like them or get the hell out of there. I mean, are you willing to blow some sweaty old man to get your face on the screen for maybe ten seconds? That's what it comes down to."

"But did you meet him?" Patty asked.

"Who?"

"Elvis!"

"Oh, he walked through the room with a bunch of guys. To tell you the truth, I doubt he knew any better than I did what was going on."

"Wasn't he sexy though?" Patty asked. "God, I could just eat him alive."

Lee shrugged. "There was a bunch of these guys together and they all looked the same. I don't even know which one was him. I guess we didn't exactly catch fire. If you want, though, I can make up a wild story about him and I swimming naked out at Malibu at midnight."

"Please do."

Onstage the singer finished and mumbled something about a break. Howard Coulter would be on his horse, Lee thought, and then she saw his approach register in Patty's eyes.

"Old times coming to visit," Patty said.

Howard swung into the chair between them, his fresh face shining. He was wearing a suede jacket and a soft felt hat, which he removed to show off his blond curls. He propped his elbows on the table and, with his hands framing his face, he looked at Lee.

"I can't believe my eyes," he said.

"How's Howard these days?" Lee asked.

"Better than I've been," he said. "Are you a sight for sore eyes. I swear, I thought an angel walked through the door."

"Damn, I must have missed her," Lee said, looking around.

"Nice to see you too, Howard," Patty said.

"Hey, Patty," Howard began to apologize.

"I know. I know. You can see me anytime. But an angel — well, I can understand."

Lee gave Patty what she hoped was a cherubic smile. Howard was too busy being enraptured to notice.

"So, you back for good, Lee?" Howard asked.

"Well, I'm back. I don't know whether it's for good or bad, Howard. You're working here now?"

"For the time being," he said. "I'm putting together a recording studio though — two-track stereo, all the latest stuff. You still singing, Lee? God, I'd love to record you."

Lee laughed easily. "Get yourself a rock and roller, Howard. You want to make money, that's the way to go. 'Blue Suede Shoes' beats the hell out of 'Ebb Tide' any day."

"Just your picture on the album would sell a million, Lee."

She laughed again. "That's it, to hell with substance. Screw the music, just give 'em pretty pictures. You oughta be in California, Howard. That kind of approach could make you a rich man."

But she couldn't even insult him. He just leaned back and regarded her fondly. Lee looked over at Patty, who batted her eyes like a lovesick cow before coming to the rescue.

"Lee's been making movies, Howard," she said. "Three of them so far."

"All classics," Lee said.

"So you're going back?" Howard asked.

"No, I believe I'll retire from film. My work there is done." She dropped her voice. "I vant to be alone."

Someone was calling Howard from the direction of the stage. He got to his feet unhappily.

"You gonna stick around, Lee? We'll grab a bite later."

She told him not tonight. She'd forgotten what a persistent bastard he was.

"Where are you staying?" he wanted to know.

She lied, said she was still looking.

"I've got plenty of room," he told her. "I'm still in the old place."

She told him she'd keep it in mind. "You better go," she said. "That man in the white jacket's about to pop a vein."

He touched her hair and backed away, hat in hand like a beggar on a street corner. Patty was watching her.

"Well, shit," Lee said.

"You hear violins?" Patty asked. "I swear to God I can hear violins."

"I never knew he was still that way," Lee said. "Christ, it was eight years ago and it never lasted a month. Why me?"

"Because," Patty said. "Everybody wants what they can't have."

Lee rolled her eyes and watched Howard by the stage. He kept looking back at her, his face bright.

"He looks like Harpo Marx," Lee said. "Did he always look like that?"

"I'm afraid so."

Lee smiled. "Well, it's too bad he doesn't have Harpo's way with words."

They decided to have another drink. Her last, Lee insisted — she wanted to be gone before Howard finished working. The waiter brought the gin, and then she told Patty about the Blue Parrot.

"Hundred a week's not bad," Patty said.

"What's this Dunston expect anyway?" Lee asked. "The guy's dumber than lint. What goes over there?"

"It's kinda uptown," Patty told her. "Be a snap for you. A little Porter, some Patti Page, maybe some Broadway stuff. You want to do Billie or Bessie, you have to bring it up a little. They don't want no sad songs, you know what I mean."

"Mel likes happy diners, is that it?"

"That's it."

"I do a funky Doris Day."

"Perfect," Patty laughed. "You got rehearsal?"

"Tomorrow. Why don't you stop by? I'm kind of lost here. Don't know what to sing, don't know what to wear."

"I'll say. What's with the longshoreman's duds? If I had that body I wouldn't wear nothin' but a smile."

Lee glanced up toward the stage. "Discretion," she laughed. "No shit, I've been leered at every day for the past two years. Guys who think grabbing your ass is a compliment."

"I doubt anybody grabbed yours and got away with it."

"I landed a couple right hooks," Lee said. "Tommy taught me a thing or two about using my dukes." She did a low-rent Brando. "I coulda been a contenda."

"You hear from him?"

"Brando?"

"Tommy."

"No."

"I guess you know he got beat a few months back. In New York."

"I read about it."

"It was too bad," Patty said. "They were talking about a title shot."

"Some things are never meant to be." Lee looked into her glass. "Maybe I didn't know that ten years ago, but I know it now."

Then she smiled quick to deflect the tone. No need for that stuff. Not tonight.

Not ever.

"I should tell you, Lee," Patty said. And she wished suddenly that she had just let it go. But she couldn't now. "There was some talk about Tommy after the fight. A lot of people around here lost money on him and they say he took a dive."

Lee straightened in her chair. "Now that's a goddamn lie," she said.

"Well, I thought you should know."

"I don't see how it's going to matter much," Lee shrugged. "From what I hear, nobody knows where he is."

Patty thought about it and then let it go. She shouldn't have been talking about Tommy Cochrane in the first place. She drank her gin and suggested one more.

"No," Lee said and she got to her feet. "I gotta be sharp tomorrow, you know how it is."

"Show business," Patty said.

"Yeah," Lee grinned. "The big time."

SEVEN

T-Bone Pike sipped the sweet coffee and looked at the Indian arrowhead on the tabletop before him. He'd had the flint only a couple days but already it was his most prized possession. This was partly because T-Bone didn't own a hell of a lot else, but mainly due to the fact it had been given to him by his friend Thomas Cochrane. As they ate breakfast T-Bone kept the flint on the table, admiring its stony beauty.

Across the table Tommy Cochrane had finished eating and now he was writing on a scrap of paper. Every so often he would squint absently across at T-Bone as he searched his memory, then go back to the paper.

"I know what I'm goin' to do, Thomas," T-Bone decided. "I'm goin' to make a hole in this arrowhead and put a string through and hang it 'round my neck. That way, I have it always."

Tommy wrote a number on the paper and then looked up.

"You can't do that, Bones," he said. "You try to drill that flint and you'll break it to pieces. I'll get you a leather thong and tie it with that, then you can wear it around your neck."

"A leather thong be fine," T-Bone said in agreement. He slipped the stone into his shirt pocket and buttoned the flap carefully. "What you so busy writin', Thomas?" he asked then.

"I'm making a list, Bones."

"What you listin'?"

"Names and numbers, Bones." Tommy turned the paper sideways so T-Bone could see. "People that owe me money. Everybody on this list borrowed money from me years ago, when things were going good, and they never paid me back, Bones. See here, at the top is Harold Stedman — he owes me fifteen hundred bucks. I lent him a thousand when he opened the Old Kentucky, and I spotted him another five hundred a few months later when he almost went under. That was eight years ago and I haven't seen a nickel since. Here's Deke Anderson, he owes me three hundred from a card game. I lent Chuck Monday four hundred to get married; his wife wanted to go to Florida for a honeymoon. I gave Teddy Joplin a hundred for this hair-growing stuff, last I seen of him he was still bald as a cue ball. There's about $3,300 on this list, and there's more than that if I could remember. But if we could collect on this, it'd be a start, Bones. I figure if we make it back to Marlow with four thousand, the farm is ours. We could get even on the other thousand later."

"Lot of money, Thomas," T-Bone said.

"It's not like I'm asking for a handout, Bones. I let 'em hold it all these years. All I want now is my money back."

"These people your friends, Thomas?"

"Used to be."

T-Bone finished his coffee. "Guess we gonna find out if used to be still is."

There was some commotion up front then. A middle-aged fat man was leading a charge through the diner; with him were a pair of younger men, one in a green zoot suit with pegged pants. Tommy knew the big man; he was Ollie Newton — Fat Ollie — who used to hang around the Dundas Street gym years ago. Ollie was a pool shooter, card player, sometime bookie, horse player, and a few other things. He was known to be a straight shooter, and Tommy Cochrane had always liked him. Tommy raised his hand in hello and the big man came over.

"How ya doin', kid?" Ollie asked and he offered his hand.

"Good to see you, Ollie," Tommy said. "This here's T-Bone Pike. Oliver Newton."

"Ah yes, Mr. Pike," Ollie said and the two shook hands. "I saw you fight at the Gardens one night. You knocked out Dundas Willie Boyd with an astounding overhand right. I can't remember which round."

T-Bone showed Tommy his teeth. "See, I tol' you," he said. "You awful good at rememberin', Mr. Oliver. That's fifteen years gone."

"It was a memorable punch," Fat Ollie said. He turned to Tommy. "Where have you been, kid? I heard you dropped off the face of the earth."

"Just got back in town. Got a little business to take care of."

"You fighting again?"

"No."

Ollie nodded. That was enough for him. Ollie was the kind of guy who understood these things. He didn't need pictures drawn like the goddamn reporters and radio people.

"You're the last mug I'd figure to see out and about at nine in the morning, Ollie," Tommy said then. "You changing your ways?"

"Not in the least," Ollie said. "In fact, I'm just heading home to bed. But first, this gentleman" — he pointed to the man in green — "is going to buy breakfast, as is the custom."

"That means he beat you at cards all night," Tommy said.

Ollie sighed with unfathomable despair. "That is precisely what it means."

Ollie then introduced Danny Bonner and Herm Bell. The pair of them were piss-ass drunk, and jammed in Herm's pockets were some $320, a hell of a run for somebody who had crawled out of bed twenty-four hours earlier without as much as cigarette money. Herm grinned and offered a salute to the two men in the booth.

"I'm awful pleased to meet you," Danny Bonner was saying to

Tommy. "I spoke to you yesterday, remember I recommended the chili?"

"That's right," Tommy said. "I remember."

"Did you try it?"

"The chili?" Tommy asked. "No."

"I don't give a damn about the chili," Danny exclaimed. "I want you to know I don't believe any of the stuff they're saying. I'm behind you all the way."

Tommy looked at Fat Ollie. "What's this?"

But the big man had his arm draped around his drunken friend and he was steering him away. "Breakfast, gentlemen, breakfast," he said and then he looked back. "Come around to see me, kid. I'm still on Queen, the old place. You been playing any poker?"

"Not lately," Tommy said. "But I might have to start."

At eleven o'clock he and T-Bone were at the Old Kentucky Tavern. The front door was locked — the joint didn't open until noon — and they walked around back through the alley. The bar was one of Tommy's old haunts — he'd celebrated here after his first professional fight. The party had taken a hell of a lot more out of him than the fight, which had gone only two rounds. The celebration had lasted three days.

The back door was open, and they walked right in. A woman washing glasses at the bar looked at them without interest, and Tommy led the way down a hallway and into Harold Stedman's office where they found the man himself, hunched over a ledger at a desk. There was a cigarette burning in the ashtray. Harry looked like a little bird, smaller even than Tommy remembered, as if in time he might just disappear altogether. But, of course, in time he would. It's what happened to everybody.

"Jesus H. Christ," Harry said when he saw them.

"Harry the Horse," Tommy said. "How's it going?"

Harry reached for the cigarette. "Well, well, stranger," he said. "When'd you arrive back in these parts?"

"I blew in with the wind, Harry. This is T-Bone Pike."

Harry was puffing like crazy on the butt. "It's sure good to see you, Tommy. Where the hell you been all these months?"

"No place special."

"Well, you look in shape. You been working out? You look like you could go tomorrow."

"I'm in walking-around shape, Harry. That's all I am."

"Well, you look ready to go," the little bird said again. "Say, you hear about this kid Brady's got, this Wilson kid? Just twenty years old, a heavyweight, and he's fifteen and oh — thirteen knockouts. How's that for a record, Tommy?"

"Depends who he's knocking out."

"Oh, he's fought some names," Harry said. "He beat up Wallace Pierce last month, knocked him colder than dry ice the third round."

"Where'd they find Pierce — the old folks' home?" Tommy asked.

Harry shook his head and pulled on the cigarette. "The kid's a hell of a hitter, I'm telling you. Brady's trying to get him ranked real quick, wants to get him a shot."

"Well, Mac will find a way to do it," Tommy said. "Not much doubt about that."

Harry butted the cigarette and flicked his cuffs once from his coat sleeves. He had bony, nicotine-stained fingers. His teeth were the same colour and huge — hence the name Harry the Horse.

"So what're you doing in town, Tommy? You looking for something? Who you with — Gus Washbone still?"

"I'm not with anybody, Harry," Tommy told him. "I'm not fighting anymore."

"Oh." And the yellow stick fingers went after another Export; there were a half-dozen packs on the desk. The bird with the horse teeth had dandruff on his shoulders and he needed a shave. As he lit up he looked narrowly at T-Bone Pike, standing in the doorway.

"You a fighter too, boy?"

"One time."

"How's business, Harry?" Tommy asked him then.

The bird eyes swung back to Tommy and they were suddenly wounded eyes — eyes that had known much misfortune. "Not good," said the little bird's voice. The little bird seemed reluctant to burden others with its woe. "Not good," it said again.

Tommy sat down then, in a chair opposite Harry. "I have to get some money together, Harry," he said. "I'm gonna have to ask you for what you owe me."

"I haven't got it," Harry said real quick. He seemed relieved, like he was thinking that maybe Tommy was going to ask for something else. What else?

"If I had it," Harry went on, "I'd give it to you. Hell, you know that. But I haven't got it. Christ, I'd be lucky to scrape together a hundred, never mind a grand."

"It's fifteen hundred, Harry."

"I remember it was a thousand," Harry said in earnest.

"It was a thousand at first and five hundred later," Tommy said. "And I remember you were awful glad to get it at the time."

"I'd have to check my books."

"It was never in your books, Harry."

Harry laced those awful fingers together and leaned over the table. "I'm not trying to pull anything, Tommy. Maybe it was fifteen. But the fact is I don't have it. And you know, the ironic thing is — part of the reason I don't have it is you, Tommy. Six months ago I was doing pretty good — things are always better in the winter, people stay in the city more."

"Tell me the ironic part, Harry."

"I'm saying I was doing good enough to lay twelve hundred on you against Rinaldi. Now if the fight goes the other way, that's twenty-four bills in my pocket, right? And when you walk in here today — bam! There's your fifteen hundred on the table, Tommy. Simple as that."

Tommy, in the chair with his hand on his chin, glanced over at T-Bone in the doorway. But T-Bone was looking at the floor, he was embarrassed for Harry the Horse and his bullshit excuses.

"But things didn't work out," Harry was saying. "I did my damnedest, Tommy, I backed you all the way. But you let me down and now I have to let you down, because I haven't got it."

"I need the money, Harry," Tommy said. "Could you get it together if I gave you some time?"

Harry put his cigarette in the heaping ashtray. "There's been a lot of talk about that fight, Tommy," he said. "You disappointed a lot of people in this town. I mean you disappointed them financially, get my drift." The yellow fingers went after the Exports. Harry went on, a little bird with nerve. "There's talk you went in the tank, Tommy. They say Rinaldi's people paid you a bundle to give him the title shot."

The accusation took Tommy hard, caught his breath in his throat. So that's what the kid in the diner was running on about.

"I've never gone down for anybody," he said after a moment.

Harry shrugged and showed his palms. Tommy was shaking his head, he truly could not believe what he had just heard.

"So you figure I took a dive and now you're welshing on the fifteen hundred?" he asked.

"I'm not saying you did, Tommy," Harry insisted. "I'm telling you the story around town."

"You're telling me you're going to welsh," Tommy said.

"It'd be a lot simpler if you'd won the goddamn fight, Tommy. I mean, that would've solved everybody's problems."

"You're telling me you're going to welsh?"

Tommy got to his feet, his big meathooks hanging at his sides. He looked at the little bird in the chair. The little bird looked at Tommy, and at T-Bone Pike.

"You're telling me that?" Tommy asked.

"I wouldn't recommend violence," the bird advised.

Tommy blinked and shook his head. "My grandfather was a great man, Harry," he said after a moment. "He told me never to hit a cripple or an old lady. I figure you're one or the other, Harry, maybe both."

Harry the Horse took a billfold from his jacket pocket and laid fifty dollars on the desk. "Take some meal money, Tommy."

Tommy had a notion to stuff the fifty into Harry's mouth, to feed the paper to the little bird, but he said to hell with it and left the office. Harry shook his head like he'd been disappointed terribly and shoved the money into his pocket. When he looked up T-Bone Pike was standing by the desk.

"What you said is a lie, mister," T-Bone told him. "And you a damn liar for sayin' it."

Harry slid his hand into a desk drawer. "Keep your distance, boy," he said.

"You ain't got no pistol there," T-Bone said. "If you did, you wouldn't be sittin' there lettin' this nigger call you down. You a damn liar and a thief and you know it."

The yellow fingers came out of the drawer and rested uneasily on the tabletop.

"Reckon Thomas right 'bout you bein' an old woman too," T-Bone said and he left.

They found Chuck Monday eating lunch in a park on Gerrard across the street from the foundry where he worked. He was sitting on the grass, reading the sports out of the *Telly* and eating a fried egg sandwich. His black flat-top was still as stiff as a hairbrush.

"Shit, Tommy, that four hundred lasted as long as the marriage," he said from the grass. "We got back from Florida and she found out we wouldn't be eating in restaurants every night and she was out the door. Hooked up with some pretty boy downtown. I hope he had lots of jack to spend on her. Right now, I'm making sixty a week and most of that goes to the finance company to pay the goddamn bills she left me with. I can give you a little here and there, Tommy, but not all at once. I'll pay you though, I swear. I never welshed in my life."

Tommy looked at the dirty hands holding the sandwich. "I wouldn't worry about it too much, Chuck," he said.

"I will though," Chuck said. "I let it go too long and I'm sorry as hell I did. I'll make it right, Tommy, I swear." He stood up and wiped his dirty hands on his dirty pants. "I'm surprised to see you back in the city, Tommy."

T-Bone saw the look come back into Tommy's eyes. "You been hearing stories, Chuck?"

"None that's any of my business," Chuck said. "But there's a lot of bullshit around town. Same as always, I guess."

"I guess," Tommy said.

"Seems there's people who always want to find somebody else to blame for everything," Chuck said. "I've made mistakes — hell, that bitch I married was the biggest one, but I never blamed anybody else for it. It was my doing and that's all there is to it. Right?"

"Right," Tommy said. "See you around, Chuck."

"I'll see ya, Tommy."

They tracked down most of the names on the list and didn't collect a thin dime. The last couple of people Tommy didn't bother to ask, just stopped and said hello and watched the faces. The word was out. Lou Dirant even tried to borrow fifty, never mentioned the two hundred Tommy had given him years earlier to buy a used Packard.

Around suppertime they were walking on Queen Street and went into the Rooster for a beer. They sat in a corner with a pair of draught each, Tommy quiet and eaten up inside, T-Bone watching quietly, not knowing what to do.

"Ain't nothing but lies, Thomas," he said at last. "A body shouldn't fret 'bout lies."

"It ain't enough that it's a lie. People have to know it's a lie."

A man in a suede jacket and felt hat hurried in the front door. He stopped when he saw them, then came closer for a better look.

"Might have known," he said.

"What?" Tommy asked.

"It figures," the man said and he walked away, to the stage where he started fooling with a microphone.

"Who that man, Thomas?" T-Bone asked.

"Damned if I know."

T-Bone took a long pull of the draught and wiped his mouth with the back of his hand. "Maybe we just leave this here Toronto, Thomas."

"No. We got to raise a stake, Bones."

"How we gonna raise that much money in jes' four weeks? That be more than a thousand dollars a week, more than a king makes."

"Maybe Harry the Horse will come through, if he's got any conscience," Tommy said. "Fifteen hundred would be a start, we could turn it into something."

"That little man ain't gonna give you nothing, Thomas. The only reason he sayin' you threw the fight so's he don't have to feel bad 'bout not payin' up. I seen men like that before, Thomas, he ain't about to pay you no fifteen hundred dollars."

"We'll get it someplace," Tommy said. "We can do it, Bones, me and you."

T-Bone put his hand on the arrowhead in his pocket and wondered what luck was there. The waiter came over with four more beer. Tommy tried to wave him off.

"No charge," the waiter said. "Gentleman at the bar sends his regards."

There was no gentleman at the bar, but Mac Brady was standing there. In his three-piece suit and grey fedora, he could have been mistaken for a gentleman, at least by someone who didn't know him. There was some kid standing with Mac, a huge farm boy with blond hair and side whiskers. The kid was drinking soda and he was showing Tommy Cochrane an insolent grin.

Mac Brady raised two fingers in salute. When Tommy nodded back Mac picked up his glass and started over.

EIGHT

I f it was true that Mel Dunston was the bad news (and it was, as far as Lee was concerned), the good news was the band. Lee hadn't been expecting much and she got a happy surprise. Teddy Foster on the piano, Ralph "Bugs" Bundy on bass, and Lee's old pal, Doc Thorne, blowing sax and clarinet. These guys weren't just good, they were a country mile better than that, and Lee was pleased as punch to have them backing her.

The first night, the Friday, went off pretty well, all things considered. The Blue Parrot was nearly full, an uptown crowd out for dinner and some entertainment. Lee waited until ten o'clock — by that time most of the crowd had finished eating — before she went on.

She opened with "Bill Bailey" to get things moving, then kept the tempo with "Sunny Side of The Street." Foster held the break on the second song to give Lee a chance to breathe; her wind wasn't good yet and she was happy for the help.

She was wearing the green velvet dress, with high-heeled pumps and dark seamed stockings. Her auburn hair looked good against the green, she knew, and she wore it down, parted at the side and brushed away from her face. Lee had always been pretty objective about her looks and she knew she looked okay tonight. Entering the club she'd received a few compliments and she'd accepted them like a bum taking coppers when he wanted quarters. *Yeah, yeah — what else you got for me?*

They'd run through maybe fifteen songs that afternoon, just her and Teddy Foster, and there were another half-dozen or so Lee knew she could wing if they had to stretch it out. Enough to get her started; she planned to keep it pretty simple for the first week.

Patty Simmons had been at the rehearsal, dispensing wise-cracks and moral support. Mel Dunston had been there too. He listened to Lee for maybe ten minutes and then spent the rest of the hour cosying up to Patty, who, in her tight skirt and beehive, must have seemed like an easy woman to Mel. As she sang Lee watched the little drama happily; she'd lay even money on how it would turn out.

"That's my knee," she heard Patty say finally. "And if your hand touches it again, I'm going to break your fucking fingers." Mel went backstage after that and waited for Lee to finish. Then he told her that her singing was okay but that he expected some "patter" between songs.

"Like the preformers do in Las Vegas," Mel told her.

"What do the *preformers* in Vegas do?" Lee asked.

"You have to develop what we in the business call *rapport* with the audience. Do you know what rapport is?"

"It's French for something, isn't it, Mel?"

Mel hesitated. "I believe so," he agreed. "Now listen, you're a beautiful-looking dame, if you don't mind me saying so. I have a lot of handsome young men come into my club, important men in this city. I want you to be nice to them when you're onstage, be their friend. Understand?"

"Gee," Lee said. "You're paying me money to be nice to men I don't know? Haven't they got a name for girls like that, Mel?"

Mel was perplexed and Lee had left him that way.

Now she finished out the first set with an offbeat version of "How Much Is That Doggie in the Window?" With the lights in her eyes, Lee had no idea what the crowd was thinking, but she knew that Doc Thorne, blowing the alto sax, loved every minute of it, his eyebrows arched happily as Lee exercised some artistic licence with the lyrics of the song.

Between sets they went backstage for a drink. The dressing room was nothing more than a hallway, blocked off at one end, with a card table and chairs scattered about. Lee took a beer and sat down. Doc Thorne, sweating bullets from the last solo, plopped down beside her, his brown face shining.

"Goddamn, that was fun," he laughed. "If this was twenty years ago, Lee, I'd marry you."

"You might have had a problem with my father," Lee said. "Hell, I was only ten years old."

Leaning against the wall, Bugs Bundy smiled and lit a reefer through the smile. The brown paper caught fire then settled into ash and ember as he pulled on the cigarette.

"Catch your breath, old man," he said to Doc Thorne. "We got a ways to go yet."

"I'm fifty-two years old and I can still kick your white ass," Doc said. He took a mighty pull on the reefer then offered it over to Lee. She declined.

"Better keep my wits about me," she said. "First night and all."

Doc gave the stick back to Bugs, and then Mel Dunston walked into the room. He went right after Bugs, his eyes popping behind thick glasses.

"I told you about that stuff," he said. "I won't have it in my place."

"This?" Bugs asked. "This ain't tea, Mel. This is just Black Cat tobacco." He pulled a pouch of Black Cat from his pocket. "See here — Black Cat."

"I thought it was whatdyacallit — maryjane," Mel said uncertainly.

"You won't find any musicians smoking that stuff," Bugs said. "Fogs up your thinking, that stuff."

Mel could never be sure if Bugs was pulling his leg or not. Most of the time he just wouldn't talk to the bass player — it seemed to Mel that it was better to be thought arrogant than an idiot. He turned to Lee; she was the reason he'd come back anyway.

"Very nice," he said, moving to sit beside her. He made a move to pat her knee, but she gave him a look of wide-eyed impropriety and he pulled away. "However," he said, "we have to work on connecting with the crowd."

Lee feigned confusion. "You're coming onstage, Mel?"

"I don't understand."

"You said that *we* have to work on connecting with the crowd."

"A figure of speech," Mel hastened to explain. He shook his head merrily at the notion. "I didn't mean that *I* — no, of course not."

"I see," Lee said. She looked over at Doc's mirthful face.

"I want you to be more chatty," Mel explained. "I want —"

"Rapport."

Mel smiled happily. "That's what I want. Make them feel at home with you."

"These people have nightclub singers at home, Mel?" Lee asked. "What the hell are they doing here?"

"Show 'em some leg," Bugs said.

"Oh, no," Mel said. "Nothing improper. Not that you . . ."

Lee got to her feet and patted Mel's balding head. "I'll try to keep my clothes on, Mel," she said. "But I can't promise anything."

She and the band walked out for the second set. Mel stayed behind. He was reasonably sure that Lee had been kidding. And he was trying not to think of Lee Charles with her clothes off.

Onstage the band went for their instruments, and Lee walked to the open mike.

"Hey, we're back," she said. She held her hand above her eyes and looked below the lights to the people at the tables. "Anybody out there?"

"Who gives a shit?" she heard Bugs say behind her. Lee turned and crossed her eyes at him, then went back to the mike.

"Yeah, we're back," she said again. "And we're here to entertain you folks tonight. First of all, I'd like to welcome you all to the . . . uh, Red Robin."

"Blue Parrot," Teddy Foster told her.

"Oh yeah, the Blue Parrot," Lee said. "I knew it was some kind of coloured bird. Anyway, I'm Lee Charles and I'm just back in town, I've been out in California the last couple years. Hollywood, to be exact. Hollywood, now that's where you go to make movies, but I guess you knew that. It's also a good place to go if you're in need of a little perspective, if you know what I mean."

Doc sounded off on the clarinet. Lee smiled.

"Anyway, I made a couple," she said. "Movies that is. And they were going to make me this big movie star with fur coats and diamonds falling out of my pockets and all that. But one day I just decided to hell with that, I'd rather be back here entertaining you good people here at the Orange Duck."

"Blue Parrot," Teddy said.

"Yeah, I'd rather be here singing to you," Lee said.

"Then sing!" The voice came from the bar.

"Well, I'm gonna sing," Lee said into the mike. "But first I've been instructed to establish some *rapport* with the audience. Now I'm not at all sure how long that's gonna take. It's been a good long while since I've established any real *rapport*, you know, and I'm kinda rusty." She turned to Doc Thorne. "Doc, how long you figure it's gonna take?"

And Doc was laughing, his lips on his horn. "I believe you damn near there, girl."

"All right," Lee said. She looked out below the lights again. "You feeling any rapport yet?"

There was a wolf whistle, again from the bar. Lee put her hands on her hips and spread her legs slightly. "There'll be none of that," she admonished. "We've been told to behave up here. Ain't that right, Doc?"

"That's a fact."

"You been behaving, Doc?"

"Yes, ma'am."

"You ain't been misbehavin'?"

"No, I ain't."

"You ain't *what*?" Lee asked and she gave him a wink.

"Ain't misbehavin'," Doc said. Then he smiled widely.

"Well, all right," Lee said. "All right." And she began to sing —

> *I don't stay out late, don't care to go.*
> *I'm home about eight, just me and my*
> *radio,*
> *Ain't misbehavin', savin' my love for*
> *you —*

They ran through forty minutes, keeping it loose and having fun, Doc laughing and egging Lee on, Bugs high as a Georgian pine on the bass, and Teddy on the keys just giving Lee her head, following wherever she wanted to go. They finished up with "Tennessee Waltz," playing it soft and melancholy, running it out like sand through an hourglass. Afterward, Lee stepped down and headed for the bar, and a man at a table stopped her and said she was better than Patti Page.

"Oh, gosh," Lee said and she went to the bar for a glass of ice water.

Half a minute later she felt a hand on her elbow and she turned to see Mac Brady's fleshy face. He showed her his gold tooth in a smile, one hand on her elbow and the other in the pocket of his vest, like some cagey politician on the stump.

"Sweet Lee drinking ice water," he said. "You taking the cure?"

"Maybe I got religion, Mac," she told him. "How you doin'?"

"I'm doing all right, for a law-abiding man," he said, flashing the tooth again. "What do you say I buy you a real drink — for old times' sake?"

"Gin and tonic," Lee said. "And I don't care for whose sake."

Lee had known Mac Brady a lot of years. He was a boxing manager, and a promoter of a lot of different things — fights, circuses, bad plays — anything that would bring in a few bucks and didn't require anything resembling good taste. Yeah, Lee had known Mac a good many years and she had never been overly fond of the man, and as such she wondered why she would agree to have a drink with him tonight. Of course, Lee wasn't real fond of automobile accidents either, but whenever she passed one, she just had to have a look.

Standing beside Mac was a sharp-eyed kid, a Viking with sideburns and wavy blond hair. He was watching Lee like a stray dog eyeing a sirloin.

"This is Nicky Wilson," Mac said. "The Nick's a fighter, the best I've ever had."

Lee wondered if he was giving her a shot with the last remark, but it didn't seem likely. Mac wasn't that quick on his feet, she decided.

"How you doin', pretty lady?" the kid asked.

"How you doing yourself," Lee said.

He gave her a quick, crooked smile, his head nodding like he was agreeing with her on something. He was a good-looking kid, she thought, built like a goddamn oak. He gave off confidence like reflected light.

"Lee used to like fighters," Mac said then. "Especially heavyweights."

"Lee used to like a lot of things that weren't all that good for her," she said and she tasted the gin.

"Well, you've never met a fighter like the Nick," Mac told her. "He is on his way. He's fifteen and oh right now — nobody can stay more than three rounds with the kid. We're looking to get him ranked and then watch out — title time. Katie, bar the door."

The kid came a little closer. "Two years," he said and he held up a pair of thick fingers. "Two years and the belt is mine."

"What'll you do 'til then — wear suspenders?" Lee asked.

"Whoa, you're still a pistol, Lee," Mac said. "I remember your lip, always getting somebody in trouble."

"Usually me," Lee said.

The kid's smile was fading a little; he was used to being the centre of attention.

"Why don't you come down to the Gardens at the end of the month, Lee?" Mac asked. "We're fighting Wosinski. Come on down, I'll get you ringside."

"You ever see a Polack fly?" the kid asked her. "You come on down, I'm gonna put that bum in the grey seats. You wanna see something, you come on down."

"Maybe," Lee told him. She finished her drink. The band was back onstage, killing time with a Joplin rag.

"I like the way you sing, pretty lady," the kid was saying now. "Will you sing for me some time?"

"I'm here six nights a week," she said.

"Have you seen Tommy?" Mac asked then.

"Not for a few years, Mac."

Mac had something to say to that but at the last minute he swallowed it. Lee noticed, but the kid was getting closer and she could feel his breath on her neck. He had strange, mottled eyes; he reminded Lee of an inbred dog her stepfather had once owned.

"I don't think you understand what I meant," he said.

Lee put her hand on his chest and backed him off. "Down, Fido. You ain't the champ yet," she told him. "And I gotta go to work."

It was the last set of the night and Lee kept it short and easy, made a point of enjoying herself for a change. Whatever else happened, she was right at home with this band. A stroke of pure luck — thrown in with a bunch of creeps, she wouldn't have lasted a week.

When she glanced beneath the lights she could see the kid Nicky Wilson watching her, his eyes arrogant, elbows on the bar behind him, hips thrust forward, a toothpick in his mouth. He was a good-looking boy, Lee had to admit.

She finished with "September Song" and then went backstage with the boys to the makeshift dressing room. The audience gave them a pretty good hand going off. Mel Dunston, who knew nothing about music but a good deal about money, took the applause as a good sign and came back to congratulate them.

"It's all you, Melvin," Bugs told, waving aside the praise. "The Blue Parrot is nothing more than an extension of your personality. You're the leader, Mel — the general — and we're just the foot soldiers. The Parrot is you."

Mel stole an uneasy look at the others. "I think that's true," he decided. He turned to Lee. "It *is* the Blue Parrot," he said. "You had trouble with that tonight."

"The Blue Parrot," Lee repeated. "I'm gonna have to write that down, Mel."

She'd been debating going back to the bar for a drink. Mac Brady was there, in his cheap pinstripe and fourteen carat tooth. And the kid with the strange eyes and the lean body was there too. What Mac's game was that night was anybody's guess, but the kid, she knew, was waiting for her, with his insolent smile and his hard-on confidence. He was a possessor, this kid, and Lee was betting that so far he'd gotten everything he'd gone after.

Doc Thorne was buttoning his jacket. "You needin' a ride, Lee?" he asked. "Got my car."

"Thanks, Doc," she said. "These heels are hell for walking the sidewalks. I don't know how the hookers do it."

"Well, they only on their feet part of the time, those girls," Doc said.

He let her off in front of the rooming house. She leaned over to kiss his brown and whiskered cheek, then went upstairs and went to bed.

NINE

Maybe the first time was accidental; anyway it was nothing you could call somebody on. The second shot was no accident — a hard left hook that caught T-Bone square in the balls and dropped him to the deck, the pain exploding through his groin like shrapnel bits. He stayed on one knee for maybe a five count, his glove on the canvas, head moving back and forth. When he got up, he looked over at the smirking Wilson kid and wiped his gloves on his trunks.

"Keep your punches up," T-Bone said to the kid. "That twice now."

"Let's go, coon," the kid said. "I wanna work out."

Mac Brady had hired T-Bone a couple days ago in the Rooster. The offer was ten bucks a day to spar with the heavyweight Nicky Wilson, who was training to fight Ted Wosinski at the Gardens later in the month. Seemed the kid was kind of hard on sparring partners, and Mac was having trouble finding anybody to work with him. T-Bone decided that ten bucks wasn't bad for maybe an hour or two at the gym; he'd been paid more, but he'd been paid a hell of a lot less, too. He figured he could put together a hundred, maybe help Tommy with the farm.

Today was the first day and Wilson was coming after him again, pawing with clumsy lefts and then throwing haymaker overhand rights that T-Bone just managed to slip. He was just trying to stay away now; the pain in his balls was still there and he wanted to make it to the bell to rest. He picked off one of the kid's candy-assed jabs, then threw a combination to the body and moved in to clinch.

"Come on, coon," the kid said in his ear. "You ain't getting paid to dance."

"Mix it up," Bert Tigers called from the corner. He was the kid's trainer and he was standing by the apron with Mac Brady.

The kid bulled T-Bone away and then came at him low, firing punches with both hands, his blond head jammed into T-Bone's shoulder. T-Bone tried to push him off and the kid hooked him low again, a hard left that missed the genitals but caught T-Bone on the upper thigh. T-Bone two-stepped the kid around so his back was to Mac Brady and then fired a vicious uppercut to the chin; the punch snapped the kid's mouth shut and stole his legs for a moment. Tigers called time then, and T-Bone went directly to his corner. The kid was giving him a mean eye, but T-Bone knew he wouldn't complain any — this kid figured he was a real hard-ass and he would never admit that T-Bone had hurt him with a punch.

T-Bone sat down alone while Bert Tigers went over the kid with a damp sponge and sage advice. Mac Brady came by to talk to T-Bone.

"Keep the jab in his face and make him move," he said. "The kid doesn't know a damn thing about defence and it's time he learned. Jab, jab. You got it?"

"You tell your fighter to keep his hands up, Mr. Brady," T-Bone said. "Three times he foul me that round. That how he gonna win down at the hockey gardens? And I ain't got no cup, either, Mr. Brady. You tell him to keep 'em up."

"Why haven't you got a cup?"

"Man there say he don't have one for T-Bone."

"Bert," Mac called over to Tigers. "This man's got no supporter — what the hell's going on?"

"I don't supply equipment to every joker who walks in here," Bert said. "Half the time I don't get it back. I don't know this boy from Adam."

"Maybe he got a cup for a white fighter," T-Bone said.

"Get this man a supporter," Mac ordered. "He's Tommy Cochrane's friend, for Christ's sakes."

T-Bone went with Bert Tigers into the dressing room and was given an ancient athletic supporter. T-Bone put the relic on and went back out to the ring, where the Wilson kid was dancing impatiently, waiting to get even.

"You get a supporter?" Mac asked as T-Bone went through the ropes.

"Yes sir," T-Bone smiled. "I got me a good one. I believe it belonged to Jack Johnson."

The Wilson kid gave T-Bone a rough three minutes then. Whatever Bert Tigers or Mac had told him, he'd forgotten; he had revenge on his mind and he went after T-Bone like a street fighter in an alley, grabbing with his left and throwing wild right hands one after another. T-Bone circled and jabbed for a while, picking off most of the punches, but the last minute he got tired and the kid caught up to him. T-Bone went down from a wicked right hand and got to his feet and was promptly knocked down again. The second time he knew he was finished, but there was nothing on earth that would make him stay down against the snot-nosed kid and, as he got up again, Mac Brady called time.

He walked away from the kid's smart face and went to his corner. He sat down to get his breath. Across the ring Wilson was catching proper hell from Mac Brady and Tigers for not listening.

After that they went a couple more rounds, but the kid did what he was told this time — worked on his defence and a little on his third-rate jab — and T-Bone had an easy enough time of it.

The kid was popping the speed bag as T-Bone went in to shower. T-Bone took a cold shower and as he was getting dressed Mac Brady came in and handed him fifteen dollars.

"We say ten dollars," T-Bone said.

"You're getting a raise, first day on the job," Mac said. "I liked the way you stayed with him, nobody else has done that. Can you come back tomorrow?"

"Yes sir."

"What about Tommy?" Mac asked then. "What are his plans?"

"He take a job being doorman at somethin' called the Bamboo Club," T-Bone said. "Start there tonight. Man gonna pay him twenty-five dollars ever' night just to stand there and say how-do to people who come in."

"That's Buzz Murdock's place," Mac said. "Buzz must figure Tommy never threw the Rinaldi fight."

"Thomas never take no dive, Mr. Brady."

"I never thought he did," Mac said. "I know Tommy Cochrane."

"He beat hell out of Rinaldi for five rounds," T-Bone said. "Then his legs start to go. Thomas thirty-five when he fight, Rinaldi ten years less'n that. When Thomas's legs went, that was it. He couldn't last past eight."

Mac nodded his understanding.

"Besides, if Rinaldi's people pay Thomas all this money to fall down, then how come Thomas flat broke today and have to come to this here Toronto to try and raise money to buy his granddaddy's farm?"

"Tommy's broke, is he?"

T-Bone would divulge anything to get the stink of a fix away from his friend.

"His purse for the Rinaldi fight, six thousand U.S. dollars," he said. "Now he have to pay his manager, his trainer, all that training money, and the guvamint. He end up with something like two thousand. And that mostly gone now."

Mac took a cigarette from a gold-plated case and offered the case to T-Bone, who said no thanks.

"Is he going to fight again, T-Bone?"

"No sir, he ain't," T-Bone replied. But he had no intention of telling Mac Brady about the headaches.

Mac lit his smoke and blew a ring into the air above him, his philosophical pose. T-Bone was dressed and ready to get out of there, but he would wait for a dismissal. After all, the man was his employer, had just given him a raise, in fact.

"Is he still ranked, T-Bone?" Mac asked.

"I wouldn't know about that," T-Bone replied. "He number seven before this las' business. Maybe he ranked now and maybe he isn't. He don't care either way."

Mac turned and made a short move toward the door. T-Bone followed and Mac stopped. "How much did you say he needed for the farm?"

"Five thousand dollars, Mr. Brady." T-Bone was at the door, his old blue sweater over his shoulder.

"My, that's a lot of money."

"Yes sir, it surely is."

T-Bone walked to the Jasper Hotel, where he and Tommy Cochrane had taken a room. The old pickup was parked out back; they hadn't used it since they'd arrived in the city.

Inside Tommy was trying on a dark grey suit he'd bought that afternoon at the Sally Ann. The jacket was a little tight in the shoulders, but other than that it fit all right. And for eight bucks it was a hell of a lot cheaper than buying off the rack these days.

"Now there's a fine lookin' suit," T-Bone said when he came in. "The folks at the Bamboo Club gonna be impressed by Mr. Thomas Cochrane, for sure."

"Yeah, I'm a regular Clark Grable," Tommy said. "How'd the sparring go?"

"Dandy fine. Got me a raise already from Mr. Brady." He sat on the bed and removed his shoes. "This Wilson a tough kid, he have old T-Bone on the canvas today. Got a right hand like a mule kick."

Tommy looked around in surprise. "He's got a hell of a right hand if he put you down, Bones. Is he dirty? He looks like a dirty son of a bitch to me."

"He got no ring smarts, Thomas," T-Bone said. "Just wind up and throw the Sunday punch, that all he know. Kids like that never bother T-Bone any, T-Bone can take care of himself with a kid like that. He pretty full of himself, but I expect he'll get that knocked out of him soon enough. That Mr. Brady a nice fella though."

"Sometimes he is."

"He stand by you, Thomas, say he know you never went down in the Rinaldi fight. Say you would never do that."

"He should know," Tommy said. "When I was a kid he offered me two hundred bucks to take a dive against this Indian he had — a guy named Willy Big Bear."

"You skin that bear, Thomas?"

"That I did, Bones. I was just nineteen and full of piss and vinegar, thought I was Jack Dempsey. But not like this Wilson kid, that moron. I had some manners, my grandfather saw to that."

T-Bone laid back on the bed and put his hands behind his neck. It felt good to be working again.

"Mr. Brady want to know if you still ranked, Thomas."

Tommy was re-tying his tie, trying for a longer tail. Years earlier Lee had always done it for him. Recent years, he hadn't worn a tie much. He looked at T-Bone in the mirror.

"If he asks again, tell him no," he said. "All he wants is to get this Wilson kid ranked. He probably figures I'm the easy way to go. Well, he can go pound salt. I don't know what's his big hurry anyway."

"I tol' him you ain't gonna fight no more, Thomas."

"Good for you, Bones. I ain't doin' that kid any favours, I don't even like the smart bastard." He gave up on the tie. "Well, I gotta go to work, I don't want to be late first night. You gonna stick around here, Bones?"

"Maybe. Maybe go shoot some snooker at that place you show me."

"Come on down to the Bamboo if you want," Tommy said. "I'll stand you to a drink."

"Ain't no place for T-Bone Pike."

"Ain't no place for me either," Tommy said. "But I need the dough."

"What we going to do about that, Tommy? Ain't both of us going to make no five thousand dollars in only one month."

"If I had a plan, I'd tell it to you," Tommy said. "We'll get together what we can and maybe we'll fall into something. We'll go gambling if we have to, maybe catch some luck."

"We gonna have to catch some big luck," T-Bone said.

Snooker was Herm Bell's game of preference, but in a pinch he would play anything — eight ball, Boston, Russian billiards. This afternoon, he'd wandered into Sully's and directly into a game of eight ball with an off-duty streetcar driver named Saunders. Reed thin and tall, Saunders was flashy on the felt; he shot with a closed bridge and a sharp eye and he was down forty dollars to Herm Bell before he realized he was in way over his head. He paid without complaint though, and promised Herm that he would beat him next time. He walked out the front door, and Herm knew it would be a long while before he'd be back.

Herm tucked the forty into his roll, then looked about the room for a game. The snooker tables were full, save for one, and there were no players willing to take Herm on. His hot hand had been elevated from neighbourhood rumour to enter-at-your-own-risk fact.

Herm bought a bottle of Coke from the machine and stood watching two oldtimers playing snooker. The old men were smooth as silk on the table; great shape players, they approached the game like a chess match, always planning three or four shots in advance, never leaving their opponent much when they missed. It gave Herm pleasure just to stand and watch.

After a time the front door opened and T-Bone Pike wandered in, loose-limbed and slow, his eyes and his walk cautious to the strange surroundings. Herm looked over; it took him a moment to recall where he'd seen the man before.

"Hello," he said then.

T-Bone nodded warily.

"We met the other morning," Herm reminded him. "Sort of. At Lem's. I was three sheets to the wind. You were with Tommy Cochrane. T-Bone, isn't it?"

"Thas' right. I didn't get your name, sir."

"Herm Bell." And Herm extended his hand.

"Nice to meet you, Mr. Bell."

Herm indicated the idle table. "Play snooker?"

"I play a little," T-Bone said. "It depend on the stakes."

"Oh — we could play straight ten dollars a game," Herm said. "Or say, fifty cents a point."

T-Bone smiled and threw his hands in the air. "That way out of my league, Mr. Bell. I believe I just make my way down the other end, see if I can't scare me up a cheaper game."

"What do you usually play?" Herm asked.

T-Bone ducked his head. "Penny a point."

Herm looked at T-bone closely; there was discolouring above his left eye and a small slit on his lip. T-Bone was still looking at the floor.

"Penny a point it is," Herm said. "But I'll warn you up front — I'm hell on wheels on a snooker table."

"Then it best I warn you, Mr. Bell. I'm from Missouri. That the show-me state." And T-Bone smiled.

Herm won twelve cents on the first game. T-Bone paid from his plastic change purse then he racked the reds for another game while Herm set the colours.

"Fat Ollie said he saw you fight before," Herm mentioned.

"Thas' right. Down at the hockey gardens."

"He said you won."

"Yes sir. I won that one."

Herm broke the rack, made nothing.

"So how long you known Tommy Cochrane?" Herm asked.

"Long time," T-Bone said and he shot a cherry in the corner. "We meet in Florida, maybe ten years back."

"Not in the ring?"

"No, no," T-Bone said and he sank the green ball. "We never fight, Thomas and me." He looked over, then shrugged. "We just meet down there."

Herm let it go then. Halfway through the second game, he was down forty points. Billy Callahan and Tony Broad walked through the front door just as Herm was making a run to get back into the game.

"It's the poker king," Callahan said when he saw Herm.

Herm nodded to the pair and went back to his game. Tony Broad flicked his cigar ash toward the ashtray, missed by two feet, then stood with his legs spread, the cheap stogie clenched in his teeth.

"Not a table to be had, Billy. We might have to toss a coupla these bums in the street."

Callahan laughed and then swaggered over to lean against the wall at the end of the table. Herm sank a cherry in the side, then the blue ball in the corner. After the spot, he made another cherry, then set up for the blue once more.

"Hey Tony," Callahan said. "You smell that?"

"What?"

"It smells like a gar."

"A cee-gar?" Tony asked on cue.

"No, a *nee-gar.*"

Herm straightened up from the table as the two men fell into gales of laughter. He glanced at T-Bone, whose eyes were hooded, watching the felt.

"I smell a nee-gar," Callahan said again. "Tell Sully to open a window."

Herm reached slowly for the chalk, looked again at T-Bone, then at Callahan. He left the blue ball alone, shot the yellow in the corner pocket instead and left the cue ball hugging the rail in front of where Billy Callahan stood. Herm walked over, glanced behind him as he lined up his next shot. Then — in a single smooth motion — he drove the fat end of the cue squarely into Callahan's testicles. Callahan screamed in pain and dropped to his knees.

Herm shot and missed, then turned. "Sorry about that, Callahan. I didn't see you there."

"You fucking prick —" Callahan managed.

"Hey, it was an accident," Herm said. "I didn't see you. Must be all this cee-gar smoke."

"Accident my ass," Tony Broad said.

Herm looked at him evenly. "These things happen," he said. "I blame it on carelessness."

Tony moved to help Callahan to his feet. Eyeing Herm darkly and muttering vague threats, the two made their way to the door and out into the street.

Herm chalked his cue, blew off the excess.

"Your shot, T-Bone."

T-Bone looked over at Herm for a moment, then bent over the table and stroked a red ball into the side pocket. He took aim at the black, then straightened up.

"You didn't have to do that, Mr. Bell," he said.

Herm took a cigarette from his shirt pocket, lit it with his Zippo. He stood looking at the door for a moment, then he blew smoke into the air above his head.

"Maybe not," he said at length. "But then, neither did he."

T-Bone looked at Herm a moment, then shot carelessly and missed. He straightened again.

"I first meet Thomas Cochrane in Jacksonville," he said. "'Cause of this here game we playing right now. Thomas down there training for a fight, same as me, but we never know each other then. One night, I gets into a pool game in a bar with this man. We playing a five-dollar game and I'm givin' him a whuppin', won thirty, forty dollars. Now this man don't like a coloured man to be takin' his money, especially not with his friends lookin' on. He get to drinkin', next thing he pulls this little pistol — no bigger than your hand — little .22 pistol. He shoot me here, two times —"

T-Bone raised his shirt to show two small round scars, just above his navel.

"Well, that was plenty enough bein' shot for me, so I got no choice but to fight. And I hit this man in the side of his head, and he get hurt real bad, and they operate on 'im, but he dies two days later. Now his friends say I be hittin' on him, *then* he shoot me. An' they say my hands be lethal weapons, on account of me bein' a fighter. So next thing I in front of the jedge for murder, and in the second degree. They give me a drunkard for a lawyer, man won't even look T-Bone in the eye. So it look real bad, then out of the blue Thomas show up. He in the bar that night, turns out, and see the whole thing. A white man talkin' on T-Bone's side. So they say it self-defence, and I go free. But the sheriff say to get out of Jacksonville and don't come back and he tell Thomas the same. So we left and we ain't been back, not so far anyway."

"I'll be damned," Herm said. "They got the death penalty in Florida?"

"They sure enough do," T-Bone said. "And they was gonna try it out on me. I sure felt sorry for that man that shoot me though, him with five children too."

"Well, you're a forgiving son of a gun," Herm laughed.

"Like the Bible says."

"So you and Tommy been friends ever since," Herm said then.

"He the best friend I have on this earth, Mr. Bell. He never treat me like a nigger. He just treat me like a human, I guess."

TEN

All over town Tony Broad had been hearing about this new singer at the Blue Parrot and, as he fancied himself a connoisseur of beautiful women, he stopped by the club Wednesday night before the card game to check things out. He had Billy Callahan with him. Callahan had been sticking pretty close to Tony Broad all week long, trying his goddamnedest to become Tony's right-hand man. In Callahan's limited vision, Tony was a smooth operator, a director of movies, and a guy who knew his way in the world. That Tony Broad represented class to Callahan revealed a hell of a lot more about Callahan than it did Broad.

For Tony's part, he always found a kid like Callahan as he moved from city to city. Somebody tough and ruthless and poor, who didn't know a line of bullshit when it was handed him. Somebody anxious to get ahead in the world without asking a lot of questions. And Tony Broad liked to have a roughneck nearby because Tony sometimes rubbed people the wrong way and he preferred to have someone around to watch his back and, if necessary, fight his battles for him. Because, as Tony liked to boast, he was an artist, not a fighter.

This Wednesday night they were at the bar in the Blue Parrot, drinking bourbon and waiting for this dame, Lee Charles, to come out and sing. Tony Broad was standing for the drinks.

"We staying here all night?" Billy Callahan asked. "I might call my girl, tell her to come down."

"We're going to the fat boy's for poker," Tony said. "I told you that."

"I got no money to play," Callahan complained. "How 'bout you spot me fifty?"

"No chance, Billy. You want money, you have to earn it."

"How do I do that?"

Tony Broad shrugged his thick shoulders. "We'll think of something for you to do." He had a drink and then wiped bourbon from his mustache. "Like tonight, for instance, when I'm ready to bet, you could wander around and give me a sign if you see a better hand than mine."

Callahan was shaking his head. "Not at Ollie's," he said. "That fat man would snap my neck for that, you don't know him."

Tony Broad backed it up a little. "Hey, just putting you on, kid. I play a straight game. Tony Broad's a winner, he doesn't need any help. The rest of those saps need the help."

While they were talking Nicky Wilson walked into the club, wearing a bright yellow turtleneck and black pegged pants. His blond hair was parted on the side and combed carefully back. Callahan said hello, but Wilson ignored him and settled in at the bar, next to the stage, and asked for a beer.

"Who's the goddamn redwood?" Tony Broad asked.

"That's Nicky Wilson, the fighter," Callahan said. "He's Mac Brady's heavyweight, everybody says he's gonna be champ someday."

"I know Mac Brady."

"Well, that's his boy."

The bartender at the Parrot was Lucky Ned — he had one eye and was missing the thumb on his left hand. When he walked down the bar with Wilson's beer, Tony Broad flagged him down and paid for the brew. When Wilson looked over, Tony gave him the nod.

"How you doin', kid?" he asked. "I'm a friend of Mac Brady's. I seen you fight once, kid. I like your style."

Nicky Wilson was the kid's favourite subject and he moved closer. "Which fight?" he asked.

"It was in . . . New York." Tony Broad was winging it now. "I can't remember the stiff's name. You laid him out."

"Archie Wyatt?"

Tony snapped his fingers. "That's who it was. At Madison Square — right?"

Nicky Wilson gave him the look. "It was the Polo Grounds."

"That's right, it was the Polo Grounds." Now Tony took a chance. "But didn't I see you fight at Madison Square?"

"Maybe last year," Nicky said. "I knocked out Stan Swartz at the Gardens."

"Oh, did you lay him out," Tony said. "Ba-boom. It was a right hand, wasn't it?"

"Yeah." Nicky was happy. "This right hand's got a lot of ba-boom in it. What'd you say your name was?"

"Tony Broad. This is my associate, William Callahan."

Callahan was pleased as hell to be elevated to the role of associate. When he shook with Wilson, the kid squeezed his knuckles until Callahan thought his hand would bust. He pulled back and looked at the grin on the kid's face. Go fuck yourself, Callahan thought, but he returned the smile.

Then Tony Broad was filling the kid Nicky with stories about the movie business and the films that he made. The kid got pretty excited and asked Tony to bring some reels down to the gym that week. As newly appointed associate, Billy Callahan decided to get in on the conversation.

"We gonna make a movie here in Toronto, Tony?" he asked.

Tony Broad took a moment to give the matter some artistic consideration. "I don't think so," he decided. "As a director, I'm always looking for new talent, but I haven't seen anybody in this city that really turns my crank, know what I mean?"

"You haven't seen Lee Charles," Callahan said.

"I've seen 'em all, Billy."

Callahan looked over at Wilson. "He knows Marilyn Monroe, personally."

Nicky Wilson had no idea in hell who Marilyn Monroe was and he just shrugged. He took a long pull on his beer and looked at his hair in the mirror behind the bar.

"You can forget about Lee Charles," he said. "Me and her got something going."

"She's your girl?"

"Good as."

She could have been listening for her cue, because at that moment Lee Charles walked out onto the stage, with the band following. Lee was wearing a black silk dress, with her shoulders bared, and she walked directly to the microphone and began to sing "Please Don't Talk About Me When I'm Gone."

At the bar, the movie director, his associate, and the boxer fell quiet as three dimwitted church mice until she finished. Billy Callahan glanced over once and saw both Nicky Wilson and Tony Broad with their mouths open. Catching flies, Billy thought.

"I'm Lee Charles," Lee said when she'd finished. "And this is the, uh, Blue Parrot Orchestra. Yeah, I just named 'em. We'll be entertaining you good people tonight with some fine musical selections and some real professional-type rapport. We hope you enjoy the show. If you have any requests, just write 'em down on a piece of paper and . . . and give 'em to your neighbour or somebody, not me. We don't do requests." She glanced backstage. "Hey, just kidding, Mel." And she swung into "Sunny Side of the Street."

Nicky Wilson wiped his mouth with the back of his hand and looked over at Tony Broad. "She's got this thing for me," he said. "You wouldn't believe it if I told you."

Tony Broad fingered his mustache thoughtfully. "You get her between the sheets yet?"

Nicky Wilson turned those eyes of inconsistent blue on Tony.

"You watch what you say about the lady," he ordered. "She ain't one of your actresses, pal."

"Hey, hey," Tony said. "It was a joke, I meant no disrespect."

"I don't like that kind of joke," the kid said. "You better remember who I am."

"Sure, kid, sure. Let me buy you another beer."

They listened to a couple more songs, then Tony Broad told Callahan they were going to the poker game.

"What's the matter — you don't like her?" Callahan asked outside.

"Like her?" Tony asked. "Jesus H. Christ — let me tell you something about Lee Charles, kid. I'm gonna put that broad in a movie, I swear by God. I'm gonna put her in a movie and I'm gonna fuck her. If it's the last thing I do, I'm gonna fuck her."

"What about that jerk Wilson? She's his girl."

"That's what he says. A dame like that isn't gonna waste time with a knucklehead like Wilson. He's nothing but a fucking farm boy — strong like bull, smart like tractor. Lee Charles wants somebody with class, somebody who can give her what she wants."

"God, she's a gorgeous woman," Callahan said. "We really gonna make a movie?"

"You bet," Tony Broad said. He waved to flag down a cab. "But right now we're gonna go make some money. Jesus, I'm hotter than a half-fucked fox in a forest fire."

Tony Broad made it five for poker, along with Fat Ollie, Herm Bell, Danny Bonner and Mac Brady. Herm's luck was holding — he'd had four winners at Greenwood the day before. Fat Ollie liked Herm and told him he was welcome to the Wednesday night game any time. Herm had broken a date with Sheila Mosconi — who had promised over the phone to fuck his brains out — to come and play cards. He'd made a date with Sheila for the following night.

"Sit on the stove and keep it warm for me," he'd told her.

"So I got this coon name of Pike sparring with him now," Mac

Brady was saying as Tony Broad and Callahan came in. "Went four rounds with my kid today, that was something. I tell you — you can't hurt a darky."

Tony and Callahan avoided eye contact with Herm and they made no mention of the earlier incident; they'd been embarrassed enough at the time.

"Tommy Cochrane's friend, isn't he?" Ollie asked. He was dealing seven card and drinking grape juice, still on the wagon.

"That's him," Mac said. "Tommy's back in town, I spoke with him the other day. Looks like he's finished with fighting."

"Well, he's smart then," Herm said. "You hang around that game too long, you end up getting beat by bums. Look at Lamotta, look at Louis."

"They miss the spotlight," Tony Broad said, sitting down and taking a mickey of bourbon from his jacket. "It's the same in my business, everybody wants to live forever. I wish I had a nickel for every dame who's begged me to put her in a movie."

"Yeah — but what can you buy for ten cents these days?" Herm asked, and Tony Broad snapped him a look.

"King bets," Ollie said.

Danny Bonner bet a deuce, and the table called. Fat Ollie delivered again.

"But it would be nice," Mac Brady said, looking at a one-eyed jack, "if Tommy Cochrane would fight one more time. I made a phone call to New York today, and it seems that Tommy is still ranked — number nine. A fight with Tommy Cochrane would fire my boy right into the top ten."

"If he won the fight," Danny Bonner said.

"Oh, he'd win the fight," Mac said. "I've always liked Tommy Cochrane, but in his prime he couldn't handle the Nick, the kid's got too much pop. And if I can get him ranked, I'm betting I could set something up with Patterson's people. To them, Nicky Wilson's just a nobody from nowhere, easy money."

"You gonna bet those sevens or just look at 'em?" Herm asked Tony Broad.

Herm had come to the decision that he didn't like the acclaimed filmmaker Tony Broad. Last time, he'd been bragging on Floyd Patterson being his friend; now, with Mac Brady sitting there, he doesn't open his mouth.

"This pair of sevens will cost you ten bucks, wise guy," Tony said.

The bet chased Mac Brady and Fat Ollie. Bonner stayed in; Herm figured him for a king in the hole to match the one on board, and not much else. Tony Broad was either working on three sevens or already had them. Herm was sitting on a four-card straight, nine high, and open both ends. He tossed a sawbuck in the pot and waited for the sixth card.

Herm drew a jack, Danny Bonner a trey, and Tony Broad — goddamn his oily soul — caught another seven. Tony touched his mustache and looked across the table to Herm, who had to be thinking four of a kind now.

Then Herm remembered that Fat Ollie had folded the seven of clubs — he recalled the card because it had been part of a three flush, possible straight. Ollie's discarded hand was lying on the table at Tony Broad's elbow. Herm reached over and swept it away.

"You got a problem?" Tony Broad asked.

"Just keeping the table neat."

"Twenty dollars," Tony Broad said.

Herm looked over at Tony's hand. There was still the possibility of a full house. Danny Bonner folded and Herm threw a twenty into the pot.

Fat Ollie dealt the down card. Herm knew by the way Tony Broad went after the hole card that he was still looking for his tight. Herm flipped the corner of his own and saw the five of hearts, filling his straight.

"Sevens bet," he said.

Herm watched for hesitation in Tony Broad's eyes, and he saw it — a flash, maybe a tenth of a second — and Herm knew there was no full house. Then Tony came at him with a smile.

"Twenty dollars," he said. "No, make it thirty."

"Make it fifty." Herm gave him the smile right back.

"Who is this fucking guy?" Tony Broad asked and he looked around the table. "Whoever taught him how to play cards? Maybe I'm holding four sevens here."

"Bet you a hundred on the side you're not," Herm said. "Ollie folded the fourth seven."

And Ollie began to laugh, his great belly bouncing with the effort.

"Fuck it," Tony said and he folded his hand. "You got lucky on your little straight — take the money, you need it more than me."

"Just the same, I'd like to thank you for contributing so generously," Herm said and he pulled in the pot.

"He's got a habit of getting lucky at the right time," Billy Callahan said. He was standing beside Herm all of a sudden, up on the balls of his feet, thumbs tucked in his belt.

Herm put his money aside and got to his feet. "Didn't I see you in the pool hall today? You got a short memory."

Without rising, Fat Ollie reached over and pulled Herm back into his chair. Then the fat man looked at Callahan.

"You want to put your mouth in this game — you put your money in this game. Right now you're just a spectator."

Callahan shifted his hard stare to Tony Broad, who closed his eyes in dismissal.

"Don't be looking over there," Ollie said. "You're dealing with me. If you ever make a suggestion like that in my place again, you'd better be able to back it up. You understand?"

"Yeah, yeah."

"And don't pull that hard-ass stuff on me," Ollie advised. "This fat man has eaten a hundred punks like you for breakfast, and he still gets hungry from time to time."

Callahan shifted his eyes. "All right."

"All right," Fat Ollie said and he let it go.

Danny Bonner wasn't much for trouble and he switched the subject right away. "How old is this kid of yours, Mr. Brady?" Danny figured Mac Brady to be some sort of legend — Mac had led him to believe as much — and as such deserved a certain respect.

"Just twenty years old," Mac said. "That's the exciting part."

"Why the big hurry to get him ranked?"

Mac was drinking scotch neat. He sipped from his glass and did a slow theatrical turn of the room, like a man suspicious of eavesdroppers. Mac was a master of such small drama. He set his glass aside and leaned forward over the table.

"I'll share a little secret with you gentlemen tonight," he began. "In the next couple of years there's going to be a new heavyweight champion — a man who is virtually unbeatable. His name is Charley Liston, but he goes by Sonny."

"I've heard of him," Danny Bonner said. Danny read every word in the sports section, never missed a day.

"You're one of the few then," Mac said. "I saw this Liston fight in Miami in April. He knocked out Big Cat Williams in the second round and never raised a sweat. He took some shots from Williams that would have hospitalized most men and he never batted an eye. He's got a shady past, so they're giving him the shuffle right now, but sooner or later he's going to get his shot and when he does — look out. It's goodnight, Lucille."

"You gonna put your boy in against this guy?" Tony Broad asked.

"I figure in a year — maybe less — Nicky will be ready for Patterson. But we have to move now — if we wait, we're going to be dealing with Sonny Liston."

"You're gonna have to deal with this Liston kid anyway."

"He's no kid," Mac said. "He's pushing thirty, some say he's older than that. Either way, we want to fight for the title before he does. Then we can put him off a couple years. By then, he'll be slowing down and the Nick will be that much better. We want the shot now — and the way we get it is through Tommy Cochrane."

"Tommy's finished fighting," Ollie said. "I got that from the source."

Mac shrugged. "Maybe he is and maybe he isn't. I hear he's trying to raise some cash. I'm going to leave it up to him though — I have nothing but respect for Tommy Cochrane."

Herm Bell was waiting for Tony Broad to deal the cards. He'd heard enough of this talk — if Tommy Cochrane didn't want to fight, that was his business. They were talking about sending him in to get his head taken off by this Wilson kid; to Herm they were talking behind Tommy Cochrane's back. Herm lost his bankroll on the fight but he still didn't figure that Cochrane went down against Rinaldi. When you bet money, sometimes you lose. Otherwise it wouldn't be called gambling.

"How 'bout we play some cards?" he suggested.

Tony Broad, deck in hand, ignored him. "What's this other guy's name?" he asked Mac Brady.

"Sonny Liston. Big man — big and black as a freight train."

Tony made a show of drawing a pad from his pocket and writing the name down. "Let me know about this Cochrane deal, Mac," he said. "I might be interested if you need some backing."

"Deal 'em," Herm said.

Tony Broad smiled. "This talk about fighting make you nervous?" he asked.

"Nothing you do makes me nervous."

"Deal the cards," Fat Ollie said, and Tony Broad dealt them.

ELEVEN

It was a long night for a man who was used to the open road, a man who wasn't big on small talk, neckties or gladhanding with strangers. A man who didn't, in Lee's words, suffer fools gladly.

A man like Tommy Cochrane. He spent the evening talking to drunks and posing with the wives of drunks for a photographer Buzz Murdock had hired for the night. He even signed a few autographs. He heard a couple of women ask their husbands, just who the hell is Tommy Cochrane anyway?

He'd had a whiskey with Buzz before he started work, but had stayed away from the stuff since. And Buzz had mentioned that he expected Tommy to double as a bouncer if the need arose. The night was pretty quiet though, and Tommy wasn't pressed into any strongarm service. For that he was happy — throwing drunks into the street wasn't Tommy's idea of honest labour.

After closing he and Buzz stood at the bar and had a nightcap, Irish for Tommy and cognac for Buzz, whose tastes were expensive enough to keep him on the verge of bankruptcy year in and year out. Buzz was a tall man, black-haired, and with a black goatee. He came from Prince Edward Island, where his family raised fat potatoes and fast standardbreds. In fifteen years Tommy had never heard him say a bad word about anyone. There were not many people Tommy could say that about.

"I don't figure it's my life's calling," Tommy said when Buzz asked him how he liked the job. "But it was all right."

"The photographer was a good idea," Buzz said. "We'll do it again next Saturday. People love to get their picture took."

"Yeah," Tommy said, "but I got a feeling that ten years from now these people are gonna be wondering who's the knucklehead mick standing beside them in the snapshot."

"Well, they say that fame is fleeting," Buzz said and he smiled. "How old are you, Tommy?"

"Thirty-five."

"How old do you feel?"

"Well . . . I don't know. I guess I never thought about it."

"I'm thirty-eight," Buzz said. "And I feel like I'm twenty-two. And I've always felt that way. Sometimes I wonder if I'm ever going to feel as old as I really am."

"You're awful philosophical tonight, Buzz."

"I guess I am." Buzz finished his Courvoisier. "You know what I'm going to do, Tommy? I'm going to go home and fuck my wife."

Tommy downed his Irish. "You twenty-two-year-olds — that's all you ever think about."

Buzz offered him a ride, but Tommy said he wanted to walk and he set out on foot. It was twenty blocks to where he was bound, but Tommy was happy with the walk, content to be alone in the city, although it had never been his city.

There were a lot of people who thought different, he knew. Fighting those years in the States, he was always known as Tommy Cochrane from Toronto. Never Tommy Cochrane from Marlow, Ontario, population twelve hundred, not counting cats, dogs, goats, and whatever else was around.

There'd been a time, he guessed, when Toronto was his city. In the early days, when he had the world by the ass, he was pretty well known around town. His face would even open a few doors that might have otherwise remained closed to a mick roughneck from the boonies. When he and Lee had been together they'd been out on the town a lot. He couldn't say why now — remembering back it seemed the best times were when they stayed at home. And he was betting that Lee, if you asked her, would say the same thing.

Tommy's first manager, Karl Krone — whose kraut soul was now twisting in hell — liked a fighter with a high profile. And Tommy, when he was with Lee, was definitely high profile. The newspapers always called her the "beautiful Lee Charles" and the papers ran pictures of them together at ball games, nightclubs, wherever they went. They were living together on Spadina Road, and the story was that they had apartments in the same building, a little lie that Lee always said stopped them all from going straight to hell.

But that was a while back. Tonight he had these empty streets and nothing much else to call his own. He walked by Oscar's Diner on Sherbourne and remembered that the first time he'd set foot in the place had been by way of the back door, delivering milk. He'd come to the city when he was twenty, fresh from his grandfather's farm and fresher yet from winning a pair of three rounders in the old Kitchener arena, fighting in an exhibition Karl Krone had set up, looking for talent.

The war was just over and people were anxious to be living again. Things were available now — gasoline and nylons — hell, you could even buy food without coupons. Entertainment was available too, and boxing fell somewhat loosely in that category. After all, two men knocking each other around a ring was pretty tame stuff compared to the horrors reported in the newspapers every day for the past six years.

Tommy Cochrane didn't arrive in Toronto as any result of these sage sociological observations. He was just a man-sized farm boy who was ready to leave the farm, at least for a while. There was nothing new in that — farm boys had been doing it since there were farms to leave and open-armed cities to run to. The difference was that Tommy Cochrane found out he could fight.

He worked at a dairy in the west end when he first came to the city, loading trucks at four in the morning with milk and cream and cheese and butter. Three nights a week and Saturday mornings he took the streetcar all the way to Cabbagetown and worked out under the trainer Gus Washbone. He won his first five fights and didn't get paid for four of them. That's when he decided to be shed of Karl Krone and he asked Gus to become his manager.

"What do I know about managing?" Gus had said.

"More than me," Tommy had told him.

"That's not enough."

"Just teach me how to fight and make sure I get paid."

Gus had looked at the clumsy kid and said all right. They went to New York together, and Gus kept his word on both counts. And Gus was in New York even now, he was managing other kids, teaching them how to fight and making sure they got paid, and Tommy was walking alone, these streets of this city that had never been his.

"We had a hell of a run though," he said to Gus and to the empty sidewalk at his feet.

The apartment — the bedroom anyway — hadn't changed one whit that Tommy could see. Same creaky bed, same dresser piled high with clothes and whatever, same clown painting (on same tilt) on same wall. Same antique hairdryer salvaged from some salon. Same lips on his cock (limp now, just recently so), same dark blonde head at his waist. Same fingernails digging into his thigh.

Same her.

Same him.

"You were one I never expected to see again," she said. Her lips on his stomach now, coming closer. Nipples sliding over his chest, legs between his legs, her wetness upon his. "What made you call, Tommy Cochrane?" Her lips on his chin, his cheek, her small tongue in his ear.

"What do you think?" he said after a moment.

"Did you miss me? After all this time, did you miss me?" Straddling him, full breasts swinging down to touch the hair on his chest.

"Yeah."

"You missed me? Tell me you missed me." Reaching behind her for his cock, her juices slick on his stomach.

"Well, yeah. I missed you."

"Why did you wait so long then?" Fingernails digging lightly into his growing cock.

"I been away. You ask too many questions."

"You never liked to talk much." Sliding down now, lifting herself up.

"You and I never had much to talk about."

"You son of a bitch." Crying out, pulling him inside. "I could fuck you forever."

She was half asleep as he began to dress. Grey light was showing through the dirty window pane. He put his tie and his socks in his jacket pocket.

"What're ya doing? You leaving?"

"Gotta go."

"Don't go. Tommy, don't go."

"See ya later."

"Stay with me. You never stayed all night."

Tommy walking to the door.

"You bastard. What about Lee Charles? You stay all night with her?"

Tommy in the doorway. "Yeah."

"Why, you fucker? Why?"

Tommy walking out. "I guess because she never asked me to."

T-Bone woke up when Tommy came into the room. Tommy turned the light on, then realized it was daylight and shut it off. T-Bone sat up in bed and ran his long brown fingers down his cheeks.

"Lawdy, what's the time?"

"It's late, Bones. Or early maybe."

"How your new job, Thomas?"

"It's a job, Bones. That's all."

"Better than no job — right, Thomas?"

Tommy stripped to his shorts and took a pint of Bushmills from the nightstand and had a drink. Then he laid down on the bed.

"Where you been, Thomas?"

"I don't know. Out visiting, I guess."

"You got some strange visiting hours."

"Get some sleep, Bones."

"Don't you worry, Thomas. Everybody do it from time to time."

"Do what?"

"Do their thinkin' with their pecker."

Later Tommy decided he would go to the gym with T-Bone. He didn't want to go but he figured he had to make sure Mac Brady and his gang were treating his friend with respect. With Tommy standing by, Bert Tigers taped T-Bone's hands and gave him freshly laundered trunks and a near-new supporter.

"Never did that yesterday, Mr. Bert," T-Bone reminded him.

"So how you doing, champ?" Bert asked Tommy. "You stayin' in shape?"

"Well, I'm still alive," Tommy told him.

Old Bert smiled and nodded like Tommy had asked him something and he was being real agreeable. Tommy knew Bert Tigers. He was an ass-kissing puke who didn't have the moxy to show the truth — and that was that he didn't much like Tommy Cochrane. Not since the time ten years ago when Tommy had put the nix on Bert working his corner in a big fight in Jersey. Tommy had always known Bert's game — he was a man who had his price and it wasn't too damn high.

Before the sparring began Tommy took a walk around the gym. The place was falling apart, but then Tommy had never seen a gym that wasn't. You never saw a *new* gym because nobody ever built a new gym; they converted warehouses and factories and sweatshops. The kind of guy who might be inclined to build a new gym was the kind of guy who would never have the money to pull it off.

Tommy walked around and he didn't touch anything and he didn't really *see* anything. What he could see and what he could hear were so familiar they weren't even there, these things. Like an old salt who doesn't notice the rolling of the ocean, Tommy didn't notice the gym, because he was — after all this time — *of* the gym.

But he noticed the kid Nicky Wilson working the speed bag in a far corner and he stayed away. The kid was all flash on the bag, showing off for a bunch of guys in suits who had to be, to Tommy's eye, sportswriters. Showing off on the speed bag was easy — any twelve-year-old could do it. The bag was a patsy; it didn't hit back and it always came back for more. The kid finished with three looping right hands that had the suits wide-eyed at his power. Tommy moved on.

T-Bone Pike was standing on the apron of the sixteen-foot ring, wearing ten-ounce gloves, his mouthpiece clenched sideways between his teeth. When he looked at Tommy he smiled happily.

When Bert came out of the back room, he had Mac Brady with him, Mac in his shirt sleeves and vest, a cold cigar in his mouth. He stopped by the reporters a minute, then brought the kid over to the ring and the sparring began. The kid Wilson and T-Bone went an easy three minutes and then broke. Mac came over to stand beside Tommy while Bert Tigers talked to his fighter in the corner. T-Bone sat alone on his stool, hands folded in his lap, like he was sitting on a park bench, watching the day go by.

"What do you think?" Mac asked of Tommy.

"What do I think about what?"

Mac gestured with the cigar. "My boy."

Tommy smiled. "He looks real good on the speed bag, Mac."

The fighters went three more rounds, sloppy and slow paced. Wilson was throwing half-ass jabs and holding back with the right.

T-Bone knew what was happening and he had himself some fun, working the kid to the body, scoring with hooks that didn't look like much but hurt like hell. Tommy knew from experience. When T-Bone went back to his corner after the last round, he winked over at Tommy. Easy money today.

Tommy watched quietly, figuring the angles, and pretty soon he was approached by Ted Sears from the *Telly*. Mac made a big production of lighting his stogie, then edged closer.

"How you doing, Tommy?" Sears offered his hand, and Tommy took it. "You made up your mind yet?"

Tommy saw Mac Brady trying to look away. One thing about Mac, Tommy thought, his schemes were easy enough to spot. Like birdshit on a windshield.

"About what?" Tommy asked the writer.

"Why — you gonna fight the kid?"

That was Mac's cue, and he came rushing in. Like most men dedicated to theatrical behaviour, he was a lousy actor. "Wait a minute now," he warned the writer. "We haven't even approached Tommy yet."

Sears looked confused and he wasn't acting.

"Somebody been telling you stories, Ted?" Tommy said and he laughed. "Now I wonder who that could be."

"Yeah, I wonder. What the fuck is this, Mac?"

Mac the actor was reluctant to reveal his plans. He agonized over his decision for maybe five seconds.

"We may offer Tommy a fight," he admitted at last. "But he's not our first choice. We've got something cooking in Miami right now, and it could be big."

"With who?"

"A name you know. A fighter in the top ten."

"You won't tell me his name?" Sears asked.

"Not at this time, no," Mac said. He made a face like he was in pain. "We're at a very delicate point in negotiation."

Tommy, watching the performance, was about to split a gut. Mac should be on the television, he was better than Milton Berle.

"If this Florida deal falls through, you might go after Tommy here?" the writer wanted to know.

Mac considered this one at length, as if the option had never crossed his mind. "I guess it's possible we could approach his people."

"I don't have any people," Tommy said.

Mac pretended not to hear. "The question is whether or not the Nick is ready for a fighter of Tommy's calibre," he said to Sears.

The writer smiled at Tommy. "What do you think about it, Tommy?"

Tommy smiled. "I see you're wearing new wingtips, Ted. I'd watch my step if I were you — there's a lot of horseshit around here, you wouldn't want to ruin those twenty-dollar shoes."

"Then you're not interested in fighting Nicky Wilson?"

"I'm not interested in fighting Nicky Wilson," Tommy said. "And I'm not interested in fighting Woodrow Wilson, and I'm not interested in fighting your old grandmother either, Ted. I'm through."

"But we heard —"

"Damn it, Ted," Tommy laughed. "You should know better than to listen to rumours from an old horse thief like Mac Brady. I'll give you a tip, Ted — if his lips are moving, chances are he's lying."

And he walked past Sears and past Mac Brady — who had skin like a goddamn alligator and wasn't in the least offended — and went into the dressing room, where T-Bone was climbing into his street clothes.

"They're playing games, Bones," Tommy said. "Let's get out of here."

When they were leaving they passed by Nicky Wilson, who was holding forth in the midst of reporters. As they went by, the kid reached out to place two fingers on Tommy's lapel.

"How 'bout you, mick?" he asked. "You want to go a couple?"

"No, thank you," Tommy smiled. "I got my good clothes on."

"You sure now? I could put you down for a nice afternoon nap. Man your age must appreciate a nice nap, eh mick?"

Tommy stopped a moment in the doorway. The kid was wearing his shitty grin, his eyebrows up, mocking Tommy. But Tommy just shook his head and went out the door with T-Bone Pike behind him.

Back in the room Tommy lay on the bed and had a drink, wearing only his pants, no shoes, no socks, nothing. T-Bone was across the room, standing at the window, his hands above the framework there, and he was looking down onto Parliament, the afternoon traffic.

"So Mac calls the papers and starts this rumour," Tommy was saying. "And these sportswriters got nothing better to do and they come down to check it out. Then Mac gets real lucky — I walk in the door. So right away, him and Tigers — that little creep — get to the kid and tell him to lay back in the ring, to fool me into thinking the kid's got nothing."

"He didn't show it today, that for sure," T-Bone agreed. "Easy fifteen dollars for T-Bone."

"Well, you'll pay for it tomorrow, Bones," Tommy said. "You were hooking him plenty hard in the ribs, I could see it in his face. He'll be out for blood tomorrow. But you knew what you were doing."

T-Bone smiled broadly. "Jus' trying to give Mr. Brady his money's worth."

Tommy decided he didn't want a drink and put the whiskey away.

"And then there's this story about a fight in Miami, which is one hundred percent Mac Brady bullshit. He's got no fight in Florida."

"You don't figure?"

"He's just getting some ink for his boy," Tommy said. "Tomorrow the papers will be full of Wilson and Florida and me, too. I'll tell ya, that Mac's a cutie — he's promoting a fight he hasn't even got yet."

"What he gonna do next though?"

"Oh, he'll let it simmer awhile, then he'll approach me with an offer. He'll lowball me at first, so when he comes with his real price, I'll jump at it. He thinks."

"What you gonna do, Thomas?"

"I'm not fighting, Bones. That's all there is to it."

Down on the street a boy in a cloth cap was running through the thin traffic, clutching something in his hand, a white-aproned grocer in hot but fading pursuit. T-Bone smiled as the kid shot between two streetcars and made his escape.

"That what the doctor tell you, Thomas?"

Tommy sat up and swung his legs around to plant his bare feet on the floor. He put his elbows on his knees and looked at the wall across the room.

"That's what he told me."

TWELVE

Most nights now you could find Tony Broad at the Blue Parrot. He liked to show up halfway through Lee's first set, with his partner Billy Callahan in tow, and he would walk through the spotlight from the stage so anybody who gave a shit would know he'd arrived. Not that many did. Tony had given Callahan a dark blue suit that he himself didn't wear anymore. If the kid wanted to keep company with Tony Broad he had to have some style.

Tony always arrived with his hair slicked perfectly, his thick mustache trimmed, and a razor crease in his trousers. There were holes in his socks, sure, but his shoes were shined and his nails were clean. He made a habit of over-tipping the waiters and Lucky Ned the bartender, ingratiating them to himself, trying to make his presence welcome and enviable. In a club where he knew he wouldn't be back, Tony never tipped at all, sometimes even ran out on the tab. Tony Broad extended himself only when and where he thought it might do him some good.

Every night he and Callahan stood side by side at the bar and drank bourbon on the rocks and watched Lee Charles. And Tony talked to Nicky Wilson the nights that Nicky Wilson was there. Which was damn near every night. And he bought Nicky Wilson drinks and he told Nicky Wilson what a great goddamn world-beater of a fighter he was.

And one night Nicky Wilson introduced him to Lee Charles, as Tony Broad had known he would all along. After that, Lee Charles talked to Tony Broad, although not as much as she talked to Nicky Wilson. That cut no ice with Tony — to him, Lee was playing games with the kid, staying near enough to fan the flame but not so close that she would get burned. The kid was a moron, a walking hard-on, and she was either fucking him around just for the hell of it or keeping things warm while she decided what she wanted. Tony Broad didn't give a shit either way — he *knew* what he wanted. For him it was just cat and mouse from here on in.

Earlier this night he'd met Billy Callahan at Pete's Grill over on Jarvis for spaghetti and meatballs. Callahan was all excited about something when they met out front and with his mouth full of meatballs, he told Tony about a botched robbery he'd witnessed that morning over on the Danforth.

"These guys broke out of the Don, I hear," he said. "So the cops are looking for them to start with. But they're sitting at the counter and all of a sudden, Jesus, they both pull guns and holler at the morning cook to empty the cash. I'm sitting there three stools away and I'm shitting my pants. So the cook's cleaning out the till, and all of a sudden this cop walks in off his beat for a cup of joe. You won't believe what happened next."

"What happened next?" Tony was stuffing a meatball into his face.

"The cop hollers and the guy standing closest to me spins around and shoots his partner right in the fuckin' head by accident. Trying to shoot the cop, see."

"No shit?"

"I'm tellin' you, by this time I'm layin' on the floor. So the cop pulls his rod and hits the other guy in the shoulder and the guy falls down right beside me. So I reached over and popped him one in the mouth."

"You did?"

"I figured there might be a reward, you never know."

"But there wasn't."

"No, but I got something just as good. I can't show you in here."

It was all-you-can-eat night at Pete's, and they finished two heaping plates each before leaving. On the way to the Parrot Callahan took Tony Broad into an alley and pulled a heavy Colt revolver from inside his jacket.

"The other guy's gun," he said. "I guess nobody knew if there was one gun or two. I mean, there's brains and blood and shit all over the place. I kicked it under the counter and grabbed it later. It's a .44. I had to clean some brains off it," he added proudly.

Tony Broad took the gun and broke the cylinder to check the load. "Not a bad piece," he said. "You got lucky, kid. You hang on to this thing, it might come in handy some day. You know what they say — God made men and Sam Colt made 'em equal."

"Where'd you hear that?"

"Seen it in a movie." Tony handed the gun back.

"I gotta go to the movies more, y'know."

"You can learn a lot of things," Tony Broad agreed.

Now they were standing at the bar in the Parrot, drinking Kentucky bourbon while Lee Charles onstage sang "It Had to Be You." Half the men in the bar sat and imagined that she was singing the song to them. The other half — the practical types — didn't dare to dream so big, and maybe it was their loss that they didn't. The lady herself could tell them — dreams will never hurt you; just so long as you didn't push 'em too hard or fall too far when they didn't come true. Even Billy Callahan knew that.

The kid Nicky Wilson was at the bar, had been there when they'd arrived. And he was in his usual spot, drinking a beer and watching Lee Charles' every move. She never looked at him when she sang, and the kid, in his blazing ego, took that to be a good sign too.

When the kid's beer was nearly empty, Tony Broad stood him another. Lucky Ned delivered the lager and then Tony moved in, smoothing his mustache with his fingertips.

"How's the Nick?" he wanted to know. "How's the training going?"

Nicky took his eyes from the stage and grinned. "You ever see dynamite, pal?" He held up his huge right fist. "That there's dynamite, pal. Knocked this nigger out cold today, laid him out like ten miles of bad highway."

"Nice to see a nigger who's good for something," Tony said. "You fight the Polack when — three weeks?"

Nicky shrugged and got cute. "Maybe the Polack," he said. "Maybe Tommy Cochrane if we can get the yellow bastard in the ring."

"Aren't you signed with the Polack?"

The kid laughed. "Yeah, we're signed with the Polack, so long as he doesn't get an injury or something."

"I get ya," Tony said and he laughed along with Nicky Wilson, a couple of half-wits being cute. There was one more to be heard from though. Billy Callahan leaned over to look at the kid.

"The way I see it," he said, "you could take Cochrane out in five rounds. Piece of cake."

"And what the fuck do you know?" the kid asked. "Five rounds — Cochrane couldn't last a round with me. He's an old man and he's scared shitless to boot. You punks off the street think you know about fighting, you don't know your ass from a hole in the ground."

Tony Broad saw Callahan's face go bad, saw the embarrassment there, watched it as it turned to rage. And right away Tony thought about the .44 in Callahan's coat and about how quick the gun could end Nicky Wilson's career and anything else he was.

Maybe somebody else would've stepped in as peacemaker, but not Tony Broad. He looked out for himself and nobody else, and the truth of the matter was that he couldn't give one lousy shit if Billy Callahan shot Nicky Wilson dead right then and there. He was a little worried about the crossfire though and he backed away a step.

But Billy Callahan wasn't ready to go that far — not yet anyway. All his young life he wanted to be accepted, and it was going to be a little while longer before he realized that what he wanted wasn't going to show. For now, he put on a hang-dog look and ate his words.

"I know you'd take him in one," he said to the kid. "I don't know what I was thinking about."

"Yeah, yeah," Nicky said and he looked away.

Tony figured things were cool enough for him to move back into the group. The band quit as he did, and Lee Charles came down off the stage to join them for a drink. She moved in between the Wilson kid and Tony Broad. That left Callahan on the outside. He stood in his ill-fitting suit and watched Lee with the same eyes that had stared longingly all those years ago at the three-speed J.C. Higgins bicycle in the front window of Fletcher's Hardware. And young Billy had schemed and pleaded and begged but he never got to touch that bike. Not once.

What he couldn't know was that Lee wasn't as distant as all that. If he wanted to talk to her, all he had to do was walk over and say hello. Lee had no pretensions about what she was — she was a saloon singer, at least for the time being, and talking to people came with the job. Besides, she liked people. People were great, as long as you didn't get to know them too well.

Of course Billy Callahan couldn't have known that — nothing had ever come that simply to him and nothing ever would.

Lee got a gin and tonic from Lucky Ned, and Nicky Wilson busted his ass to pay for the drink before Tony Broad could beat him to it. Tony could buy the kid beer all night long, but when it came to Lee Charles, Nicky paid the shot.

"You sure get out a lot for somebody who's supposed to be in training," Lee said when she had her drink.

"I'm a fighter, not a monk," Nicky told her. "Besides — fighting's not my only talent."

"So I keep hearing," Lee said.

"Speaking of talent," Tony Broad spoke up. "Your voice is sounding sweet as brown sugar, Lee. Why haven't you ever recorded anything?"

"I made a couple singles, a few years back," Lee said. "They each sold ten million copies."

The kid was impressed. "You're kidding," he said.

"You're goddamn right I'm kidding."

Nicky didn't like to be jerked around, especially in front of Tony Broad and the punk Callahan. He straightened up from the bar and put his wall eyes on Tony Broad.

"Records are nothing anyway," he said. "Lee's been in the movies, out in Hollywood, California."

"That right?" Tony asked.

Lee laughed. "One of these nights I'll bring my Academy Awards in, line 'em up on the bar."

Nicky moved a little closer. "You know — Tony's in the movie business too."

"I didn't know that," Lee said.

Nicky, in the centre of things again, was smiling. "Tell her about the movies you make, Tony," he said.

And Tony Broad smiled right back at him. That's it, kid, do my work for me. Fucking pea-brain.

"What kind of movies you making, Tony?" Lee asked.

"Oh, you know — love stories."

Nicky laughed and leaned closer. Lee could feel the length of his thigh along her leg. She waited a moment then shifted away.

"I get the feeling these aren't Doris Day movies," she said to Tony Broad.

"These are films for the mature audience," Tony said. "But if Doris is interested. . . ." He gave her what he considered to be a charming smile.

"When are you gonna get me some of these movies?" Nicky

demanded. "I like to watch them. What about you, Lee — you like to watch those kind of movies?"

"Not really."

"Why not?" The kid was actually leering now, leaning over her.

"Oh, I don't know," she said. "When I was a kid, I always wanted to drink beer. Once I started though, I never had the urge to sit around watching other people do it."

Tony Broad laughed out loud. In a second Callahan joined him, but he didn't know why.

"You got a mean lip, lady," Nicky told her. "Someday somebody's gonna take that out of you."

"There's been a few that tried."

"Well, somebody's gonna do it," the kid said. "And you know what? When it happens, you're gonna love it — you're just gonna lay back and love it, 'cause it's what you've been looking for."

Lee stepped back. "My, aren't we full of it tonight?"

The kid touched her again. "You know what I'm full of," he said. "That's why you're standing here. You know exactly what it is I'm full of."

Lee smiled sweetly. "Shit?" she said.

She left her drink on the bar and went backstage. Broad and Callahan and the kid watched her walk, each resenting the fact that the others had eyes.

"You having a little trouble getting to first base with that girl, kid?" Tony said. "Hell, you even up to bat yet?"

Nicky was pissed off. "What the fuck business is it of yours?" He looked like he would take a swing at Tony Broad.

"Hey, hey," Tony said, backing off.

"Maybe I should remind you who I am, asshole."

"I know who you are, kid," Tony said quickly. "You're going to be the heavyweight champion of the world and that's a fact. I think we should drink to that right now. Lucky Ned!" he called to the bartender.

Nicky Wilson smiled. "Sure, I'll drink to that."

Tony Broad brought out his billfold and thought to himself — Jesus, it was like petting a stray dog, pleasing this kid. What an idiot, what a goddamned, self-centred, shit for brains idiot. And he smiled at Nicky Wilson.

"Listen, kid," he said when they'd drunk. "I got a couple of movies and a projector in my room. You can have 'em for tomorrow night if you want. You got some friends who want to watch?"

"Sure I do."

"I'll drop 'em at the gym tomorrow."

"All right," the kid said. "You gonna watch 'em with us?"

"No," Tony Broad told the kid. "I got business tomorrow night."

Herm Bell finally kept his date with Sheila Mosconi. His luck had been holding all week and he'd flogged it all over town, knowing that sooner or later the lady would leave. That morning though, over breakfast at Lem's, he realized he'd turned down a sure piece of ass three nights running and he was suddenly concerned that he was losing his sex drive. He didn't want to become one of these guys who prefer filling an inside straight to good old-fashioned fucking. He'd phoned Sheila right away and, getting a hard-on just talking on the phone, he'd walked back to his breakfast knowing he was okay.

That afternoon he bought a new brown suit, with a striped shirt and tabbed collar, a silk tie, and new brown bucks. He got his hair cut at a new place on Parliament, and the barber cut it okay but fucked it up when he combed it and it took Herm fifteen minutes back home to get it right. His mother came in as he was walking out, paper bag full of groceries in her arms, cigarette hanging from her mouth. She looked tired. Shirley Bell had embraced the working life these thirty years and she was at a constant loss to understand her son's reluctance to do the same.

"Well, Mr. Big Shot with the new clothes," she said when she saw him. "Did one of your horses come in for once? Or are you robbing banks these days, Mr. Moneybags?"

Herm took the bag from her and set it on the counter. Then he grabbed his mother and planted a huge kiss on her cheek. "I did it, Ma. I robbed an armoured truck today. Shot the guard and half a dozen coppers. You gotta hide me, Ma, the cops are coming."

"You stop that nonsense, mister," she scolded, pulling away from him. "You're not too old for the flyswatter, you know."

"I'll buy you a gold flyswatter, Ma. I'm rolling in it."

She shook her head and began to put the groceries away. "I suppose you won't be here for supper? I suppose you got big plans again tonight."

Herm bounced around her, jabbing like a featherweight. "Got a date, Ma. Got a date with an angel."

"Who is this angel?"

"You don't know her, Ma. Sheila Mosconi, she's from the east end."

Shirley Bell began to cut up a chicken on the counter top. "You can't take out a neighbourhood girl? What about Eddie Jones' daughter, Linda. She always liked you, Herm."

"Ma, she's got a mustache like Ernie Kovacs."

"They can fix that these days."

Herm threw another jab. His mother held the knife out in defence. "Get away, mister."

Herm kissed her cheek again. "I gotta go, Ma. By the way, I think I saw a big rat in your bedroom. You better do something about it." And he was gone.

Shirley Bell put down the knife and went into her room. The box on the bed was from Eaton's. Inside was a silk scarf. Navy blue, her colour.

"Mr. Moneybags," she said.

Herm took a cab to pick up his date. She was a crazy girl, was Sheila Mosconi, with a bit of a reputation and a healthy appetite for any number of things. She'd been half in love with Herm Bell off and on for maybe five years. Sometimes Herm was in love with her too, but it usually only lasted a couple hours.

Tonight he'd brought along a mickey of lemon gin, a proper drink for a lady, and they tipped it back crossing the viaduct heading back into town. In a minute she had his cock out in the back seat of the cab, squeezing it in her hand and running her red fingernail across the tip.

"Easy now," Herm laughed as he watched the cabbie in the mirror. "I thought we were going to eat first."

And she dropped her head and put her lips on his cock, running her tongue wildly over the head just long enough to drive him crazy, and then she straightened up and sat primly, hands in her lap, on her side of the cab.

"I'll be a good girl," she promised.

Herm caught his breath and zipped his pants. "If I thought that was true, I'd have left you at home," he said.

They went to the Bamboo Club for dinner. Herm was surprised to see Tommy Cochrane greeting people at the door, wearing a sorry-looking suit and looking about as comfortable as a priest in a whorehouse. Herm didn't think Tommy would remember him.

"Sure, Lem's diner," Tommy said. "You were with Ollie."

"We were a little tight," Herm admitted. "Up all night playing cards."

"Ollie got a regular game?"

"Wednesdays," Herm said. "You want to sit in this week?"

"Maybe not this week," Tommy told him. "I'll have to see how things go."

"I'm hungry," Sheila said.

"She's hungry," Herm said to Tommy and they moved off to their table.

Herm had a sirloin and Sheila some sort of chicken dish that didn't look to Herm like anything that ever walked around in a barnyard. They had a bottle of wine, some French stuff that even the waiter couldn't pronounce, and by dessert Sheila had her shoe off and her nyloned toe in Herm's crotch. Herm paid the bill and they walked out of the club, stopping a second in the doorway to speak to Tommy Cochrane.

"Heading out?"

"There's a new singer at the Blue Parrot we're going to catch," Herm told him.

They said goodbye and went into the street. While they waited for a cab, though, Sheila pointed to the Duke Hotel down the street and they walked over and took a room. They fucked the first time on the floor inside the door, with Sheila's dress hiked up and Herm's pants around his ankles. She screamed like a banshee when she came and Herm burned both elbows on the cheap carpet. They lay there panting for a while.

"What do you say," Herm suggested at length, "we take our shoes off."

They stayed in the room a couple of hours. They broke the bed, and the lamp beside the bed, and Sheila bit Herm's earlobe until it bled. Then they got dressed and wandered into the street. It was past midnight; Sheila leaned back into Herm's arms beneath the street-light and announced it was time to go home.

"I'll get you a cab," Herm said.

"Ain't you coming?"

"Think I'll stay downtown awhile."

"Take me home," she said. "You can stay on the couch, my parents don't mind. We can stay up awhile. My parents sleep real sound," she smiled.

"I'll get you a cab, baby."

"I want to stay with you."

He managed to get her into the taxi and paid the driver to take her home. She called him a son of a bitch as she left, but that was okay — Herm wasn't going to her house or anybody else's, not at this early hour and him with a new suit and money in his pocket.

He decided to go back into the Bamboo for a drink. The place was largely empty now — it was a club that thinned out early, which meant that the food was okay but the orchestra was lousy. Tommy Cochrane was at the bar by himself, nursing a short whiskey. Herm walked over and ordered scotch for himself and another Irish for Tommy.

"How was the singer at the Parrot?"

"Well," Herm said. "We got sort of sidetracked."

"Waylaid?"

"The last part anyway."

"Beats listening to a nightclub singer," Tommy said.

Herm took a drink of straight scotch and made a face. "How long you have to stay here?" he asked. "You want to go over to the Parrot with me?"

"I have to stick around 'til closing," Tommy said. "What's this singer's name anyway?"

"I don't know. But I hear she's a real looker." Herm had another drink and felt it smoother this time, nothing like liquor for fooling a person. He looked over at Tommy a moment. "Don't take this the wrong way," he said cautiously. "But how come a guy like you is doing this kind of work?"

"Well, I'm broke," Tommy said.

Herm nodded. "I've played snooker with your friend T-Bone a couple of times. Over at Sully's."

"He told me," Tommy smiled. "Penny a point."

"Penny a point," Herm agreed. "He told me you guys are trying to raise some dough."

Tommy took a slow drink of the Jameson's and let it rest on his tongue a moment before swallowing. He looked over at the kid beside him — a good-looking kid, dressed to the nines, hair oiled and combed back, silk tie. Kind of a gambler, but polite — not a wise guy like most of the punks you see. What the hell, Tommy

BRAD SMITH

thought. So he told Herm Bell about his grandfather's farm in Marlow and the money he needed to buy it. And he told him how much time he had to raise the dough.

"That's why I'm working in a place like this," he said.

"Five grand is a lot of jack to raise in three weeks," Herm said.

"I figure I can swing it with four."

"Well, we both know you're not going to make it here," Herm said. "What've you got in mind?"

"I don't have what you'd call a plan," Tommy said. "Right now I'm trying to put together four or five hundred for a stake. Then maybe I'll go gambling. That's why I was asking about Ollie's."

"You need a bigger game than Ollie's for what you want. The most you could take out of there is a few hundred. Besides, you got that much confidence in your poker playing?"

"I'd have to get lucky," Tommy said. "I know that. I'm not looking for a sure thing, I don't believe in 'em."

"I do," Herm said.

"Yeah?"

Herm smiled. "That dame I was with tonight."

Tommy smiled back. "What're they charging for a room at the Duke these days?"

Herm signalled to the waiter, and this time Tommy paid for the drinks. The club was empty now except for a couple in a corner booth, the woman bent over a rye and coke and the man asleep with his drunken cheek on the tabletop, his hand on the woman's thigh.

"Does Mac Brady know you're looking for money?" Herm asked.

"There isn't a stray dog takes a crap in this city that Mac Brady doesn't know about it," Tommy said. Then he nodded. "I tried to collect some old debts. Mac knows. Why?"

"He's been talking a fight between you and Nicky Wilson."

"Well, talkin's what Mac does best."

"I'm guessing the money's there for you," Herm said. "So you must have your reasons for deciding against it. I'm not going to ask what they are."

"Fair enough."

Herm drank his scotch and made to leave; he could still catch the last set at the Blue Parrot if he hurried. He asked again if Tommy wanted to go along, but Tommy said no, he was heading home.

Herm slid down from the stool. "You ever play the horses, Tommy?"

"Sure. It's been a while though."

"I been hittin' them pretty good lately," Herm said and he wasn't boasting. "I don't know what it's worth, but I got friends at the track — my old man worked the ponies for thirty years. Sometimes I hear when a horse is ready to go. Once in a blue moon — you know? I was thinking — if I hear about something going off, say, eight to one, ten to one — and you had four or five hundred to bet, you might get lucky."

Tommy was listening with interest.

"I'm not talking about a fix," Herm said. "It's just sometimes they'll hold a horse back a few races, to get the odds where they want 'em. Then they'll let him run, and if he wins, it's square. Sometimes he does, and sometimes he doesn't. But it's a better chance than cards, and maybe you'd get your whole roll in one shot. But it's no sure thing, mind you."

"I don't believe in sure things — remember?" Tommy said.

"I remember."

Tommy was thinking it over. "And you'd take a cut, is that it?"

Herm looked him straight in the eye for maybe ten full seconds.

"No, that's not it," he said. "I like your friend and I thought maybe I could do you a favour, that's all."

Tommy looked down at his drink. Herm turned to leave.

"Wait a minute," Tommy said and Herm stopped. "You'll have to excuse my big mouth. I been hanging around with creeps so long I'm starting to think like 'em."

Herm just shrugged it off.

"I guess you're one of the few people in this town who didn't lose money on me in the Rinaldi fight," Tommy said then.

"Shit," Herm said. "If everybody in this town lost what they say they lost on that fight, the bookies would be living like Howard Hughes."

Tommy smiled.

"But I had you for two hundred," Herm added.

"And you're not sore?"

"What right have I got to be sore?" Herm asked. "I listened to the fight on the radio. You went eight tough rounds with that fuckin' gorilla and in the end you got beat. Who the hell am I to be sore about that? I figure you fought your fight and that's it."

Tommy narrowed his eyes and looked at the sharp-dressed kid a moment. "All right," he said at last.

"I'd like to see you get your farm," Herm said then. "Think about the horse angle. Sure, it's a long shot. They say long shots are for suckers, but every time one comes in, somebody's got his two dollars on it."

"That's true."

"What the hell, life's a long shot," Herm said. "That's what makes it fun."

Tommy laughed and drank off his whiskey. "I haven't been think-ing that way lately," he said. "I guess I forgot about the fun part."

"Oh, Jesus," Herm said. "Don't ever do that."

THIRTEEN

Lee grudgingly decided that it was time to make the trip to Rosedale and visit her mother, at least to announce that she was back in the country and still drawing breath. Friday she went down to Simpsons to pick up a gift of some sort but she couldn't find anything she even suspected the old girl would like. What do you give somebody who has everything she wants and doesn't like any of it?

When she ran into Patty Simmons leaving the store, she abandoned the idea of the visit and she and Patty went for lunch at the Hungarian Cafe. They took a table by the windows in front and sat down. A waiter wearing a bad toupee and a pencil mustache brought menus and then scurried off to the kitchen.

"Hope he doesn't drop that rug in the soup," Lee said, watching him.

"So what's new?" Patty asked. "Hey, Bobby and I have been meaning to get down to the Parrot, but he's working a lot and everything. How's it going?"

"Well, Ed Sullivan hasn't called," Lee said, "but we're having fun. The band is great — if it wasn't for those guys, I wouldn't be there. Doc's in his second childhood, Bugs is smoking tea like there's no tomorrow. Good times."

"What about Dunston?"

"Mel is in seventh heaven, we're packing the joint every night. The old bastard doesn't know Hoagy Carmichael from a hoagy sandwich, but he likes what he sees in the cash drawer. And he misses you terribly, Patty. I think you gave him his first hard-on in ten years."

"He's lucky I didn't turn out his lights, the pervert."

Lee shook her head in profound and feigned disapproval. "That's my boss you're talking about, honey," she said. "So what's new with you, anyway?"

"Still trying to make a baby," Patty said. "The old man is so serious. He bought a book on reproduction, believe it or not. So that's what we're doing in the bedroom now — trying to *reproduce*. Kinda takes the romance out of it, you know what I mean? I remember when it was just fucking and we did it on the kitchen table if we wanted."

"Do we have to talk about sex?" Lee asked. "I been abstaining."

Patty arched her eyebrows. "I see. How long's this been going on?"

"Couple centuries, I think."

"What's the matter — no men in California?"

"I met some great pretenders."

"And no relief in sight?"

The waiter returned then and took their lunch orders. Lee stared at his greasy hairpiece while he wrote on his pad. For some reason she had a sick desire to touch the thing. She ordered a chicken sandwich and Patty had the goulash. When the waiter left Lee tried to get off the subject.

"I like your hair that way," she said.

"Oh, do you?" Patty asked. "Since when did you give a damn about anybody's hair or shoes or anything else? Look at you, girl — walking around in those pants and Tommy Cochrane's old jacket. Yeah, I recognize it. Shit, if you don't want that body, give it to science. No, give it to me."

"You can have it. I ain't using it."

"But you're thinking about it," Patty laughed. "Don't give me the con — who is he?"

Lee made a face. "There's this kid, a boxer, been hanging around the Parrot. And he is on my trail, I mean he's sniffing like a bloodhound." She laughed at herself. "Another fighter — can you believe it?"

"With you I believe anything, Lee," Patty said. "So you like this guy?"

"Good question — I don't know the answer. He's got weird eyes and he's so full of himself he's about ready to pop open. He's kinda strange, to tell you the truth."

"But — ?"

The waiter brought iced tea and Lee poured and took a drink.

"He's sexy, for some reason," she said then. "I mean, I think he's kind of a jerk at heart, but there's something there. Anyway, I guess I'm going out with him tonight after work."

"You guess?"

Lee shrugged. "Probably just gonna get myself in shit. But what am I supposed to do — dry up?"

"Heavens, no."

Lee pushed the bitter tea away. "Goddamn it, I wish Tommy was around."

"Well, Tommy ain't around," Patty said. "And you are. So you better get on with it."

"Thank you, Dear Abby."

"You're welcome. Here's the food."

Patty tucked into her goulash like a starving woman. Lee just nibbled at her sandwich, watching for strands of toupee in the chicken. After a minute she set it aside and told Patty about the last she had seen of Tommy Cochrane.

"Gus Washbone was trying to talk Tommy into going to England to fight this guy Smythe. Turned out the limey wasn't much of a fighter, but he could punch, and people over there were talking him up to be the guy to beat Marciano."

"Who?" Patty asked, goulash on her chin.

Lee handed her a napkin. "Just listen. So Gus figures Tommy to get a name if he beats this Smythe. Except Tommy doesn't want to go to England because, believe it or not — Thomas Andrew Cochrane is afraid to fly. But he and I were going through some rough times about then — he was away a lot, fighting in the States, and there was this singer, Johnny Dillon, who was after my ass —"

"I remember Johnny Dillon," Patty said. She was eating Lee's sandwich now.

"Yeah, well — Tommy gets the bright idea that I want to go out with Dillon. And he thinks that maybe Dillon can help my career and that he's holding me back by hanging around. So one day he announces he's going to England to fight and he says that maybe we should just cool it for a while and kinda go our separate ways. He's telling me this in the gym, for Christ's sakes, while he's hitting the heavy bag, and he's not even looking at me, it's like he's firing his goddamn manager or something. So I got pissed off and said fine and walked on out of there and that was it. He was pounding that bag like it was his worst enemy when I left and that's the last I saw him. Six years ago. And I was too young and stupid to know what was going on."

"So he did it?" Patty asked. "He flew to England?"

"Naw, he took a boat," Lee said. "Knocked the limey cold in forty-eight seconds. Three weeks to get there, three weeks to get home, and he spends less than a minute in the ring. Dumb mick."

"But he did it for you," Patty said. "God, that's kind of romantic, you know."

"Yeah, the dumb son of a bitch did it for me and all I ever wanted was to be with him. Everything was going along fine, and the one time he decides to get analytical about us, he fucks everything up."

"What about Johnny Dillon, did you ever go out with him?"

"Yeah, but it was long time after," Lee said. "He turned out to be a crying drunk, a real mama's boy. One night with him was lots for me. He was probably a lousy fuck anyway."

"He was."

Lee laughed out loud. "Why, you little tramp."

There was no hot water today, but T-Bone went into the shower anyway, soaping himself down and rinsing off quick as he could before the cold spray tightened his muscles. He'd just had another bad day in the ring with Nicky Wilson, had been down on the canvas three times and had his upper lip split. Something was eating at Wilson and he was getting meaner every day. Today he'd been taunting T-Bone like usual, but he'd been calling T-Bone's friend Thomas Cochrane down too, calling Thomas a coward and an old woman. And yesterday Wilson had actually knocked T-Bone cold for a few seconds with an overhand right thrown after Bert Tigers had called time and T-Bone had dropped his gloves.

The kid was twenty years younger than T-Bone and the difference was beginning to tell. But T-Bone needed money for the farm and he would keep on with the sparring as long as Mac Brady wanted him. T-Bone had never quit anything in his life and he wouldn't start now, especially not at the hands of this punk Nicky Wilson. So he took the abuse and he never told Thomas about the kid's mean mouth and he never told about the knockout either.

T-Bone Pike believed in justice in this world and he believed that someday somebody would make Nicky Wilson believe in it too.

When he came out of the shower Mac Brady was there with his fifteen dollars. There was another man with Mac, a short, thick guy with a black mustache. He was carrying one of those movie projectors and a couple of tin cans about the size of an apple pie. The chubby guy was smiling at Mac Brady like he was selling something.

"Told the kid I'd drop these off," he was saying. "I figured it might help you out — keep the kid at home for a couple nights anyway."

"Well I've about given up on keeping that kid home at night," Mac said. "He figures the world's his goddamn oyster and he's out every night proving it. Good thing is, the knucklehead is young and strong as a Clydesdale so he can get away with it for a while. One of these days, though, I'm going to lay the law down."

T-Bone was putting his clothes on, holding his teeth against the split in his lip to stop the bleeding there. All he wanted was to get back to the hotel and lie down for a time. For the first time in his life T-Bone Pike felt old.

"The kid's been making the Blue Parrot his home," the short man was saying now. "He's got his eyes full of Lee Charles."

"What?" T-Bone said.

Tony Broad turned to look at him. "You say something, coon?"

"No, sir," T-Bone said. "I just thinking 'bout something out loud, I guess."

Tony Broad looked at Mac. "I think your coon's been taking too many punches to the head," he smiled.

"T-Bone is a good man," Mac said. "He's the only fighter in the place who'll go more than a round with the Nick. He's been doing a good job for me."

"Sure," Tony Broad said. He gave Mac a smile that suggested that he was familiar with the foolish ways of the Negro. Mac was having none of it though — Mac Brady was a lot of things, but a bigot wasn't one of them. When he got up in the morning he figured there were only so many people in the world to take advantage of, and if you began to discriminate against one group or another, you were cutting your own percentage.

None of this touched T-Bone Pike this day. He was hurrying now, tying his shoes and taking his jacket from the hook on the wall, nodding to Mac Brady as he went out the door, past the ring and the mats, around the heavy bag, and through the scarred wooden door and onto the sidewalk where he began to walk in long strides, not feeling like an old man now, hurrying for the Jasper

Hotel where he hoped he would find his friend Thomas Cochrane.

Back in the gym, Tony Broad was after Mac Brady for a little information.

"So who you gonna fight — the Polack or Cochrane?"

Mac looked Tony over. "Cochrane," he said.

"Does he know it?"

"Not yet. But it's as good as done. It'll take a week or so to sign him, but Tommy's going to fight. He'll have no choice, because I've got something he wants. I've got his farm."

"*You've* got his farm?"

"In a manner of speaking, I do," Mac said. "You see, I understand Tommy Cochrane — he's a straight-ahead, stubborn son of a bitch, but he's smart enough to recognize facts when he's faced with them. He's got no choice but to fight."

Tony Broad was turning it over in his mind, wondering if there was a dollar with his name on it somewhere in all of this.

"You got the dough?" he asked.

"Now why would you ask a question like that?" Mac asked. "You looking for something?"

Always, Tony Broad thought to himself. "Let me know what happens," he said to Mac. "I've always got an eye out for a good investment. Tell the kid to enjoy the movies."

"Sure," Mac said. "He's out running, I'll tell him when he gets back."

When Tony Broad was gone, Mac went out into the gym to find Bert Tigers, the trainer. Bert was working with a young welter, a cream puff who couldn't punch a hole in a cloud of smoke, and whose only chance to win a fight would be if his opponent dropped dead of a stroke during the ring announcements. Still, the kid's old man was paying Bert Tigers twenty dollars a day to teach his kid how to box, and Bert was collecting the double saw and going through the motions. Once the old man saw his kid on the deck a couple times, that would be the end of it.

"What's with this Tony Broad?" Mac asked, walking up beside Bert. The kid was skipping rope like some schoolgirl.

"Beats me," Bert said. "I only seen him around the last month or so. He's from the States, I hear. Claims he makes beaver movies, that's the story."

"So I've heard," Mac said. "Keep on eye on him, Bert. He's a little too slippery for my liking. Son of a bitch reminds me of myself when I was younger."

Bert stone-eyed his boss a moment, then turned his attention back to the gangly youth tripping over the rope.

"Feet together, kid," he called. "Feet together."

When Tommy Cochrane walked into the Bamboo that night, Mac Brady was already there, waiting for him at the bar. Tommy didn't bother to wait to be invited, he just went over and sat down. Mac offered a drink and Tommy told him no.

"Somehow I figured you to show today," Tommy said. "You're getting awful damned predictable, Mac."

"You get old enough, there's no such thing as a new trick, Tommy. That's the tragedy of life."

"The tragedy of life," Tommy repeated. He laughed and shook his head. When he looked up, he saw himself and Mac Brady in the mirror behind the bar, an unlikely pair, as much now as it always had been. Yet somehow they seemed to fit together, and maybe that bothered Tommy a little, but not much. He knew which one of the two he was.

"What the hell, might as well cut to it," Mac said and he reached into a pocket and brought out an envelope. "No sense bullshitting each other. There it is, two thousand dollars."

Because Mac Brady said there was two thousand dollars in the envelope, Tommy knew that there wasn't. He opened the flap and counted fifty twenties inside. Then he smiled at Mac.

"I make it a thousand."

"That's right," Mac agreed. "A thousand now and a thousand later, after the fight. Two grand."

Tommy placed the envelope gingerly on the bar. "First of all, Mac — if I'm dealing with you, I get everything up front. And second of all — I'm not dealing with you."

"What do you mean, you're not dealing with me?" Mac asked. "You're not being realistic, Tommy."

"I'm not fighting, Mac. Now I've told *you*, I've told that peckerhead you call a fighter, I've told your newspaper hacks, and I'll tell it in church if you like — I'm not fighting."

"Why not?"

"Because I'm *not*."

The bartender came near to freshen Mac's drink, but Mac waved him off.

"I have information which indicates that you are in need of money," Mac said then. "Something to do with a farm once owned by your beloved grandfather."

"Leave my beloved grandfather out of this, Mac. My financial affairs are none of your damn business. Never were. All you need to hear from me is one word, and that word is *no*."

Mac pushed his glass away and then reached reluctantly for the envelope. His jowly face was downcast, a chastised bulldog. Beside him, Tommy was enjoying the performance.

"The least you can do is tell me why not," Mac said.

"Because I don't want to, Mac. Do you hear me?"

"I can't believe you're afraid, Tommy."

"You believe what you want."

Mac shook his head like a man greatly confused and got to his feet. He jerked his vest over his gut with both hands and made an ineffective pass at his tie.

"How much money do you need for the farm, Tommy?" he asked.

"A million dollars, Mac."

"Okay, Tommy," Mac said. "If that's the way you want it. I come here as a businessman, and all you want to do is make jokes about a million dollars. And me just trying to do you a favour."

"Oh yeah, you're a real philanthropist, Mac."

"No need for name calling, Tommy."

"See ya around, Mac."

Bert Tigers was waiting in the car outside. Bert had a habit of popping off at the wrong time — Mac always said that Bert couldn't get laid in a Mexican whorehouse — so Mac had made him wait in the car while he went in to talk to Tommy Cochrane. Now Mac came out of the Bamboo and got in the passenger side. It took him a moment to adjust his bulk in the seat of the Nash.

"Well?" Bert asked.

"He'll fight."

"That was awful goddamn easy," Bert said. "How'd you get him to say yes?"

"He didn't say yes. But he will, it's just a matter of time and money." Mac laughed. "Mostly, it's a matter of money."

"He's a bullheaded mick," Bert said. "What makes you so sure?"

Mac indicated the street with a wave of his hand. "Drive," he said. As usual Bert pulled into traffic without looking, causing horns to blow and brakes to screech. Mac waited for things to calm down.

"I'll tell you a story, Bert," he said then.

"A story?" Bert asked.

"There's this pretty girl," Mac said, "sitting at a bar, and this guy comes up and says, 'Will you go to bed with me for a million dollars?'

"And the girl says, 'For a million dollars? Sure.'

"So the guy says, 'Well, will you go to bed with me for one dollar?'

"And the girl tells him to take a hike. 'What kind of girl do you think I am?' she asks.

"And the guy says, 'Hey, we've already established what kind of girl you are. All we're doing now is talking price.'"

Bert Tigers didn't have much going for him, and what he had didn't include a sense of humour. He regarded Mac unhappily a moment and then went back to his erratic driving.

"I swear, I don't know what the fuck you're talking about sometimes," he told Mac.

Mac sighed. "We already know what Tommy wants," he said. "All we have to do now is agree on a price."

FOURTEEN

Tony Broad had staked his claim at the bar. He was drinking hundred proof bourbon and running his fingers over the coarse bristles of his mustache. He was watching the stage, listening to Lee Charles sing "Tennessee Waltz." He was thinking of what it was going to be like to have the smell of Lee Charles on his fingers, to have her sweet juices on his mustache, to have those tits in his mouth and in his hands.

Tonight Tony was dressed in his best pinstripe and he was wearing his stick-pin with the imitation diamond and his gold-plated cufflinks. His mustache was clipped close and his thick hair Brylcreemed back. Best of all, he had that moron Nicky Wilson sitting in a hotel room somewhere, watching third-rate stag movies and polishing his cane, no doubt.

Tony had a handful of hundred-dollar bills in his wallet, with fifty or sixty singles stuffed in between. It looked like he was carrying ten grand. It was an old trick, but then they were the tricks Tony knew.

And he had one of his famous movie contracts tucked away in his jacket. He was prepared tonight, was Tony Broad, and he took another hit of bourbon and listened as Lee Charles finished the song.

"Thank you," Lee said from the stage when the audience had responded. "That was "Tennessee Waltz" — song made famous by the renowned singer — um, Satchel Page."

Doc said behind her, "*Patti* Page. It was Patti Page sang 'Tennessee Waltz.'"

Lee turned. "You sure about that, Doc? What'd Satchel Page sing?"

Doc smiled. "'Take Me Out To the Ballgame' maybe?"

"Naw, that wasn't it," Lee said. "We better take a break and find out. We'll ask Mel Dunston, the man knows his music."

She came down off the stage and walked to the bar, where Tony Broad was standing. As usual, the Callahan kid was with Tony, but tonight he was hanging back a little farther than usual. A fringe player if she ever saw one, Lee thought. She pushed back her hair and said hello to Tony Broad.

"I got your note," she said. "Thought it was a song request at first. What's up?"

"Let me buy you a drink. Lee."

"Sure. Rum and coke, we'll drink a toast to Castro."

"Who?"

Lee shook her head and smiled. "Don't you read the papers?"

When Tony Broad paid for the drinks he left his billfold open on the bar long enough for Lee to see, then he carelessly put it away.

"I was talking to Mel Dunston," he said, handing her the *libre*. "He said the gig's going good here."

"Mel actually admitted making money?" Lee asked. "Gotta be a blue moon."

"He kinda let on that he was breaking even anyway," Tony said. "What've you got — three more weeks?"

"Depends," Lee said. "Maybe more."

"You figuring on staying longer?"

Lee sipped at the cheap bar rum. "It hasn't been offered. I'd have to think it over if it was. I mean, we're having a good time, but I don't know if I want to take my pension here."

Tony adjusted his stick-pin, that gorgeous rhinestone. "What else you got in mind?"

"Nothing."

Tony was actually getting nervous, the skin at his hairline was moist, and his pulse was racing. He took a drink of bourbon.

"Ever think about getting back into acting?"

"I just got out of it," Lee said. "And I think I know where this conversation's heading."

Tony had a look that he liked to think was sincere and he tried it on Lee. "Oh no," he said. "It's not what you think. I have this property."

"Yeah?" Lee said. "How many acres?"

Tony smiled. "Seriously, Lee, I'm moving away from the other stuff. This movie is experimental, there's nothing like it out in Hollywood."

Lee drank some rum and turned her back against the bar to look at the people sitting and eating. The joint was putting out truck-loads of food, ignorant slobs with their mouths full applauding and telling Lee what a wonderful talent she was. Thank you, ma'am, just don't be spitting those peas at me, if you don't mind.

"You telling me there won't be any screwing in this movie?"

"God, but you're the bluntest woman I ever met."

"What do you want me to say — lovemaking?" Lee laughed. "Tell me, Mr. Movie Director, is there any lovemaking in this movie of yours?"

"Only if it falls into the context of the story."

"Holy smokes," Lee laughed. "You really are in the movie business. Nobody else could come up with a line of shit like that."

"Listen to me, Lee —"

"Hey, I'm sorry, Tony, but I think you got the wrong woman here. I'm not passing judgment, you understand, it's just that I don't think I'd be very good at this kind of . . . artistic endeavour." She laughed again, then apologized for it.

"There are girls from my films who have gone on to be very big in Hollywood," Tony told her.

"Name one."

"I can't do that. Most of 'em have changed their names, and they wouldn't appreciate me offering this kind of info around. After all, I'm a professional too."

"Really? You belong to the director's guild, Tony?"

"Sure."

"Where's your card?"

"Back at the hotel. I don't carry it with me as a rule."

"Why? Is it heavy?"

Tony was getting pounded and he knew it. He managed a smile. "You're one fast dame," he said.

Lee finished her drink.

"Listen," Tony said quickly. "You can pick up some real easy money doing this. I know what you're making here a week, I could give you twenty times that for one night's work."

"I just broke a contract, Tony."

He was pressing and he caught himself. He fell back and leaned casually on the bar, his pudgy hand curled around his bourbon.

"It'll be a couple weeks before we hold auditions," he said. "Take some time and think it over."

"You hold auditions?" Lee asked. "What do you do — rent a church basement?"

"You're a pistol," Tony Broad told her.

"No, my daddy was a pistol," Lee said. "I'm a son of a gun." And she went back to work.

When she was gone Billy Callahan moved closer; he'd been told to keep his distance while Tony talked to Lee Charles. Now he put his empty glass on the bar, a hint for Tony Broad, and moved in to lean against the railing there. He had the .44 stuck in the side waistband of his pants — out of sight but not out of mind, at least not where Billy Callahan was concerned. Since picking the pistol from the greasy linoleum of the diner he'd become a different man. He was nobody to fuck with anymore and he was looking forward to the day when people would find that out.

"So what's Miss Hollywood got to say for herself?" he asked now.

Tony had a drink. "We're negotiating," he said. "The lady wants to think it over."

"That what she said?"

"Did you ever see lips like that, Billy?" Tony asked. "A man could make a movie of those lips and nothing else. That mouth is a masterpiece on its own."

"Aw, you just want to fuck her like everybody else," Callahan said. "We gonna have another drink or not?"

Tony waved to Lucky Ned then turned back to the stage.

"Yeah, but I'm not like everybody else, because I'm gonna get her. What you have to learn, Billy my boy, is that everybody in the world has got something they want. All you have to do is find out what that something is, and you own that person. They'll do anything you want. Anything."

Callahan dunked the ice in his newly arrived drink. "What do you figure Lee Charles wants?"

"I don't know yet," Tony Broad said. "But there's something she's not telling. She's got a smart mouth, and she acts like she don't give a shit, but she's hiding something."

"Maybe not."

Tony looked at Callahan. "If there's one thing I know, it's people. Everybody's got something eatin' them."

"What's eatin' you, Tony?"

"Right now?" Tony took a drink of bourbon and smiled at the stage. "Lee Charles."

For a man who liked to brag that he never took no for an answer, the truth for Tony Broad was far from that. Growing up in Cleveland during the thirties, he heard the word every day. His father was an out of work railroad man, a mean drunk with no money to drink who took to imbibing wood alcohol, aftershave lotion — even melted-down 78 records when the need grew strong enough. Tony was the oldest of eight kids and when he was thirteen, his father killed his mother in a drunken fit, clubbing her to death with an axe handle. When the old man went to prison the kids were put into a home; Tony lasted maybe a month and then left forever. He hadn't seen his brothers or sisters since. He hadn't seen his father either, couldn't remember what the old man looked like.

Tony became a small-time hustler, but not a good one; a petty thief who lacked nerve; a runner for bookies, pimps, and operators who needed a bum boy. Then one day he and Mike Boston hit a small studio in Philadelphia and made off with fifteen thousand dollars' worth of film equipment, and Tony Broad became a movie maker.

It had been Mike Boston's idea to make stag movies. He'd seen enough of the flicks to know that there wasn't much skill and even less imagination involved. For women, they hired prostitutes and for men, whatever hard-luck kid or wise guy they could find in whatever city they were in.

One day Tony got lucky and connected with a man in Newark who offered to buy copies of whatever Tony and Mike Boston turned out. The man called himself Mr. Jones and he had a network of buyers all over North America. He was crying for new material and he didn't give a shit about quality.

So Tony moved into what he considered the big time. He began to stay away from the whores, who were always a problem, and started to cast his films, as he called them, from the legions of would-be actresses, singers and models he found in every city. They were all either on their way up, looking for a break or heading back down and looking for a buck. Whatever their direction, Tony had a line for them; he had cards printed up, with his name and a Beverly Hills address, and he dressed well and groomed himself carefully. Sometimes he snuck out of hotels in the dead of night, but it didn't cost a nickel to keep the mustache trimmed.

Mike Boston had what little imagination there was in the partnership and he always took charge of the actual shooting. One night in Cleveland — Tony's return home — Mike was filming an eighteen-year-old who wanted to be Ava Gardner, in bed with Bobby Dean, the washed-out actor and singer who'd lost his voice to whiskey and was doing stags to make enough money to stay permanently drunk, when the girl's father crashed into the hotel room. Mike Boston took a .38 slug in the forehead, and Bobby Dean would have received the same had he not jumped out of the second-storey window into the alley below where, like a typical drunkard, he landed unhurt.

Tony Broad left his buddy to a county funeral and headed out of town, this time for good. After that he put on the director's hat himself, but before he did he always made sure he had a punk like Billy Callahan on hand to watch his back. And if he had any eighteen-year-old girls around, he preferred that they be orphans.

Lately Tony Broad had been dreaming about going to Hollywood. He didn't have any illusions about his talent as a film-maker but from what he saw when he himself went to the movies he doubted that would be a problem. What he wanted, as usual, was something to back him up, something that would get him respect and allow him to walk in the front door. Maybe, just maybe, that something was Lee Charles.

When the woman in question finished her second set Tony tried to get her to join him at the bar again. He wasn't about to bring up the other matter. He would let it simmer awhile, get to know her better. He would find out what it was that Lee Charles wanted.

But she walked past him, shaking her head.

"Have another drink," Tony Broad said.

"How ya doing, kid?" Lee said to Billy Callahan, but Callahan in his surprise couldn't manage an answer.

"I believe I'll have a beer backstage with the band," Lee told Tony Broad.

"Why don't we have a drink and forget about the other business?" Tony suggested. "We're friends, I shouldn't have brought it up."

He had his hand lightly on her elbow, beseeching her to stay.

"It's forgotten," Lee said. "But I'm going back to have a beer with the guys."

"Is there a problem here?"

Tony knew the voice. He figured he had that voice locked away in a room with a projector and some sweaty palms. Tony fixed his smile, tied it on with baling wire and then turned to look at Nicky Wilson, who was presently looking at Tony's hand on Lee Charles' elbow.

"I said is there a problem?" Nicky asked again.

Tony had the presence of mind to release Lee's arm. He gave Callahan a quick look.

"We were just gonna have a drink here, Nick. You want to join us?"

Tony was aware that Lee Charles was amused and it pissed him off.

"I'll buy the lady a drink," Nicky said.

"I'm going for a beer," Lee told them both. "Catch you Romeos later."

"We on for tonight?" Nick asked.

She looked at him a moment. "Depends. Where we going?"

Nicky had put himself between Lee and Tony Broad now. He stood there with his legs spread and his thumbs in his belt loops. Tony Broad wished the son of a bitch was dead, wished that Callahan would pull the .44 right now and destroy that smirking blond face forever.

"I know a place, Solly's, where we can go eat," the kid was telling Lee. "It's an all-night joint. Then maybe we'll go for a drive." He smiled. "Unless you got something else in mind."

Lee saw the dark expression of Tony Broad and thought, oh shit, not another one.

"Maybe we'll go for a bite to eat," she said to Nicky. "Okay?"

"Okay."

Lee went backstage, and Nicky tried to get Lucky Ned's attention.

"I thought you were watching movies," Tony said.

"I already watched 'em," the Wilson kid said. He smiled in the direction Lee had taken. "Maybe I'll watch 'em again later, you know what I mean?"

Backstage Lee took a beer from Bugs and sat down beside Doc. She was wearing heels and she slipped them off and propped her feet in Doc's lap.

"Let's do one sitting down, boys," she suggested. "You got no idea what it's like in these pumps."

"Shoulda been a piano player, girl," Teddy told her. "Get to sit all night long." He winked at Doc. "Of course, you don't get the spotlight, all that glory."

"Oh yeah, I just live for the glory," Lee said.

"All those sharp-dressed cats waiting for you at the bar."

"Right, I'm the luckiest girl in the world." She lifted Doc's tie with her foot. "What're we smoking tonight, Bugs?"

"Fresh out," Bugs told her. "The city is dry, for some reason. Reefer madness, know what I mean? Since when did you want to blow anyway?"

"I figured maybe just tonight," Lee said. "Got a date with Nick Wilson later and I thought a little boo might loosen me up. I been kinda out of this scene, feel like a schoolgirl."

"No dates out in Hollywood, Lee?" Teddy asked.

"I kept waiting for Cary Grant to call."

"This Wilson cat is the fighter, isn't he?" Bugs asked.

"Yeah."

"He beat up a pal of mine in the Rooster one night," Bugs said. "Never had a reason for doin' it either."

"Never liked a boxer who fought outside the ring," Doc said. "Don't show no class. You be careful of this dude, Lee."

"Don't you worry about me, Doc," Lee told him. "I been out in all kinds of weather. If I can't handle a kid like this, I'd better hang 'em up."

"You be careful," Doc said again.

"Yes, father."

"We need a name tonight, Lee," Bugs said then. "You're slipping, girl."

"God, I don't know," Lee said. "I'm running out of lies to tell. So much for my dream of becoming a politician."

"Oh, you history, child," Doc said. "And we gonna be history too, we don't get back out there. Five'll get you ten Mel's sitting in his office with a stopwatch on us."

Lee wasn't looking forward to the last set being over, so naturally it flew by. She deliberately kept it uptempo, starting with "All of Me" and swinging into "Ain't Nobody's Business If I Do," trying to be goofy and loose in between, pushing the sexy stuff aside.

At the bar Nicky Wilson stood with a horny Elvis sneer and watched her happily. Beside him Tony Broad had pulled it in a little, in deference to Nicky, but he was still there with his own threadbare ambitions, his own little schemes. And then there was Callahan, the wild-eyed skittish one — God only knew what was going on in his muddled head. If there was a wild card in the deck, he was it.

"What a crowd, what a crowd," Lee said to Doc between songs.

"They here for you, child."

"You make 'em sound like the men in the white suits with the butterfly nets, Doc."

Doc grinned around his mouthpiece and nodded his head. Lee made a pistol with her hand and shot him dead, then turned to the mike.

"We got one more," she said. "Gonna do a political song. It's about this grasshopper, see, and — well, never mind, you'll get the picture. Oh, by the way, I'm Satchel Page and this is the Blue Parrot Country and Western Revue Band."

"Yippy-i-ay," Bugs said and Lee began to sing —

There's a grasshopper sitting on a
*   railroad track,*
Singin' polly-wolly doodle all the
*   day,*
Pickin' his teeth with a carpet tack,
Singin' polly-wolly doodle all the
*   day —*

"What the hell is that?" asked Tony Broad at the bar.

"Who cares?" Nicky said.

Lee and the band really stretched it out then, kicked the famed grasshopper all over the stage, bringing it down and starting it up again, Doc coming in at the end with a solo on the tenor sax, the sweat pouring from his forehead, eyes tight, cheeks blown out full. Lee brought it down at last in a Louis Armstrong growl and just let it lie.

She was ready to step down when she saw him. He was standing in the half-light at the far corner of the bar, behind Nicky Wilson and Tony Broad and the Callahan kid. He must have come in during the last song, slipping unnoticed back into her life, back into a world that had been only half there since he'd left.

She nearly lost her balance when she saw him, but even in this she was cat quick, and she forced herself to look away. She called to the band, who were heading off, and then walked back to the mike.

"Maybe we'll do one more," she said. Doc and Teddy looked at one another, then shrugged and went back to their instruments. Bugs was still standing by his bass — for the first time in a month he was out of tea and he didn't quite know what was going on.

"This is a Billie Holiday song," Lee said into the mike. She hesitated. "And I . . . haven't sung it for a long time, so you'll have to hang in with me. It's called 'My Man.'"

She looked at the band a moment and then turned back to the mike again. "I don't know if I remember all the words," she said. "But I remember what it's about."

Back in the lights now, she couldn't see him as she began to sing. They'd never rehearsed this one, but the guys fell right in, following her when she led and pulling her through when she slipped up. Lee knew they'd be okay — Doc had even played some sessions with Billie back in the forties.

> *— just want to dream of a cottage by*
> *a stream,*
> *with my man,*
> *where a few flowers grew*
> *and perhaps a kid or two,*
> *with my man*

She kept her eyes on that corner of the room, where he was just a shadow now, as she sang. What if he wasn't there, what if she'd invented him because she wanted him to be there?

But no — he was there — she could feel him in the room. And not only was he there, he was the only one who was.

> *— oh, my man, I love him so,*
> *he'll never know,*
> *All my life is just despair,*
> *But I don't care*
> *When he takes me in his arms,*
> *The world is bright, all right —*

At the bar, Nicky Wilson was cocksure she was singing to him and he was puffed up like a heavyweight peacock just thinking about it, standing there elbows on the bar, thumbs tucked in his pockets. Beside him, Tony Broad had saturated his brain with enough bourbon by now that he dared to consider the possibility that she was singing to *him*. Nicky elbowed him in the ribs and showed him wolf's teeth beneath the inconsistent eyes.

"You know what this song is about, don't you?" he laughed. "She ain't singing about grasshoppers now."

Lee made it through the song, remembering all the words or at least all the words worth remembering this night. The song faded out on instrumental; she set the mike aside while the band was still playing and walked off the stage and across the room. Nicky Wilson straightened from where he'd been slouched at the bar.

"Sorry, kid," Lee said and she passed him by without a glance.

He was standing there without a drink along that last bit of bar. End of the line, she thought, where else would she find him? He was wearing a dark suit, his tie loosely knotted, sandy hair mussed as always (was that grey in the hair?), big hands hanging at his sides awkwardly — like the only place he ever knew what to do with them was inside a ring — and it seemed he was barely breathing, his eyes on her as soft as she remembered his touch.

She stopped in front of him, almost as tall as him in her pumps, knowing full well that everybody in the joint was watching her and not giving one thin damn.

She could only stand there a moment though, and then she had to touch him; she put her arms around his neck and her cheek next to his, just to feel him after all this time, to smell of him after these years. And then he put those hams of his around her, and they stayed like that, not saying anything, for maybe a minute. And Lee thought she would cry, but she knew she wouldn't because he would say it was sentimental nonsense, even though he was the sentimental one, not her.

Finally she put her lips against his neck and then on his mouth and she stepped back to look at him again.

"Oh, you goddamn mick," she said. "Where you been?"

FIFTEEN

He was awake before she was — like always — and he rolled on his side and lay for a moment in the scant light that showed beneath the blind and he watched her face as she slept. If it was possible, she was even more beautiful asleep than awake; in sleep she dropped her guard, there was nothing in her face of the fast tongue or razor wit she used to keep the world away. Her dark red hair was tangled on the pillow beneath her head, falling across one shoulder to reach her nipple. Tommy leaned over to put his mouth there for a second, but pulled away before she woke.

He got out of bed and put on his pants and went barefoot down the hallway to the communal bathroom, watching out for the landlady along the way. He'd been advised his presence in the rooming house was not welcome. Well, if the old girl hadn't heard them last night, she was either deaf or legally dead.

He took a leak and washed his hands and face and then went back to her room. She was awake and watching as he stepped out of his pants and got back into bed.

"Hey," he said.

"Sweet Jesus," she said. "I got drunk and brought home another stranger."

"Hey, think how bad I feel."

She pulled his face to hers and bit his lip lightly. "Where you been?"

"Oh, having a look around."

"You do like to ramble. You see anybody in the hall?"

"Not a soul, ma'am."

"I'd hate like hell to get thrown out of such a luxury joint, lose my standing in the community and all."

Tommy smiled and rolled onto his back, pulling the sheet with him. Lee moved beside him, hooking her leg over his.

"I was thinking that maybe you'd quit your rambling ways by now."

"I been kinda thinking that way myself lately."

"Yeah?"

"Yeah, little bit."

She pulled back from him then, looked in his eyes.

"Hey, you know that kid Nicky Wilson?" she said. "I was supposed to have a date with him last night."

Tommy shrugged.

"I wanted you to know," Lee said.

"Okay."

"He's supposed to be some hot-shot heavyweight. You heard of him?"

"Not 'til I got back in the city," Tommy said. "But then I never read a newspaper or even listened to the radio for six months. Bought a DeSoto in Albany a few months back, never turned the radio on once. T-Bone'd sing to me while I drove."

"T-Bone's with you?"

"Yeah, we got a room at the Jasper."

"You didn't tell me that last night."

"Last night I had my mind on other things."

"More than your mind." She reached for him.

"Mac Brady's been trying to get me in the ring with this Wilson. They're after my ranking and they know I'm trying to raise some cash."

He had told her about the farm the night before. "So what are you going to do?" she asked.

"I can't fight, Lee. It's over."

She put the backs of her fingers on his cheek. "You need a shave, mick. I'll get some water and a razor and fix you up."

"Now?"

"Maybe later," she smiled. She ran her palm down over his chest; she found that even after all this time she couldn't keep her hands off him. "Listen, I'd give you the money if I had it, but I don't. I broke my contract out west and I left there with a couple hundred bucks."

"I'm not after your money, ma'am."

"Oh, yeah?"

"Maybe your ass, but not your assets."

"Well, maybe we can work something out," she said. She looked at him in the half-light. "What're you going to do?"

"It's probably gonna come down to some one-shot gamble. If I win, I win, and if I don't, then the farm is gone. Don't be feeling sorry for me, I should have taken better care of my money back in the good days."

"I was hoping these were the good days."

"They're getting better," Tommy said. "You know, T-Bone's been sparring with this Wilson; he'd never say, but I know he's tucking his money away for the farm. Bones has got this picture in his head of us living the good life up there, raising chickens and beef cattle, maybe a couple horses, living better than a couple old palookas like us have any right to."

"You telling me you don't have that same picture?"

"I guess maybe I do," he admitted shortly. "But I know it's only a picture and that's maybe all it's ever gonna be."

She put her hands on his chest suddenly then, and moved to straddle him, allowing the sheet to fall from her shoulders. Naked, she looked down into the grey eyes she thought she might never see again.

"I think you should be a farmer," she said. "I can see that."

He slid his hands over her flat stomach, felt her ribs beneath his touch, moved his hands so that the weight of her breasts rested in his palms. Keeping her eyes on his, she moved her hand down. She was still wet from the night before and she shifted herself upward and then lowered herself onto him. She smiled and closed her eyes as he entered her — sweet memories of the best days of her life — and then she looked down at him again.

"Where the hell you been, mick?"

T-Bone Pike was standing in the centre of the hotel room and he had his hands on his hips and he was fixing his grandmother's admonishing eye on Thomas Cochrane.

"Least a body can do is send some sort o' message," he said again.

"Western Union?"

"The telephone or such."

"We got no telephone here, Bones. How can I phone you with no phone?"

"Out all night," T-Bone exclaimed. "Got me so worried I don't sleep. How I know you not in some alley with a knife in your thick head? Lawdy, I never see anything like it."

"You knew where I was, Bones. You sent me there."

"I don't know no such thing. All I ask is for a little respect, so I can sleep at night." He moved to sit on the bed. "How is Lee Charles these days anyhow?"

"She's all right. She was asking about you."

"She remember T-Bone?"

"Sure she remembers you. We're going to meet her for a beer this afternoon. Unless you figure you're too upset to go for a beer with Lee Charles."

"I go for a beer with that woman any day. You the huckleberry I upset with. I don't know what a beautiful woman like that ever see in a huckleberry like you anyhow. I swear."

"Me either. Come on, Bones, we'll walk downtown, it's a nice day for it."

"Well, listen to Thomas Cochrane, talkin' 'bout what a nice day we havin'. You in a awful damn good mood."

"Maybe I am."

"Wonder why that could be."

"Let's go, Bones," Tommy said. "Where's your shoes?"

"Right here 'neath the bed." T-Bone reached for his shoes, then looked up. "Thomas?"

"Yeah."

"Never mind."

They walked together, down Parliament, then west on Queen, T-Bone Pike striding scarecrow loose, hands dangling at his sides, head bobbing, eyes avoiding contact with people he met, a habit gained from growing up coloured in the south.

In the cold light of day Tommy could see the bruised skin beneath T-Bone's right eye. And there was the cut on his lip from a couple of days earlier.

"Looks to me like you're getting beat up, Bones."

"Nothing that ain't happened before."

"Why don't you pack it in, tell Mac Brady you're not interested. No sense getting your brains rattled for that kid."

"Man's got to earn his way in this world, Thomas. That's a natural fact. Grandma Pike used to say idle hands be the devil's workshop. You wouldn't want old T-Bone in the workshop of the devil, would you?"

"I guess not. But Grandma Pike never had to dance with a punk like Nicky Wilson either."

T-Bone smiled. "The devil come in many disguises, Thomas."

When they got to the Rooster, Lee Charles was already there, sitting at a table with the blond kid in the felt hat. The kid was leaning close to Lee and, in spite of the kid's serious face, Lee was laughing.

"Do you use that line a lot?" she was asking.

"I've never said those words before," the kid assured her. "I've been waiting years to say them to you."

"I think," Lee said, "you should have held out a little longer."

She got to her feet when Tommy and T-Bone came in. She took T-Bone Pike's face in her hands and kissed him.

"Hello, Thibideau," she said. "God, it's good to see you."

"Thibideau?" Tommy asked.

"Thas right, Thibideau," T-Bone said. "Where you think T-Bone come from, you think I get my name from a piece of meat?"

Lee turned to the kid at the table. "This is Howard Coulter, gentlemen."

Howard was looking unhappily at Tommy. "How ya doing?" he said and he moved off. Lee shrugged, and the three of them sat down and ordered a pitcher of beer.

"How life treating you, Miss Lee?" T-Bone asked.

"Good enough, Thibideau. I see you haven't shook yourself clear of this mick yet."

"He need somebody to look out for him."

"He sure as hell does."

"I hear you singing down at some club, Miss Lee. You still sing that 'Stormy Weather'?"

"You come in and I'll sing it for you, Thibideau," she told him. "Like the old days."

So Tommy poured the beer, and they sat and talked a little about those old days, about songs sung and fights won and the good times in between. T-Bone was happy as a clam to be sitting with these two people and he got to thinking that maybe that arrowhead held a little luck after all.

When they had the second pitcher in front of them, the front door opened and Mac Brady rolled in, looking dapper in a grey serge suit and a black bowler hat. The bowler he tipped to Lee Charles.

"Whatcha doing, Mac — following me around now?" Tommy asked.

"Let's just say I'm a man who knows the whereabouts of all the important people in this town," Mac said.

"In that case, you got the wrong table," Lee told him.

"A familiar sight, the two of you," Mac said, inviting himself to sit down. "Gives a man a sense of déjà vu."

"What the hell is that?" Tommy asked.

But Mac just smiled and looked at T-Bone. "How are you, Mr. Pike?"

"I'm fine, Mr. Brady."

"You gonna have a beer with us, Mac?" Tommy asked.

"A beer would be nice," Mac said and he signalled to the waiter for another glass. "I can only stay a moment though, I'm out tying up loose ends this afternoon. That's what happens when you're chief cook and bottle washer too."

Tommy smiled. "You got some loose ends here in the Rooster, Mac?"

Mac grinned; he never could bullshit Tommy Cochrane. "No, I just stopped in for a cool drink."

"Well, you're welcome to it."

Mac drank and winked for no reason across the table to T-Bone. Then he turned to Lee. "What are you up to, Lee Charles?" he asked. "Are you going to finance this farm of Tommy's?"

Lee raised her eyebrows. "I beg your pardon?"

"You know, Mac," Tommy said, "every time you come close to being a nice guy, you ruin it by sticking your nose into things that are none of your damn business."

"Maybe your financial welfare is my business, Tommy. At least, it could be."

"I doubt it."

Mac took a drink. "Three thousand, Tommy. Now, that's a hell of a price and you know it to be true. You couldn't draw that kind

BRAD SMITH

of money anywhere else, and that includes New York and Miami. Maybe a year ago, but not now, Tommy."

"You're right, Mac."

"But you're turning it down," Mac said. "Look at you, you haven't got a pot to piss in — excuse my French, Lee — and yet you're saying no. Show some sense, man. You're looking a gift horse in the mouth."

"I'm not so sure which end of the horse I'm dealing with," Tommy said.

Lee looked over at Mac and smiled. But when Mac got to his feet, he didn't look particularly unhappy and she wondered why that would be.

"Smart talk like that won't buy you many farms, Tommy," Mac said. "You buy farms with money . . . and you don't have any."

Mac tipped his bowler and left. Tommy watched him go through the door, then he got up and said he was going to the gents'. He left Lee and T-Bone sitting there.

"That Mr. Brady a uncommon persistent man."

Lee was looking at the door just exited by Mac Brady. "He's used to getting what he wants." Then she glanced over at T-Bone. "He's going to keep upping the price until Tommy fights. You know that, don't you?"

"No, he can't fight, Miss Lee. The doctor tell him."

"What, Bones? What did the doctor tell him?"

"I'm not supposed to be talking on this, but I guess it all right being it's you, Miss Lee. He got somethin' in his head, Thomas, some sort of blood vessel or such, and if he get hit, it like to bust and kill Thomas. He ain't supposed to be doing no more fightin', Miss Lee, don't matter if it be this Wilson kid or nobody else."

"Jesus," Lee said. "He never said anything to me."

"He never say nothin' to nobody 'bout it. Only ways I know is one night Thomas have too much of the Old Bushmills and he get to talking 'bout all manner of things, you included too, Miss Lee."

154

Lee saw Tommy coming from the back of the room. She looked over at T-Bone.

"We both know what he's like," she said. "If he decides to fight, we're gonna have to stop him."

"Yes, ma'am. I been knowing that all along. Sayin' it is a easy thing though. Easier than doin'."

Tommy came back and sat down and had a drink of beer. Lee shook her head when he offered her another glass.

"That's it for me," she said. "I got work tonight, can't be showing up sloppy drunk."

"I should be moving along myself," Tommy said.

"You're at the Bamboo tonight?"

"Yeah."

"You coming by later?"

Tommy looked at her narrowly across the table. "Unless I get a better offer."

Lee got to her feet and kissed T-Bone again and then looked over at Tommy Cochrane.

"There *is* no better offer."

SIXTEEN

He turned the corner of the familiar street and saw the familiar decay and smelled the familiar odour — of stale beer, of laundry soap, of garbage rotting in alleys. There was a sweetness in the air too, though — cheap perfume from girls growing up too soon, cologne from the boys doing the same, the scent of flowers springing from boxes outside the windows of the old brick walk-ups.

Here and there the bricks had shaken loose and fallen from the building. The boys and girls who lived inside sometimes did the same. And it was the same and it was different to him as he strolled — tough-looking teenage boys giving him the eye, all of them dressed in black pants and white t-shirts, belt buckles fastened on the hip, this year's style down here. The girls in their tight skirts and pony-tails, red lipstick by the yard. In his day, they'd been bobbysoxers.

Cabbagetown.

The building was closed down, locked up tighter than a Scotsman's purse. He went around back, grabbed the fire ladder and pulled himself to the second floor. The screwdriver was (incredibly) still above the sill; he jimmied the window (like a thousand times before) and was inside in a heartbeat. He went down the wooden stairs and into the main room. Most everything was gone — moved away or reduced to dust. A heavy bag rested in the corner, its sides split, its insides spilled. There were a few mats, not worth hauling away, he guessed, and some filthy towels, not worth the laundering.

He had a thought and walked into the back room to the apartment. There was a light showing through the transom. He smiled as he knocked and walked in.

The apartment was not an apartment and never had been. It was one room, maybe ten by twelve, and it contained a cot, a chair, a radio and an icebox. The radio was on the icebox, Sinatra was on the radio, and Jimmy Mack was on the cot.

Jimmy's eyes widened and he jumped to a sitting position, putting aside the paperback novel he'd been reading. Recognition took a few seconds.

"Well, I'll be dipped in shellac," he said. "Tommy Cochrane come to call."

Tommy smiled and offered his hand. "How you doing, Jimmy? I didn't figure anybody was here anymore."

Jimmy had taken on the absurd body of a bone-thin man with a pot belly. His hands were liver-spotted and his face was creased like ten-ounce gloves left too long in the sun, but his hair, though white, was thick and full as a teenager's. There was an open mickey of rum on the floor.

"Jesus, it's good to see you, Tommy. Sit down, just move those newspapers, I been gonna throw 'em out."

Tommy sat and refused a drink from the rum. He watched as Jimmy drank and then capped the bottle.

"What the hell you doing here, Jimmy?"

"Why, I live here. Always have."

"You lived here when the gym was open. How long you been closed?"

Jimmy blinked at him. "You know, I got no idea. Been a while though, been quite a while."

"I'll say it has. Place smells worse than it ever did, and that's saying something. What the hell you doing here, Jimmy?"

"A man's got to be someplace," the old man said. "How 'bout you, I could ask you the same question. You out lookin' for ghosts?"

Tommy crossed his legs and ran his hand through his hair. "Maybe I am, Jimmy. I don't know, I just had a notion to stop by."

Jimmy Mack took another shot of rum. The paperback teetered, then fell off the bed onto the floor. Tommy saw it was *Hondo*, by Louis L'Amour. Tommy looked out the open door into the gym.

"I sure spent some time here, Jimmy. I can remember when this place felt like home."

"You were awful damn green, those days. Your first week here, I figured you'd break your neck tryin' to skip rope, and that'd be the end of you. Used to wonder what I'd tell the cops when they came to pick up the body."

Tommy smiled, still looking out the door.

"What'd you do, come up the fire escape?" Jimmy asked.

Tommy nodded over the smile. "Old dogs remember old tricks, Jimmy. Used to be half the neighbourhood went in and out that window."

"No more. Them days are done. Now I don't see nobody; the owner pays me fifty a month to keep the place up, that's all."

Tommy surveyed the disaster that was the gym. "You're overpaid, Jimmy."

The old man snorted into the mickey. "Where's Gus these days?"

"Gus is in New York. He's got a gym there, little hole in the wall, but he's doing all right. Gus is one in a million."

"He did all right by you, for sure. Him and Karl Krone, too."

Tommy turned quickly in his chair. "Krone was a thief, don't pretend otherwise."

"He was my friend. Don't you talk like that about my friend."

"Your friend was a son of a bitch. He cheated every kid he ever handled. If he was all right with you, it was because you never had a nickel for him to steal, don't you understand that?"

Jimmy got clumsily to his feet. "I'll punch you right in the god-damn nose!"

He took a step and threw a weak right hand, missed Tommy by three feet and fell forward. Tommy grabbed him before he split his head on the icebox. He sat Jimmy back on the bed and handed him the rum. The old man began to cry.

"It's all right, Jimmy. Jesus, I know he was your friend. I didn't mean anything by it."

"Nobody gives a shit about me," Jimmy cried.

"Sure they do."

"Bullshit! Nobody ever comes around anymore. I used to be somebody here, I used to be in charge."

Tommy picked up the paperback and looked at the buckskinned figure on the cover.

"I guess maybe you're right, Jimmy. I don't know why people just throw the past away like yesterday's papers, but they do. I guess everybody just figures that the future looks a little better."

Jimmy looked up. "I got no future, Tommy. I got nothing."

Tommy looked at the runny eyes and the shaking hands and he couldn't think of a thing to say to the old man. After a time he just got up and said goodbye.

Herm spent the morning at the track, watching the grooms work the mounts for the afternoon's card. He hung around all morning, drinking coffee and shooting the breeze with people he knew, train-ers and grooms and jockeys. To Herm it was one of life's pleasures to sit back in the morning sun, cup of joe in his hand, the smell of manure in his nostrils (he loved the smell of horseshit — to his gam-bler's nose it was Chanel No. 5), and the knowledge that the lady was with him even yet; she was by his side, whispering in his ear, worshipping his every move.

Herm's old man had been a groom at this track, and others, and although Frank Bell had never said as much to his son, Herm was certain that his father had loved the smell of horseshit too. He'd ridden some great horses, Frank Bell had, and he used to come home and tell of this horse or that, and of how he knew when a horse was ready to run. He'd even sat on Man o' War, took the stallion for a fast mile one day back when both horse and man were young and full of piss and vinegar. That the horse fulfilled its promise more than the man was of no great surprise — people remembered horses, they remembered jockeys, they even remembered trainers — but nobody knew a groom from one year to the next. There was Man o' War and Citation and Hard Tack and Meade, but for every one of those there were countless guys who had no names, who got up at four in the morning to brush coats and clean stalls and dig out hooves. Guys like Frank Bell, who was too big to be a jockey and too much in love with the track to walk away and be something else.

Yeah, guys like Frank Bell, who loved horses and the track so much he drew his last breath in a horse stall, settling down one day in some clean straw, pitchfork still in his hand, with a heart that stopped beating, maybe because it had been broken so many times in the very place where Frank Bell finally laid his body down.

Because of that Herm never got close to the horses like his father; although he loved them from a kid, he loved them from afar. And when they broke his heart, it hurt only for a little while, because to Herm they were like streetcars and women — there would be another one coming along directly. And another after that.

So this morning he sat in the sun and talked with the people he knew — people like his father — and he was happy because the thoroughbreds brought him nothing but joy, and if he never had another winner the rest of his life, it didn't matter, because just the notion that he *might* have a winner tomorrow was enough to make him content.

When he left the track he went to Lem's for lunch, sat himself in a corner booth with the day's *Telly* and ordered a toasted western sandwich with a side order of fries and a cherry coke.

As he was eating Danny Bonner came in and joined him. It was Wednesday, and Danny was there for the chili. He was wearing a white sports coat and a pink shirt and a fucked-up tie that looked about a foot wide and had a picture of a Buick on it.

"Where you been — Hollywood?" Herm asked.

"The threads?" Danny asked. "You wouldn't believe the price on these duds. You might as well say I stole 'em."

"I'd say there was definitely a crime involved."

"I've been upgrading my wardrobe a little," Danny said. "I was reading in *Reader's Digest* where it says that clothes make the man, that it was like a statement, or something like that."

"You're making a hell of a statement, kid. Don't spill any chili on that Buick, you'll have to take it down to the carwash and get it cleaned."

"Very funny, Herm. You playing at Ollie's tonight?"

"Yeah. How about you?"

"I'll be there. Told the girlfriend I'd be tied up tonight. A fellow's got to have his night out with the boys, right?"

"I didn't know you had a girl, Danny."

"Sure, I've been pretty steady with Sheila Mosconi for a month or more now. She thinks I'm the cat's ass, wait'll she sees these threads, she'll fall over."

"She'll swoon, all right."

A month or more, Danny had said. And three nights earlier Herm and Sheila had fucked each other silly in an eight-dollar room at the Duke Hotel. She had called his place just that morning, Herm's mother had given him the message.

"So you two are hitting it off?"

"Pretty good," Danny said. "We haven't hit the sheets yet, you have to take it slow with certain girls. She's a Catholic, you know how it is. She told me she knows who you are. You know her?"

"A little."

"We should double some night. I'm thinking about buying a car, maybe a Caddy."

He saw Herm's eyes rise and he turned to see Tony Broad and Billy Callahan walking through the diner. They were dressed the both of them like movie gangsters and Callahan was walking with the same swagger he'd shown in Sully's pool hall. Herm had caught a rumour that the kid was carrying a rod, although Herm couldn't figure out why. Now he saw that the two planned to join him and Danny in the booth.

"Move over, you mugs," Callahan said.

"Who we got here — the gang from Ollie's?" Tony Broad asked. He removed his coat and sat down. "You guys going steady? What do you say you spring for lunch, Bell? You been taking all our money lately."

"You want a free meal, go to the Sally Ann."

"Touchy, touchy," Tony said. "How's the chili, kid?" This to Danny Bonner.

When Danny started on about the chili, Herm turned to look at Callahan beside him. And Callahan showed his bad teeth and reached over to take a cold french fry from Herm's plate.

"You don't mind if I help myself? You owe me after that stunt you pulled at Sully's."

"Go ahead," Herm said. "They were going out in the alley to the dogs anyway."

The two men ordered the special, and then Danny Bonner went after Tony about the movie business. Herm wasn't too interested — he figured Tony Broad was to the movie business what Danny Bonner was to the world of fashion. But Danny was hot to hear about it.

"How often do you make 'em?" he wanted to know.

Tony Broad shrugged and lit his cigar. Danny was a dumb kid, but more to the point, he was a dumb kid who had nothing to offer Tony Broad. Danny, of course, didn't know he was being snubbed.

"You gonna make one in Toronto?"

"We're gonna make one with Lee Charles, what do you think about that?" Callahan said to Danny.

Herm saw that Tony Broad was pissed off at Callahan for the remark. So when Tony tried to change the subject, Herm stayed with it.

"Lee Charles the singer?" He was looking at Callahan. "You're gonna make a movie with Lee Charles?"

"We don't discuss the film business with the local jokers down at the diner," Tony said. "We might be making a film in Toronto and we might not. Nobody said anything about Lee Charles."

"He did," Herm said, indicating Callahan.

"I didn't hear him." Tony looked at Danny Bonner. "Did you hear him say anything about Lee Charles?"

"Who the hell is Lee Charles?"

"Ha, now that's a good question," Tony said. "She's just some torch singer, they're a dime a dozen where I come from."

"I hear she's Nicky Wilson's girl," Herm said.

"She's got a funny way of showing it then," Tony said. "Last night she stood Wilson up and walked out of the Blue Parrot with Tommy Cochrane."

"No shit?" Herm said. "Good for Tommy."

"I'll lay you odds there's nothing to it," Tony said. "Cochrane's a bum, he probably owes her money."

"Fucking Wilson went nuts," Callahan said. "He wanted to kill Cochrane, said when he got him in the ring he was going to put him in the hospital for a year."

"I wouldn't want to tangle with Nick Wilson," Danny said.

"He's not going to get Tommy in the ring," Herm said.

"Then he'll get him out of the ring," Callahan said. "I don't give a shit either way — they're both a coupla creeps to me."

"You wouldn't tell them that," Danny said.

"I'd tell 'em anything I fucking please," Callahan said. "I grew up on the streets, these guys with their padded gloves don't scare me none."

"You," Tony Broad said to Herm. "How come you know what Tommy Cochrane's going to do? You his big pal all of a sudden?"

"Sure," Herm said. "You can understand that — you being so tight with Floyd Patterson and all." He pushed Callahan aside then and stepped out of the booth; when he did he felt the pistol under Callahan's jacket.

"See you gents around," Herm said. "Watch you don't shoot your dick off with that thing, Callahan."

On his way out of the diner Herm called Sheila Mosconi from the pay phone and told her he wouldn't be seeing her anymore. No reason, he said when she asked why, it was just that he wouldn't be seeing her anymore.

He was having a beer in the Bamboo when Tommy Cochrane came in for work that night. Tommy stopped to talk to Buzz Murdock for a few minutes, then made his way over to the bar.

"Got a nag for you," Herm said.

Tommy asked for a glass of water from the bartender.

"I was down to the track this morning," Herm said then. "There's a four-year-old named Bobby Pin in the seventh on Saturday. He's just up from the States and he's ready to run, so I hear. They figure maybe ten to one, give or take a point."

"Bobby Pin." Tommy tried the name on his tongue, as if that would tell him something about the horse.

"There's a couple others this week," Herm said. "But not at the kind of odds you're looking for. Maybe two to one, something like that, but not what you need, not for a one-time score."

"You figure he's ready?" Tommy asked.

"One of the trainers, friend of my old man's, practically guaranteed me this horse will run in the money. But then, place or show won't give you what you need."

"I have to go for the win," Tommy agreed.

He pulled his billfold from his coat pocket and counted what was there. A hundred and seventy and some change. Buzz owed him fifty, and fifty more by Saturday. T-Bone was making fifteen a day and living like a monk; he'd have something salted away. But still he was going to be short.

"When's the game at Ollie's?" Tommy asked.

"Tonight."

"Can I get in?"

"I don't see why not. The fat man speaks highly of you."

Tommy pushed the water away and asked the bartender for a beer for himself and one for Herm. For the first time the chance that he could raise the money — however slight — had appeared and he was nervous even thinking about it. Sometimes it was easier to want things than to have them.

"Who's at this game?"

Herm shrugged. "It changes from week to week. Ollie, of course, and Mac Brady, once in a while. A kid named Danny Bonner, good kid."

"I met him."

"That's right, you did. Who else? Myself. Some slime, calls himself Tony Broad and his pal, a punk named Callahan. Tony Broad makes stag movies, at least that's what he says. A one-eyed jack for sure. He probably doesn't play a square game, but I doubt he's got the moxy to cheat at Ollie's."

"Can I make a hundred?"

"You get the cards, you can make a hundred. Or you can lose two hundred."

"Well, life's a long shot, that's where the fun is," Tommy said. "You know who told me that?"

"No."

"You did."

"I did?" Herm laughed. "Well, what do you know — I'm a goddamned philosopher."

———————

Tommy worked until eleven, drew the fifty that Buzz owed him on wages, and then walked the six blocks to the Blue Parrot.

When he walked in the front door, Lee was onstage. She made a face at him and went on singing "Anything Goes." Tommy went to the bar for a shot. Nicky Wilson was standing there alone and he mouthed the word "coward" at Tommy, and Tommy laughed in his face and walked on by. He ordered Irish and then looked down the bar and laughed at Wilson again. The kid was so mad he could barely stand still.

It was a trick Tommy had learned from Gus Washbone years ago. You can love a man or hate a man, and he'll take it in stride, but the one thing that a man can not tolerate is being laughed at. It makes him feel inferior and left out and it just plain pisses him off.

Lee came to the bar when the song was finished. Tommy called to Lucky Ned, but she waved the bartender away. "I'll sip at yours," she said.

"Yeah, drink my liquor. Spend my money."

"Jump your bones," she said and she kissed him quickly, her mouth smelling of the Jameson's and of her.

"I won't be around when you get done," Tommy said. "There's a card game at Ollie Newton's, I'm gonna try to raise a little cash."

He told her about the tip from Herm Bell.

About a horse named Bobby Pin.

"Jesus," Lee said when she'd heard. "It's awful flimsy."

"Flimsy ain't the word for it. But it's all I got. I can either sit by and watch the farm slide away or I can take a flyer and hope to get lucky. I'm a little overdue in the luck department, but I feel like maybe it's changing."

"Why's that?"

Tommy shrugged. "No reason."

"Come on, mick," she said. "Tell me why."

"Well —" he said. "Because two days ago I didn't know where you were and today I do."

She kissed him again, this time on his ear, her teeth sharp against his lobe. "I declare, you old country boys can be real charmers . . . when you're forced into it," she said. "I believe you're turning my head."

"Have a drink, Lee," she heard and when she turned, Nicky Wilson was standing there with a gin and a grin.

"No thanks."

"I got your usual," Nicky said. "Whatsa matter?"

"No thanks." She could see now the kid was drunk.

"How about you, grandpa? You want a gin — nice ladies' drink?"

"No thanks, kid," Tommy said, real polite.

"What're you drinking — that Irish shit? I'd drink horse piss before I'd drink Irish whiskey."

"Well, if a horse happens by, we'll draw you a glass," Lee said.

Nicky showed red. "You know your boyfriend's afraid to fight me? He tell you that?"

"Oh, leave it," Lee said.

"He's an old man and a yellow mick," the kid said then. "If he fucks like he fights, it can't be much fun for you, lady."

For maybe a five count Tommy thought he would do it — his hands on the bar were clenched, and his breath was quick. But in the end he let it go. In a moment he was laughing in the kid's face again and he kept laughing as Lee took him by the arm and led him backstage. He could hear the kid, in a rage, screaming at Lucky Ned to take the drink away.

"You're going to hook up with him," Lee said. "He's the kind to keep pushing."

Tommy smiled. "Well, I'm not gonna oblige him."

The band was backstage and Lee introduced Tommy around. Doc Thorne was an old pal, and he put Tommy in a bear hug.

"Where you been all this time, Tommy C?"

"I been everywhere, Doc. Like the song."

"I bet you have. I say, it does the heart good to see you two together again."

"I never figured you had a heart, Doc," Lee said.

"Big as a washtub, girl. And you know it's true."

They talked a few minutes and then Tommy said he would be going. Doc asked after his destination, and Tommy told him.

"Want to come along, Doc?"

"Does I *want* to come along?" Doc asked. "Of course I *want* to come along. But I am not *going* to come along, 'cause things have changed since the old days, Tommy. Nowadays, I got me a hard-headed woman at home who'll kick my ass six ways from Sunday if I'm out gambling away the rent money. You hear me, Tommy C?"

"I hear you, Doc."

Lee walked outside with Tommy and they stood by the back door, in the alley where the garbage cans sat and where Doc Thorne's old Packard was parked.

"You stay out of trouble, mick."

"Yup."

She stood there looking at him in the light from the doorway. Six years was a long time to be apart and she hated to see him go now, even for a few hours. Feeling this way surprised her, because Lee had never admitted anything to anybody, not even herself.

"You know, I could ask my mother for a loan," she told him. "God knows she's got the money."

Tommy laughed. "Your mother wouldn't pay money to see me eaten by wolves."

"Oh, she'd pay to see that."

"Yeah, I suppose she would."

"I wouldn't tell her it was for you," Lee said then.

"You're forgetting something," Tommy said. "Your mother wouldn't lend you money either."

"Probably not."

He kissed her. "Well, I'll see ya."

"You better."

"You're supposed to wish me luck."

"You don't need luck," she told him. "You got me."

SEVENTEEN

anny Bonner was in seventh heaven. Here he was, sitting in at
Ollie's weekly game, wearing new threads, money in his pocket, a song in his heart. Because who should be sitting across
from him but Tommy Cochrane himself. Danny had never really
socialized with anybody famous before, but this night here he sat,
playing a little poker, shooting the shit, having a hell of a time. Wait
until the boys at Lem's heard about this.

What's more, Danny was sitting on aces over tens and he was
betting ten dollars on the hand. And it was just him and Tommy
Cochrane left.

Tommy checked his cards and called the bet. Danny showed the
two pair, and Tommy tossed his hand.

"Tough one, Tommy," Danny said, and Tommy smiled. At least
the kid had stopped calling him Mr. Cochrane.

They'd been playing for three hours, and Tommy had been up
and down like a toilet seat. He was sitting between Fat Ollie and
Herm Bell; across the table were Bonner, Tony Broad and Billy
Callahan. Mac Brady had been there, but he left when he saw
Tommy in the game.

"You don't want to play poker with me, Mac?" Tommy had
asked the promoter.

"You won't get my money that way, Tommy."

"Sit down, Mac. Play some cards."

"No, the one throat I never cut is my own," Mac had said. "I'll have a shot of Ollie's good scotch and then I'm heading home, boys."

When Mac was gone, Callahan scoffed and looked over at Tony Broad. "Going home, my ass," he said. "Mac's going down to Sherbourne for a little paid pussy. The man spends more money on whores than I spend on clothes, for Christ's sakes."

Fat Ollie laughed. "I hope he gets better value for his dollar."

Callahan glared at the fat man, but kept his tongue. Herm Bell was shuffling and he began to deal.

"Straight seven, gents."

"So Mac likes the pros, does he?" Tony Broad said, checking his hole cards. "Well, that's the way to go, just fuck 'em and pay 'em and that's it."

Tony and Callahan had shown up drunk and had been hitting the bourbon pretty good ever since.

"The queen is high," Herm said to Danny, and Danny bet a buck.

"Seen a lot of guys take a fall over some skirt," Tony went on. "The only thing a dame wants to do is change a man. Don't matter what you are, they want to change you into something else. It's like branding cattle. If they can change you — they own you."

"Buck to you," Herm told him.

"I know it's a buck to me," Tony said irritably and he threw in a dollar. "What about you, Cochrane? You must have had your fair share of the dames. Famous boxer and all."

"About the same as everybody else, I guess," Tommy said.

"Yeah?" Tony Broad asked. "Well, everybody else doesn't waltz out of the Blue Parrot with Lee Charles on his arm."

"No, but everybody else is minding their own business," Herm said.

Tony took a moment to pour more bourbon and then he turned a bad eye on Herm Bell.

"Back off, sonny," he said. "All I'm doing is asking the man a question. Is Lee Charles a good fuck or what?"

Ollie pushed his chair back; he'd had enough of Tony Broad. But Tommy smiled and shook his head, and Ollie decided to wait. Tommy looked at Tony Broad, who was noisily lighting a cigar. His shaky hands, though, betrayed his cocky pose.

"I came here to play cards, friend," Tommy said. "If you have something on your mind, we can go out back and talk about it." He paused. "But I'd rather not because that's not why I'm here."

Ollie couldn't figure why Tommy was taking it easy on Tony Broad. Neither could Herm Bell. Tony, squinting at Tommy through the smoke and Jack Daniel's, took it the wrong way.

"Hey, you wanna play cards, let's play cards," he said to Tommy. "I don't know what the big deal is, I just asked a simple question."

"Ask it again," Tommy said.

"What?"

"Ask it again."

Tony looked nervously about the table. Now Ollie was smiling and in a minute Herm was joining him. Callahan was looking at his feet and Danny, as usual, didn't know what was going on. Tony put a finger under his collar and realized too late how he looked.

"Well?" Ollie said.

"I don't think I will," Tony said quietly.

"Then let's play cards."

Tommy won the hand on three eights, and his luck began to swing. By dawn he was up over a hundred. He won the last pot when Ollie called the game, then he and Herm, who was up a hundred himself, took Fat Ollie and Danny Bonner to Lem's for breakfast. Tony Broad and the Callahan kid had left earlier, both whining about their luck.

In the rest room at Lem's Tommy counted up and found he'd won a hundred and forty-two. With two nights' wages coming, and whatever Bones had stashed away, he could scrape enough together for the bet.

Never bet money on a bobby pin before.

Never bought a farm before, either. First time for everything.

Herm lived in the neighbourhood and he walked with Tommy to the Jasper after breakfast. They agreed to meet there Saturday at noon and go down to the track together.

"This Tony Broad is a class act," Herm said.

"I'm used to those guys," Tommy said. "Been a lot of years since I let a mouth like that bother me."

"That shit Callahan is carrying a heater."

"I figured."

"How'd you figure? He never took his coat off."

"That's why. It was eighty degrees in that room."

They were walking up to the Jasper now. The swamper was out front, sweeping the steps, or at least leaning on his broom. It was eight o'clock in the morning.

"Well, it was a lousy thing to say about your girl," Herm said.

"What the hell," Tommy said. "He just wants something he's never gonna have."

"Well, I'll see ya, Tommy."

"See ya, kid."

When Tommy went up to his room, T-Bone was in the bathroom, his face lathered and a straight razor in his hand.

"Out all night again," he said.

"Don't get started, Bones."

T-Bone smiled into the mirror. "Just teasin', Thomas. I know you been with Lee Charles."

"I wasn't with her this time, Bones."

T-Bone pulled the blade from his face. "Then where in hell you been?"

"Playing poker."

"Poker? Lawdy Jesus, what the hell you thinkin' 'bout now? Out playin' poker all night like some damn kid. And me sittin' here worryin' so that I don't sleep. I never seen nothin' like it."

Tommy got undressed and got into bed and fell asleep while T-Bone was tearing a strip off his hide. T-Bone was still talking as he put his shoes on and went out the door and down to the gym.

Mac Brady reached into his pocket for another antacid pill. Every time Mac had bacon and eggs and orange juice for breakfast, he ended up with an acid stomach. This morning he'd had Post Toasties and skim milk for breakfast and he still had trouble with his stomach. He had trouble with his stomach this morning because his fighter was being a pain in the ass.

"He said he ain't gonna run," Bert Tigers said again.

"I heard you the first time," Mac said. "Where is he?"

"Out talking to the guy from the paper."

"Which paper?"

"How the hell do I know?"

"Well, what're they talking about?"

"Tommy Cochrane."

Mac went out into the gym to find his fighter.

"Just write that he's afraid," Nicky was telling the reporter. "That's all. Just say he's got no guts."

The reporter was a new guy, and Mac didn't know him or what paper he was with. "Hey, can I have a minute with my boy?" Mac asked as he approached.

The reporter was scribbling away on a pad and he made no move to leave.

"I wouldn't be writing that Tommy Cochrane is afraid," Mac told him.

"Why not?"

"Ask your editor."

The reporter walked away then. Mac looked at the thick kid in front of him and took another tablet.

"Bert says you won't do your roadwork."

"Bert's got a big fucking mouth, that's what Bert's got."

"He's got a job," Mac said. "What's this about the roadwork?"

Nicky Wilson put on a schoolgirl pout. "I'm sick of running, it ain't doing me any good anyway. I'm ready to fight. And I don't mean some dumb Polack. I want Tommy Cochrane."

What you really want is Lee Charles, Mac thought to himself, that's what this is about. He sighed and moved over to sit on a bench along the wall. He indicated that Nicky should join him there, and the kid did, trying to hold his rebellious pose the best he could. It worked better standing up.

"I'll tell you what, Nicky," Mac said. "You don't want to run, you don't have to. Why don't you get showered and changed? Then we'll go down to my office."

Mac Brady didn't have an office. But he had a hotel room that he called an office, when he wasn't calling it whatever else he wanted it to be.

"Well . . . sure," Nicky said slowly.

"I'll show you a piece of paper I've got," Mac said then. "It's got a bunch of fancy words and legal mumbo jumbo on it, and at the bottom it's got your signature. You know what that paper means?"

Nicky was staring off across the gym.

"It means," Mac told him, "that you are going to fight *when* I tell you to, and it means you are going to fight *who* I tell you to — but more than anything it means if you start acting like a jackass and telling me you don't want to train — then you're not going to fight at all. You can go sit in the corner with your head up your ass or you can go back to Manitoba and throw grain bags for the rest of your life. You think you'll get rich that way, you think you'll get your name in the newspaper by bucking barley, you goddamn ignorant punk?"

Nicky's eyes were blinking, his lip turned. For a minute Mac thought the sorry son of a bitch would cry.

"Is that what you think?" Mac asked again.

"No."

"Then what are you going to do?"

Nicky's voice was quiet. "I'm gonna go running."

Mac looked at him for a minute more, just stared at the big kid without an ounce of sympathy. There were people who said that Mac Brady didn't do much to earn his money. Well, those people didn't know. How would they like to babysit a two-hundred-and-twenty-pound baby with the brains of a medicine ball?

"All right," Mac said.

Nicky got to his feet. He had to save face. "But I want Tommy Cochrane," he said. "The son of a bitch has been laughing at me."

"Well, gee whiz, I had no idea," Mac said. "Listen, you'll get Tommy Cochrane, but you leave it up to me. You hear?"

"Yeah."

"Go run your five and get back here to spar."

When the kid was gone Mac pulled the racing form from his pocket and went over his day's picks. As he was finishing up T-Bone Pike came into the gym. He was singing —

> I been workin' on the railroad
> All I do all day,
> I been working on the railroad,
> Don't care what you say —

Mac waved him over. "Nicky's out on the road," he said. "Have a seat a minute."

"Yes, sir."

"How long you been coming down to spar, T-Bone?"

"'Bout two weeks now, Mr. Brady."

"Well, you've done a good job for me."

"Why, thank you, sir."

Mac reached into his jacket for his wallet. "And I know you've been taking some hits, and you haven't complained one bit. I'm going to give you a twenty-dollar bonus, T-Bone."

T-Bone took the twenty and put it in his pocket. "Thank you, sir."

Mac looked down at the form in his hand. "Which horse do you like in the tenth, T-Bone?"

"Oh, I don't know nothing 'bout horses, Mr. Brady. 'Cepting that they like to kick a body if they get a chance."

Mac laughed. "They sure as hell do, in more ways than one." He set the form aside. "How's Tommy doing, T-Bone?"

"Just fine. He got a job down at the Bamboo Club, greeting people and like that. And Lee Charles is back in town, look maybe like they sparkin' again."

Mac looked at the fighter and smiled. T-Bone Pike had a habit of telling Mac things that Mac already knew. And not much else.

"How's Tommy coming with the money for the farm?"

"Couldn't say, sir."

"I can't see him putting together too much cash the way he's going at it. Tell me, how much more do you figure he needs?"

"Couldn't say that either, sir."

Mac smiled again and looked at his Timex. "You better go change." He watched the coloured man stand up. "You know something, T-Bone — you're a hell of a friend to have."

"Same as ever'body else, I reckon."

"No, I don't think so," Mac said.

When T-Bone came out of the dressing room, Nicky Wilson was already in the ring, dancing in his corner, showing off to the slugs at ringside. T-Bone took one look at the crazy eyes and he knew it was going to be bad.

"Get your black ass in here," the kid called to him. "Life ain't all watermelon and fried chicken."

T-bone went easily through the ropes and had a look around. The usual bunch was standing along the apron. Tony Broad was there too, along with a bad-looking kid in a hood suit.

"Come on, Rastus."

"I'm T-Bone."

"Where's your pal, T-Bone — trying on dresses?"

T-Bone didn't say anything else, just stood and waited for Bert Tigers to call time.

"You know your friend's a chickenshit?" Nicky asked.

"Time!"

T-Bone took a couple steps, then moved to his right as the kid charged him. The kid was all mouth today, talking on Tommy Cochrane, then T-Bone's mother, and anything else that popped into his addled brain. T-Bone kept going to his right, away from the kid's big punch, and he stuck his left in the kid's face every time the kid came close.

The strategy worked okay for two rounds, but in the third T-Bone's legs began to go, and the kid caught up, trapped T-Bone in a corner and hammered away at his ribs with both hands.

"I hear your mother fucks pigs, Rastus," the kid said, and T-Bone reached inside with an uppercut that snapped the kid's head like a whiplash.

The kid threw a deliberate hook to T-Bone's balls and T-Bone, in pain, pushed Wilson away and spoke in the ring for the first time in two weeks.

"You nothin' but a pussy, Wilson."

The kid went over the edge; he pulled T-Bone into the centre of the ring and knocked him to the deck with a wild right hand. A split second later T-Bone felt the kid's shoe crash into his nose.

Bert Tigers jumped into the ring when he saw the kick. Even the punks at ringside couldn't believe what they'd seen.

"Are you crazy?!" Bert screamed at his fighter. "What the fuck are you doing?"

Nicky was staring at T-Bone, still on the canvas. Bert was on his tiptoes in front of Wilson and he was wailing on his fighter.

T-Bone's nose was bleeding as he got up and went through the ropes and down to the dressing room. The place was pretty quiet when he walked by, but there was snickering as he passed and he saw Tony Broad with a grin on his face. It'd been a long time — so long that T-Bone thought that maybe he'd never have to feel this way again. But it was the same now as when he was a kid — he wanted to sit right down and cry, but he knew he couldn't.

He wouldn't show it to them.

In the ring Bert Tigers was still bawling out Nicky Wilson.

"You better get your ass in there and apologize," he ordered.

Nicky looked at Bert a moment and he smiled. "No."

"You have to," Bert told him. "Goddamn it — you know what you did?"

"Leave it the way it is," Nicky said. Smirking yet, he climbed out of the ring.

EIGHTEEN

Tony Broad ran into Mac Brady outside the steambaths on King Street. So Tony invited himself along for a steam and a massage, figuring that Mac would pick up the tab.

It was early in the day, and they were alone in the sauna, two fat men in towels and sweat, neither of them too free and easy with the truth where the other was concerned.

"Looks like you're fighting the Polack," Tony started.

"Maybe. Maybe not."

"What're you saying? It's too late to pull a switch now."

Mac just smiled and felt his pores leak.

"You saying that maybe the Polack gets an injury?" Tony asked. "Like a hernia from lifting his wallet?"

"I wouldn't know about that."

Tony pushed the sweat away from his eyes with his fingertips. He didn't care much for steambaths and never had. It was his understanding though that it was the kind of place that men of class and stature patronized.

"But you still don't have Tommy Cochrane," he said then.

Big Mac shrugged and threw more water on the rocks.

"Tommy Cochrane needs money and he needs it now. He's not going to get it shaking hands at the Bamboo, he's not going to make it playing cards, and he won't get it from Lee Charles — my information indicates that the lovely Miss Charles is broke — so Tommy's in a bind and he knows it."

Tony leaned away from the steam coming off the rocks. His eyes were filling and he was having trouble breathing. Beside him on the bench, Mac was pink and restful as a baby in a bassinet.

But Tony's ears were working just fine.

"You say Lee Charles ain't too flush?"

"That's the story. She's pulling down a hundred a week at the Parrot. She'd have to sing a lot of songs to cure what ails Tommy Cochrane."

"What kind of dough is Cochrane looking for anyway?"

"A few grand would be my guess. And there's only one man in town who can make him a deal for that kind of cash and right now that man is sitting with his pores open and a hard-on and he's getting ready to go down the hall to get the once-over by that German girl in the massage parlour."

"You can get a little extra here?" Tony asked.

"You got money, you can get anything you want. You ought to know that." Mac stood up. "Cost you twenty for a little mouth."

"Damn, all I got is small change," Tony said. "Left my billfold in my other jacket."

"You'll have to stay here and jack off," Mac told him. "Next time bring your money." And he went smiling out the door.

Tony was out of there right behind him; he grabbed a quick shower and went down the backstairs to the alley, leaving Mac to spring for the sauna. As for the blow job, that could wait. Tony had other things on his mind.

He found Billy Callahan pitching nickels in an alley behind Sully's pool hall. Dumb shit — tossing coins with a mob of fifteen-year-olds, on a good day you might come ahead a couple bucks.

The minute Callahan saw Tony, he quit acting and talking like a teenager, picked up his change and gave the kids the bum's rush.

"We might not be out of the running with Lee Charles after all," Tony told him as they walked down the street.

They went into a diner off Dundas and ordered coffee. Billy Callahan had a big raisin bun to go with his brew.

"We got to raise some money," Tony said.

"I thought you had money."

"Not enough, I don't."

Callahan ate one of the raisins off the top of the bun. "How much do we need?"

"I don't know. Two, three grand anyway. I got a little stashed away, but we got expenses — film, money for the lady. An actor."

"I bet I could be an actor," Callahan told him.

"Yeah, you'd like that," Tony said. "We need a pro. Bobby Dean, if I can find him. Works cheap and he's hung like a mule." Tony spooned more sugar into his coffee. "Your job is gonna be getting the money to pull this thing off. You're the financial backer."

"Financial backer." It was Billy's second title in less than two weeks and it made his head swim. "How am I gonna do that — raise the money?"

"With that friend you've been carrying around," Tony told him. "Unless you're afraid to use it."

"If I was afraid to use it, I wouldn't be carrying it."

Tony nodded and put his fat nose in his coffee cup a moment. "You know," he said surfacing, "this is a wide-open town compared to places south of the border. You don't got half the cops here as they do down there. This town's easy pickings — clubs and clip joints. Pick the right one and you could be in and out in two minutes with enough jack to bankroll the whole deal."

"Sure," Callahan said. "I know that."

Tony smiled big. "Then what're we waiting for?"

"I'm trying to figure just what the hell I get out of this," Callahan said. "Seems like I'm taking all the risks."

Tony put his chubby hands on the table and leaned forward in sombre conspiracy. "This ain't gonna be some run of the mill flick, kid. Not with Lee Charles, it ain't. We're taking this baby to Hollywood. And you *know* what's in Hollywood, don't you?"

"What?"

"Everything you ever dreamed about, that's what."

"Yeah," Callahan smiled and took a big bite out of his bun. "But what about Lee Charles?"

"What about her?"

"Do I get to fuck her?"

Tony grinned crookedly and leaned back in his chair. "In these movies, kid, everybody gets to fuck the broad. All we do — we hold back the money 'til the shooting's finished. Then we tell her she's got to jump you and me, it's part of the movie. If she wants her money, she's got no choice. And by that time, she's already been fucked every way but up, so what's a couple more?"

Callahan had his dumb smile fixed in place. "You got everything figured out," he said in admiration.

"You bet," Tony Broad said. "That's why I'm the boss."

The landlady caught Tommy walking out of the bathroom, wearing only his pants — no shoes, no socks, no shirt. She was a thick, muscular woman who looked to Tommy like she should be unloading trucks somewhere. Her grey hair was pulled back in a pony-tail and she had forearms like Popeye.

"See here!" she shouted when he tried to retreat. "What are you doing here?"

Tommy had no choice but to say that he was visiting Lee Charles. "But she's my sister," he explained quickly.

"That so?" the thick woman said. "Where's your shirt?"

Tommy thought for a moment then finally held his hands up in surrender, like the villain in a western movie.

"We got rules here," the woman said. "No cooking, no alcohol, no men. That means you."

"Yes, ma'am."

"I don't want to see you here again."

"You won't." Tommy turned to walk away.

"And Mr. Cochrane?"

Tommy spun round at the sound of his name. The landlady stepped closer.

"The next time you fight a chump like Rinaldi," she admonished, "put him away early, for crying out loud. None of this fancy-dan stuff. Slug the son of a bitch and get it over with. I lost a dollar on that fight to the grocer."

"Yes, ma'am. I'm sorry."

When Tommy got back to the room, Lee was lying on the bed, wearing his shirt and laughing like she would die. Tommy stood inside the door and shook his head.

"You coulda come and rescued me."

Lee tried to catch her breath. "No chance," she said. "The woman scares the hell out of me."

"I screwed it up now. I won't be able to come back here."

"I was getting kinda sick of you anyway," Lee told him.

"That a fact?"

"Yeah, that's a fact. All you want to do is screw. Is that any way to treat your sister?"

"I was under the impression you enjoyed it."

"Hey, I'm a better actress than I thought." Then she grabbed him by the belt and pulled him onto the bed.

Later they were hungry and they left the rooming house and went down to the market, where they bought cheese and crackers and smoked sausage at a Greek place. The owner knew Lee by now and called her by name.

"I see you've found yourself a young man already," he smiled.

"This guy?" Lee said. "He's my brother, that's all."

There was a small park off Spadina, and they sat on the grass and ate the lunch. There were maybe a dozen kids playing softball in the park. Before the game began, a fight nearly broke out over who was going to be Mickey Mantle.

"You figure on staying at the Parrot?" Tommy asked.

"I don't know," Lee said. "The job was supposed to be for a month, but we're packing 'em in. I got a feeling Mel's going to offer me a contract."

"Well, that's good."

"I guess."

A kid at the plate hit a long foul ball that landed in the grass near them. Tommy got up and tossed it back into the game, fired a perfect strike to the third baseman.

"You didn't tell me you were a ballplayer, mick," Lee said.

"Hey, we had a good ball team in Marlow," Tommy said. "Went to the provincial finals when I was fifteen, lost in extra innings. I still got my old jacket somewhere."

Lee took a bite of the cheddar cheese. "Why did you never take me to Marlow?"

Tommy looked at the kids playing ball. "You know, I used to wonder that myself. I guess I never wanted to look like some hick, figured you wouldn't like me if you saw where I come from."

"And now you want to go back there."

"I sure as hell do. I hate to think about losing that place, Lee." He fell quiet for a full minute, watched the kids playing ball. "It just seemed like it would always be there."

"Can you make a living from it?" she asked.

"Oh yeah, you can make a living. I mean, you won't get rich, but you can get along all right. It's nice to get your hands dirty, believe it or not. Been a while since I did any work that actually felt like work."

He took his jack-knife and sliced the sausage.

"Mind you, it's nothing fancy," he said. "But it's a place where you could . . . put your feet up."

"It sounds nice."

"You're right," he said to her then. "I should've taken you to Marlow."

"Well, we're not dead yet."

Tommy turned to look at her. "Could you ever live on a farm?"

"I never have."

"You ever think about it?"

"Sure," she said. "Lately."

"Well, what do you think?"

"Sure."

NINETEEN

When Herm was in the chips, he liked to have breakfast every morning at Lem's Diner. Poached eggs and ham, pancakes, brown bread toast, coffee, juice and marmalade. Eggs beside the toast, not on top, thank you ma'am. Who the hell wants soggy toast?

It was Saturday — *the* Saturday — and he settled into a booth and ordered his usual, then opened up the daily racing form, which he'd picked up sixty seconds earlier from the kid at Sully's. Herm turned at once to the seventh race and looked for the horse Bobby Pin. And there he was — out of the six hole — not a great post, but it could have been worse. Besides, at a mile and a sixteenth the post wasn't all that important. The dope on Bobby Pin — and who knew if it was true — was that he'd been running in the Finger Lakes and he had a place and a show in ten outings. A brown gelding, sixteen hands. High horse.

Oh, Bobby Pin.

Sometimes there were things to be learned from a racing form and sometimes there was nothing. The problem was, you never knew which was true until the race was run. Hindsight was a wonderful thing but, to a betting man, about as useless as tits on a boar.

After breakfast he went back to Sully's and shot some eight-ball with Stan Jones the elder until noon. Stan wasn't too flush, as usual, and they played for ten cents a game. Herm was off his stick and he lost a dime after five games. He gave Stan the elder a dollar bill and told him to invest in a meal, although Herm knew it would never happen, unless barley and hops could pass for lunch.

At noon Herm walked over to the Jasper Hotel. Tommy Cochrane and T-Bone Pike were sitting on the steps out front when he arrived.

"Hello, T-Bone," Herm said. "How are you?"

"Just fine, Mr. Bell," T-Bone said. "Look like a fine day for the horse races."

"Are you coming with us?" Herm asked. "Or are you sparring?"

"No, no," T-Bone said. "Got the day off. Got a snooker game down the way with a man from down Arkansas, he a hillbilly guitar picker whose daddy knew a man who might have known my daddy."

Herm looked at the coloured man's face, cut and bruised like damaged fruit, and thought that T-Bone Pike deserved a day off.

While they were talking Herm noticed a stocky man in a black flat-top approaching through the alley. As Herm watched, the flat-top walked directly up to Tommy and extended his hand.

"I heard I could find you here."

"How you doing, Chuck?"

"I'm all right," Chuck Monday said. He held a bill in his hand. "It ain't much, I know, but here's ten on what I owe you. I'll try to give you ten every two weeks from here on, 'til I pay it off."

Tommy looked at the sawbuck, and at the earnest face behind it, for maybe a three count. To refuse the money would be an insult to Chuck Monday.

"Thanks, Chuck," Tommy said. "I appreciate it."

Chuck nodded quickly. "Well, you take care. See you in a couple weeks."

Tommy watched until Chuck had rounded the corner and passed out of sight. "Well, let's go," he said then.

Herm and Tommy walked to the streetcar stop on Gerrard. Tommy had his wallet in his front pocket and he checked its safety as he walked. He was carrying four hundred and eighty dollars (four-ninety now), what he'd earned from the Bamboo and made at the card game, along with a hundred from T-Bone Pike. Now all he needed was a horse that would run.

"Looks like T-Bone's having a rough go down at the gym," Herm said as they stood and waited for the car.

"Nick Wilson," Tommy said. "That kid's got a lot to learn about respect. Something happened down there yesterday that Bones won't talk about, that's where he got the cut."

"It's a hell of a way to earn a living."

"Don't worry, Wilson is getting his, too. Bones may be forty years old, but he's as strong as his word and he's smart. He knows more inside a ring than Wilson could learn in a hundred years."

On the streetcar Herm showed Tommy the form. Herm had already made his picks for the first six races, the seventh he'd left blank.

"Early line shows fifteen to one, but that'll drop when they start to bet him. You won't be the only one."

"What about you?"

"I didn't figure to bet him to win, it'd just knock your odds down," Herm said. "Unless you want me to as a show of faith."

"I figure you've shown faith."

Herm nodded. "I'll bet him a few bucks to place, that'll do. This horse is going to run in the money."

It had been a lot of years since Tommy had visited Greenwood. The place hadn't changed though, the same mix of high rollers and society's dregs, bee-hived blondes and bag ladies, men smoking Havanas and bums picking discarded tote tickets off the floor.

And a well-dressed kid with a nose for gambling and a finished-up fighter looking for acreage.

It was a long afternoon for Tommy, waiting for the seventh to arrive. He didn't bet the first six, didn't want to hurt his bankroll, didn't want to jaundice his luck.

Herm bet all the way through and he had the winner in the second and the show horse — a long shot — in the third. By the end of the sixth he was up over eighty dollars. He and Tommy walked down to the rail to watch the horses as they came out for the seventh. Bobby Pin was wearing black and blue — colour of a shiner, Tommy thought, good sign or bad? — and he was a tall horse, with a good head and full jowls, like a stallion, although he wasn't.

"What do you think?" Tommy asked Herm Bell.

Herm just shrugged. "He's a horse, that's all I know," he said. "Now, if my old man was here, be a different story. He could tell you things about a horse that the horse himself didn't know. How its tendons looked, how it was blowing, what it had for breakfast, how much it shit this morning. He knew more about horses than he did about everything on earth put together. More than he knew about people, that's for sure, that's why my mother left. She used to tell my aunt she was gonna start wearing a saddle and bridle, that way my old man might notice her."

Tommy watched the chestnut fighting the bit, prancing sideways, eyes wide and strung out. Typical thoroughbred, wrapped a little tight. Hey, hey, Bobby Pin, Tommy thought. You gonna run for me today, gonna help me catch some luck? I've got ninety acres of better than average farmland riding on you, not to mention a white stucco house and a solid barn of pine and oak, put up by the strong Irish hands of James Cochrane.

And more than that, Bobby Pin, you ringer, you thief of dreams, you side-stepping, bit-fighting chestnut son of a bitch. A lot more than that.

The odds on the board went from fifteen to eighteen to twenty to one. It was an eleven-horse field and the favourite was Baxter's Beauty, showing three to two at the present. Herm turned to Tommy.

"I'm going to go bet," he said.

Tommy stayed by the rail until two minutes to post and then he went and put four hundred and fifty dollars on the nose of the chestnut gelding Bobby Pin.

When he rejoined Herm at the rail all bets were down and the odds on the six horse had dropped to eleven to one.

"The late money knocked him down," Herm said. "But eleven is good, you can't squawk about eleven."

Bobby Pin came out of the gate in the middle of the field and he stayed right there until the three-quarter mark. Baxter's Beauty settled along the rail in second and he appeared to be coasting. The leader was a bay mare named Tammy Too and she was setting a mean pace she wasn't likely to hold.

At the rail neither Tommy nor Herm said anything, but kept their eyes on the black-blue colours in the midst of the pack. Herm was praying for Tommy Cochrane's horse harder than he'd ever prayed for one of his own. For Herm, winning was just money — money to spend on good food and better liquor, nice clothes and nicer women. But this was different, this was something Herm had never dealt with before. This time it was somebody's dream out there. The possibility made him happy, but it scared him a little, too.

At the three-quarter post Bobby Pin found a hole and broke through on the outside. As he began to move, Tammy Too shot her wad and fell away to give Baxter's Beauty the lead. Bobby Pin came on to challenge at once and coming out of the clubhouse turn he was neck and neck with Baxter's Beauty. The chestnut had the momentum though and the favourite began to fail. Down the stretch it was Bobby Pin by one and a half, then two lengths.

At the rail Tommy had crumpled the racing form into a ball without knowing it and he hadn't drawn a breath since the clubhouse turn. He kept his eyes on the number six of the saddle cloth, afraid that the horse in the lead wasn't his. Herm Bell had his head back and he was laughing out loud.

And then a rank bay filly name of Fiery Kate came out of the pack like the devil himself was chasing her. She was tight to the rail, and flying. The jock on Bobby Pin kept his horse wide, hunched over the gelding's neck, working the whip stride for stride. At the wire it looked as if Bobby Pin had held on.

When they went to the photo, it was Fiery Kate by a nose.

They took a cab back downtown, Herm's insistence. Tommy hadn't said much since the race. Herm sat and looked out the window at the traffic on Queen.

"I feel like a son of a bitch," he said.

"No," Tommy told him.

"Should've kept my goddamn mouth shut right from the start. It was a dumb idea."

"It was about three inches away from being a great idea," Tommy said. "Things don't always turn out. Were you mad at me for the Rinaldi fight?"

"It's not the same thing."

"Well, it's close enough," Tommy said. And he laughed. "Jesus, didn't we have a hell of a two minutes though? You gave me a good horse, kid, he ran a game race."

But Herm couldn't be happy with it. He kept turning it over in his mind.

"A place bet wouldn't have helped," he said out loud. "Only paid five bucks to place, they had him bet from here to Tuesday for second."

"I had to go for the win," Tommy said. "I knew that."

"Goddamn black-hearted, plowhorse son of a bitch," Herm said. "You want to go for a drink? I'm buying and for as long as you're drinking."

Tommy was looking out the window. He didn't know how he felt. "Okay, let's go for a drink," he said. "But we have to go to the Parrot, I told Lee and Bones I'd meet 'em there after the race."

Herm told the driver. "What're you going to do now, Tommy?"

"Well, I got ten days. Could be I'm screwed, blued and tattooed. You know any jobs that pay five hundred dollars a day?"

"What about Mac Brady?"

"Mac Brady and that prick he calls a heavyweight can both take a long walk off a short pier," Tommy replied.

Herm went back to looking out the window. He wouldn't ask about things that were none of his concern. Tommy turned to look at the honest face beneath the pompadour and decided that Herm Bell was a good kid. He was a good kid and today he'd nearly turned Tommy a hell of a favour. He'd tried, anyway.

"I've been advised by the medical profession not to fight again," Tommy said to the kid. "I've got what the doctors call an aneurysm. There's a good chance that if I go back in the ring, I won't get out alive."

Herm looked over. "Holy shit. Does Mac Brady know this?"

"Nobody knows it. Just me and Bones. And now you. I'd appreciate it if you'd keep it quiet, though."

"You got my word."

"Good enough."

Tommy let it go at that and turned to look out the window again. It was hot July on Queen Street, and the women were dressed in shorts and halters, wearing sandals on their feet as they went about their errands. There were a million people in the city who never heard of a horse named Bobby Pin and wouldn't care if they did.

"Ten days," Tommy said out loud.

Lee was standing at the end of the bar when they got to the Blue Parrot, having a beer with Doc Thorne. Lee wasn't wearing shorts or sandals, she was wearing a loose cotton shirt and khaki pants, and she was the best thing Tommy Cochrane had ever laid eyes on. When she saw him she watched his eyes and then she knew. She didn't ask any questions.

Tony Broad and his sidekick Callahan were standing down the bar a ways, drinking and joking with an off-duty waitress. They were polluted for five in the afternoon, and they were pissed off because Lee Charles had minutes earlier turned down their offer of a drink.

Herm ordered beers all around and laid a twenty on the bar. Tommy introduced him to Lee and the horn player. Doc Thorne laid some skin on Herm.

"You boys been down to the ponies, Lee tells me," Doc said. "How you make out?"

"Well," Tommy said. "We got beat by a filly named Fiery Kate. I should know better than to bet against an Irish handle like that, Doc."

"Win some, lose some," Doc said.

"That's a fact."

Lee squeezed Tommy's hand a moment.

"No sign of Bones yet?" Tommy asked, and she said not.

Down the bar Tony Broad was getting loud. Tommy heard his own name and when he turned he saw that Broad was directing the waitress's attention his way.

"That big fella, now that's Tommy Cochrane," Tony was saying. "A real live heavyweight fighter."

The waitress smiled uneasily, and Tommy just looked away. But Tony Broad wasn't watching Tommy, he had his eyes on Lee Charles. Who the fuck was she to turn down a drink with him?

"But you gotta see this fighter Mac Brady's got," Tony kept it up. "This Nicky Wilson. The kid's a goddamned redwood and he's going places. Ain't that right, Billy?"

Billy Callahan said that it was right. If Tony Broad said the square root of nine was four, Billy Callahan would say that was right, too.

Herm Bell saw what was happening and he was watching the action happily. He was feeling low and shut out and he was in the mood to waltz with a couple of morons if he got half a chance.

"Let it go," he heard Tommy say.

Now the waitress was asking about the wondrous Nicky Wilson, saying she'd seen him in the Parrot.

"Oh, he's something," Tony Broad, who didn't give two shits for Nicky Wilson, was saying. "Like yesterday down at the gym, he smashes this nigger. Puts him on the canvas and — boom! — kicks him right in the mug. Nigger's bleeding all over the deck."

"Never saw a nigger bleed like that," Callahan said. "Red blood too — just like you and me."

Lee tried to hold on to Tommy, but she had no chance. For a thirty-five-year-old finished-up boxer, he could still move. When he got to Tony Broad he took him by the thick throat and leaned him backward over the bar.

"He kicked him?" Tommy asked.

Callahan stepped away from the bar, his hands out in front. But Herm Bell braced him there, blocking him off from Tommy.

"You put that hand inside the jacket and I'm gonna rip your head off," Herm told him. "And throw it in your face."

Tony Broad was losing air, but indignant, demanding that Tommy unhand him.

"He *kicked* him?" Tommy was still asking.

Tony pushed with his forearms and managed to roll free of Tommy's grip. He started to scramble away. Herm stayed tight with Callahan, daring him to go for the heater in his coat. It wasn't likely though, not with a room full of spectators.

Tony ran like a fat rabbit behind the bar and stood beside Lucky Ned, the bartender.

"Phone the police," Tony demanded. "This man has assaulted me."

But Lucky Ned was a man who made his decisions in his own time. He just looked at Tony Broad, then at Tommy, and stood where he was.

T-Bone Pike chose that moment to stroll into the Parrot. He'd just come from winning three dollars in a four-hour snooker game and he was feeling damn good. Luck was on his shoulder and he'd convinced himself on the way over that the lady smiling on him today was smiling on Thomas Cochrane too.

But then Tommy had him roughly by the arm and he was pushing him into the room behind the stage. T-Bone's eyes were jumping.

"What happened at the gym yesterday?" Tommy asked.

"Nothin' happen."

"Goddamn it," Tommy snapped. "What happened?"

"Nothin'," T-Bone said again. "Just sparrin', is all."

Tommy caught himself then, took a breath. After a moment he reached out and ran his thumb gingerly over the cut on his friend's chin.

"Oh, Jesus. Did he kick you, Bones?"

"Wasn't nothin', Thomas."

"Oh, Jesus."

T-Bone was ashamed and he looked down at the floor. "How your horse do, Thomas?"

Tommy turned and walked back out into the bar. Things had quieted down. Callahan and Tony Broad were back at their end of the bar, but they weren't so noisy now; they were nursing fresh bourbons and looking uneasy. Tommy took his place between Lee and the Doc, and he drank down his draught and said nothing. Herm ordered another round.

Occasionally, as he drank, Tommy looked up into the mirror behind the bar. Once when he did, he caught Lee's eyes, but he looked away quick, wouldn't let her get involved there. It seemed to her that he was looking for something in the reflection.

Finally, Tommy straightened and looked down the bar to Tony Broad.

"You," he said.

"Stay away from me," Tony told him.

"You a friend of Mac Brady's?" Tommy asked.

There was enough bar between the two of them that Tony could find a measure of confidence.

"What's it to you?" he asked.

"I want you to give him a message for me," Tommy said. "Tell him the price is five grand. Tell him he's got a fight."

TWENTY

The house was a phantom, an aberration, as strange as a house could be. There was nothing she could recall with any semblance of accuracy — the rooms were smaller or bigger, the colours redder, bluer. A breakdown of memory. At the front door Lee hadn't known whether to knock or not. Either action seemed a great exaggeration. In the end she walked right in, stepping bravely into her past, into the delicately furnished front room with the Persian carpets and teak carvings and the picture of the bob-haired teenage girl over the fireplace.

A voice called down from upstairs, promising (threatening?) an imminent arrival. Lee sat down and then stood up again. A long-haired white cat with a pinched face sauntered into the room, eyed Lee with disdain and then scooted away when she tried to pet it.

"Fuck you, too," she said to the cat and then her mother came down the stairs and into the room.

"Hello, Lee," she said, and they kept their distance, mother and daughter. There would be no hugging or pecks on the cheek. Thirty-year-old habits were not broken, not that easily, not in this house.

They had tea and some sort of hard English biscuits that only her mother would dare serve to humans. The petulant cat sat in her mother's lap as the old girl sipped her tea and inquired casually about her daughter's life the past couple of years.

"I been kicking around a little bit," Lee told her.

"*Kicking* around?" her mother asked, her eyes registering her tired dismay at the demise of the language. "But I heard you were in California."

She'd *heard*. She'd heard because Lee had written three or four times her first year out there. Of course, her mother hadn't replied — she'd obviously decided against sending mail to that land of ill-mannered decadence. She'd probably boiled Lee's letters before reading them. This was assuming that she *had* read them. A smart bookie would give you five to one against.

"Yeah, I was in California," Lee said.

"And now?"

"And now I'm not."

"I can see that. How long have you been back?"

"Couple days." A small lie, maybe not a lie at all. How long *had* she been back?

"And you have a place to stay?"

"I've got an apartment downtown," Lee said. A bigger lie. They came easier, that much she remembered. "I'm singing at a club, a place called the Blue Parrot. Do you know it?"

They both knew goddamn well that her mother didn't know it, and never would. It was a question that didn't rate an answer, and didn't get one.

Lee took a drink of the bitter tea, set the hard cookie aside. The cat in the lap looked at her with eyes of lime green, a hideous animal, the kind of thing her mother liked.

"Where's Walter?"

"He's not here."

"No shit."

"Must you talk like that?" Lee thought the old lady would cover the cat's ears. "He's spending time at the cottage this summer."

"You two have separated then," Lee said.

The ice blue eyes flashed, warning Lee that certain questions wouldn't be answered here today. No wonder Walter had taken a powder — he may have been a glad-hander and a drunk and an all-star shit at times, but at least he had a certain capacity for enjoying himself once in a while. He was probably in Coboconk right now, tossing back ale in the Paddy House and telling everyone who would listen how much money he made last year without lifting a single finger of either of his baby-soft hands.

While here, back in the city, sat his second wife, who was at least as wealthy as he, with her hair dyed a new colour this year — purple approaching black — and her face powdered white, a death mask.

Today she was facing her only child, Lee, whom she'd borne only to please her first husband. Lee's father had been a tough son of a bitch, who'd made a fortune in silver in northern Ontario and who'd died in a barroom fight over a hockey game. As far as exits go, you can't get much more Canadian than that. In any event, the old girl hadn't had much use for barrooms or her daughter since.

"It's nice that you could drop by," she was saying now. "I've wondered about you."

Not enough to answer my letters, Lee thought. Well, let's cut to it, then, it seemed unlikely that things would be warming up, not in this life. Probably not the next.

"I have a favour to ask," Lee said.

"Oh?"

"I need to borrow some money," Lee said. She was quick to clarify. "I'm asking for a loan, not a handout. I'll pay you back, at whatever rate of interest you decide."

"How much money?"

"Five thousand dollars."

And her mother actually laughed at her. Laughed and looked at the goddamn cat, as if asking if the animal had heard. Still smiling as she took a bite from one of the granite biscuits.

"Oh, Lee."

"This is important," Lee said, holding her temper. "You know I wouldn't ask otherwise. Do you realize how hard it is for me to do this?"

"It didn't appear difficult."

"I'm in trouble and I need the money," Lee said flatly. "You know you can more than afford it, I'll pay you back with interest, it'll be no different than if the money was sitting in the bank."

The cat jumped down and left the room, casting its vote on the matter. Lee's mother asked after the nature of her trouble.

"Isn't it enough that I'm your daughter and I've come to you?"

Her mother considered this for a long time. "No," she said.

Ah, yes. Home sweet home. Lee set the vile tea aside and got to her feet. Her mother seem relieved that the visit was over and followed her to the door.

"Why do you need the money?"

Lee stepped outside into brilliant sunlight. There were roses blooming in the yard, red and yellow, huge beautiful blossoms. Lee hated to see them in this place, it was a cruel contradiction, an insult to nature.

"There's a chance that the money could save Tommy Cochrane's life."

"Well," her mother said smiling. "That man is a hoodlum and I would not spend five cents to save his life."

Lee stood looking at the flowers a moment.

"You know," she said, "I can't for the life of me figure why Walter would want to spend the summer at the cottage."

Her mother closed the door.

Mac Brady had his fight, but he was on short notice and he had some ground to cover if he was going to pull it off. Luckily he already had the card — so he had the Gardens booked, he had the licence, the vendors, everything in line on that end. Now it was a matter of changing opponents and making it look good. Not that anybody on the money end was going to complain — after all, Tommy Cochrane was a better draw than the Polack.

As for Wosinski, the Pole went down with a herniated disc the day after Mac got the okay from Tommy. It was an unfortunate injury and it paid Wosinski almost as much as the fight would have, with the bonus that he wouldn't have to get his brains rattled to collect.

Mac took care of the medical report on the Pole and went to the commission to request a change in the licence. There were a few clever remarks, and some head shaking, but everything went smoothly enough. What was going on was obvious, but it wasn't necessarily bad for boxing. Wilson butchering Wosinski might have been.

It was testimony to Mac's influence — and the number of people who owed him favours on one level or another — that he managed to accomplish all this in one day. And when he'd pushed whatever buttons needed pushing, he went looking for Tommy Cochrane. He found him shooting snooker at Sully's with T-Bone Pike. Mac showed a contract and an offer of four thousand.

"You didn't get my message?" Tommy asked.

"Four is the best I can do, Tommy."

"Then you haven't got a fight. Now you're really in a spot, Mac — I heard today that Wosinski's down with a bad back. Imagine that."

Tommy grinned at Mac and then leaned over the felt. He dropped a cherry in the corner but hooked himself on the pink. The only shot he had was a bank on the blue and he tried it and made it. Then he looked at Mac.

"Maybe I'll go shoot pool for a living," he said.

"If I can call some debts," Mac said doubtfully, "I can go to forty-five hundred."

"Five grand, Mac. Don't you hear good?"

"How the hell can I pay you five thousand dollars? It's bad business."

"Then walk away from it, Mac. Just leave it alone and walk away."

"Okay, smart guy, that's what I'm going to do," Mac said and he strode out of the pool hall.

Tommy tried a combination and missed. He looked up at T-Bone.

"What do you figure, Bones?"

"I say fifteen minutes, Thomas."

"Less," Tommy said and he checked the clock at the front. "Bet you a nickel."

T-Bone bent at the waist and proceeded to run the table, beating Tommy by forty points. As Tommy was racking again, Mac Brady came through the front door. Tommy looked at the clock. Eleven minutes. T-Bone placed a nickel on the rail.

"Well, I made some calls," Mac said.

"What's the matter — you don't like the phone in here?" Tommy asked. "Bust 'em up, Bones."

T-Bone miscued on the break. Mac watched, then drew the contract from his pocket.

"Well, call me a goddamn fool, but five thousand it is," he said. "I'll be the laughing stock of the town if this gets out."

"Oh, it'll get out, I can guarantee you that," Tommy said. "It'll get out because you'll let it out first chance you get, Mac. It sells tickets, and you know it. I'll probably read in the newspaper tomorrow that I'm getting *ten* grand."

Mac shook his head and spread the contract on the green felt.

"You think you know me, Tommy, but you don't. I'm just doing a job here, just like everybody else. Now let's get your chicken scratch on this contract, and I'll leave you to your game."

"You get my signature when I get my five thousand, Mac," Tommy said. He blasted the cue ball into the pack, scattering reds all over the contract. "Now you *know* that. Why don't we quit playing games?"

"You think I'm walking around with five grand in my pocket? I don't carry that kind of cash."

"Then get it," Tommy said. "And while we're talking money, you better know you're picking up my training expenses. Looks like I'm stuck using Bert's gym. I'll train in the afternoons and I don't want that jackass Wilson anywhere near me. I mean it, Mac — he better be out of there when I show."

"Who the hell are you — Doc Kearns all of a sudden?"

"You know who I am, Mac — I'm the one in the middle. Now you get the cash together and bring it over to the Jasper and I'll sign your paper. Otherwise, it's no deal and you got no fight. Now what do you say to that?"

Mac tugged at the contract, sliding it out from under the snooker balls like a magician pulling a tablecloth from beneath china.

"You'll get your money, Tommy. I'll send it over tomorrow or the next day. But you'd better hold up your end, you'd better give me a show. I'm not paying for some two-minute performance."

"You couldn't care less if it's two minutes or two hours," Tommy told him. "All you want is the ranking, Mac. But don't you worry about me, I'll give you a show. In fact, I'll go you one better. I'm gonna whup your boy, Mac. I'm gonna beat him until he begs you to throw the towel."

"Maybe you will," Mac said, tucking the contract away. "But I doubt it."

He left the pool hall again. Tommy watched after him, then went back to his game. T-Bone was looking on narrowly.

"You sure 'bout this, Thomas?"

"Sure enough."

T-Bone put his hand on the arrowhead around his neck. "What about the doctor, Thomas? You know what he tole you."

"Forget about that, Bones. I mean it, I don't want you to mention it again." He dumped the eight in the corner. "Besides, doctors are wrong all the time. I feel good."

"That an easy person to fool."

"Who?"

"Yourself."

Tommy lined up a cherry, then straightened from the table. "This is the farm we're talking about, Bones. Remember that. This is the farm."

"It a lot more than that," T-Bone Pike said. "And don't be tellin' this nigger any different."

TWENTY-ONE

Monday Herm was back at the track, looking to get even with the nags for what they did to him (or to Tommy Cochrane, at least) on Saturday. He got there early and he wandered down to the stables to pass the morning with the boys there, maybe pick up a horse or two. The talk today wasn't about thoroughbreds though — the news was out that Tommy Cochrane was going to fight Nicky Wilson, and expert opinions on the outcome were forming as thick as the flies on the manure pile out back.

Herm didn't want to talk about the fight — what he knew he couldn't say anyway — so he sat in a tack room with a cup of coffee and stayed pretty quiet. What he heard, though, told him there wasn't much support for Tommy Cochrane.

"Cochrane's had his day," a groom was saying. "He's over the hill, and the kid's a banger."

"Tommy's smart though," somebody else said.

"If he was smart, he wouldn't be fighting Nicky Wilson."

After a while Herm went out and strolled down to the paddock where Red Lamare, who'd been Frank Bell's best friend, was watching a grey gelding walk.

"Hi, Red."

"Lookit this horse, Herm," Red said. "I can't let this horse run on that tendon. How can I let this horse run on that tendon?"

To Herm there was nothing wrong with the tendon, but he knew that there was, because Red had said so.

"I don't know," Herm said. "Don't let him run."

"Ha," Red told him. "I have to let him run, on account the owner says so. His wife's family is up from Montreal and he wants to show off, big thoroughbred owner and all. Dumb son of a bitch, the horse'll run last, maybe cripple itself doin' it."

"Thanks for the tip," Herm said. "That cuts one field for me anyway."

"Think about the horses, Herm," Red said. "Didn't your father teach you nothing? You have to care about the animals."

"My father cared too much about the animals, that's what he taught me."

Red shook his head — the hair white now, the nickname still Red — and leaned his small hands against the top rail of the paddock fence. "Well, this horse is not running today. Not with me as trainer. I've quit better people than this asshole before, and I'll do it again."

"You got a tip for me today, Red?"

"Yeah, always be your own boss."

Herm left him there and went out and had a terrible day at the wickets. He stayed for nine races and never cashed a ticket, never really came close until the ninth, when he put fifty to win on the favourite, figuring to double up before leaving — that at least — and got beat by a photo. He took a streetcar into town and went to the Rooster for a beer. Herm never drank at the Rooster and he hoped that he wouldn't see anybody he knew there. He wasn't in the mood for conversation.

He stood at the bar and drank a pair of draught, taking them down slow, drinking just for the drinking, not for the taste or the effect or the companionship of the hops. When he was empty he called to the bartender for two more.

"How do you like this new draught?" the man asked. "Gold Label."

"Just set 'em up," Herm said. "It's no different than any other beer."

The bartender placed the beer on the bar. "Ain't you the friendly bastard."

"What I am is none of your fucking business," Herm said. "I ain't looking for conversation, bub."

"Too bad," the bartender said. "You're a joy to talk to." He walked away and picked up a cloth to wipe clean some drink glasses, a real bartender's move. Herm stood with his fresh draught and thought about this lousy Monday. The money didn't bother him, never had. But he wondered if the streak had run its course.

And he was wondering about Tommy Cochrane too — if he was going to be alive when Monday rolled around again.

When Lee Charles walked in, Herm was glad to see her. Of course, any man with the strength to blink would be glad to see Lee Charles, but it was different with Herm today. She was looking about the room as she came over to say hello.

"I'm supposed to meet a friend," she said. "Patty Simmons — you know her?"

Herm said that he didn't. He offered to buy Lee a drink while she waited, and she asked for a beer.

"I'm damn sorry about that race the other day," Herm said. "I was pulling for Tommy to get his farm."

"Well, he's not sore, if that's what you think," Lee assured him. "He went in with his eyes open."

"So now he's going to fight."

"I guess he is." There was something about the kid's tone though, and Lee looked at the green eyes beneath the pompadour and in a moment she knew.

"He told you."

Herm put away his third draught and reached for number four. "Yeah, he told me. I didn't know he told you."

"I heard from T-Bone."

Herm looked at her. "So you're going to spend the next week holding your breath."

"I'm going to spend the next week trying to raise five thousand dollars. He can't fight, that's all there is to it."

"You got any ideas?"

Lee shook her head. "I asked my mother for a loan, and she laughed at me." She took a drink. "At least, she claims to be my mother. Be nice to find out different someday."

"Close family."

"You got it."

The front door opened and Howard Coulter — Lee's luck running today — came in. In a moment he was beside her, eyeing Herm suspiciously and whispering sweet shit in Lee's ear. At first she was polite.

"For God's sakes, just tell me," he said, his breath too close on her neck. "What can I do to make you happy?"

"You can fuck off," she said, loud enough.

Howard stole a look at Herm and then followed the advice.

"Problem?" Herm asked.

Lee shook her head. "Some guy I held hands with once — hundred years ago."

Patty came in then, and Lee waved to her. "See you later," she said to Herm. "Thanks for the beer."

"What're you gonna do?" he asked.

"I got a hole card, but not a good one," she told him. "I'm going to talk to Mel Dunston at the Parrot, see if I can swing something long term with him."

"What's your chances?"

"Shit," Lee said. "You thought the ponies were a long shot — you don't know Mel Dunston."

She went off to join her friend at a table. The bartender came by. "Another draught, chief?"

"I'm going to the Bamboo," Herm told him. "This beer is horse piss."

Billy Callahan waited in the shadows in the alley behind the Old Kentucky Tavern long enough to smoke a cigarette. The light from the window above him came from the manager's office. At least Callahan was pretty sure of the fact; it may have come from the dames' washroom, in which case the next window over was the manager's. Either way, he was pretty close.

He smoked his Export down to a nub, then turned his watch to the light. Ten past twelve. Any stragglers would be gone by now. He grabbed the knob on the rear door and it turned in his hand. Security wasn't a priority at the Old Kentucky.

He checked the load in his pistol and walked right in, down the short hallway, past the washrooms and into the office, where Harold Stedman was sitting at a desk, counting receipts and writing lies in his ledger.

Young Billy came into the room like Eliot Ness on the television, feet spread apart, both hands on the pistol, barrel at eye level.

"Stand and deliver," he said, a line he'd long admired.

"What?" Harry the Horse asked.

"The money, you old fuck. This is a heist — what'd ya think?"

Billy took a cloth sack from his coat pocket and tossed it on the desk. "Put it in the bag."

Harry shook his head and began to stuff the cash inside.

"You might as well hit the newspaper stand as hit me," he said. "You think you're making a score here?"

"Shut up," Billy told him. He'd been expecting the old man to show some fear. "I'll shoot you," he reminded Harry.

"Go ahead."

"You're one brave son of a bitch," Billy said. "Talking to me like that."

Harry threw the bag on the desk and motioned to it with his chin.

"I don't have to be brave," he said. "You got nothin' I'm scared of. The worst you can do is shoot me and that'd just be doing me a favour."

Billy put the sack inside his coat. Then he just stood there; he was green at this and he didn't know what to do next. It seemed though that there was something he should say or do before taking his leave. Like Cagney in the movies. Top of the world, ma.

He pointed the gun at the manager again. "You better forget my face, pops. If you know what's good for you."

Harry stood up and showed his long yellow teeth. "Go fuck yourself, punk. I'll forget your face all right. Just like everybody else who's ever met you. You're just a piece of shit and you'll end up face down in the alley soon enough without my help. Now get the fuck out of here."

Harry the Horse was no gelding anyway. Billy bounced on the balls of his feet a moment, weighing what the little man had said. Then he leaned over and whipped the barrel of the gun across Harry's face, opening a gash there and knocking Harry back into his chair.

"Take that in the alley," Billy said and he left.

Outside he began to run, through the parking lot and out onto Montague Street. On the sidewalk he forced himself to slow to a walk, his hands in his pockets, hat pulled low. Any cop driving by would have pulled him in on looks alone.

He made it to Tony Broad's hotel on Isabella, walked past the desk clerk, who knew his face by now, and went up to Tony's room on the third floor. Tony was sitting on the bed, with bourbon in a pint and the radio on. Billy Callahan was laughing as he came through the door.

"Piece of cake," he said and he tossed over the bag. "The kid comes through."

Tony grabbed for the bag. "Nobody saw you?"

"Just the creep running the joint. I gave him a little Sam Colt to shut him up."

"Christ, you shot him?"

"Naw, just roughed him up a little."

Tony dumped the bag on the bedspread and began to count. Callahan moved over easily to pick up the bottle. He was feeling cocky and indestructible. The night had gone smooth as silk, and it was just the beginning. Times had changed for Billy Callahan.

"Three hundred and seventeen dollars," Tony Broad said then. He looked at Callahan in disgust. "What the fuck is this — cigarette money?"

"Gotta be more than that," Callahan said, but he knew there wasn't.

"Three hundred bucks," Tony said. "Can you do it ten times a night? 'Cause that's what we're gonna need."

He came over and took the bottle away from Callahan. "Who'd you rob — an ice cream vendor?"

"Shit," Callahan said.

Tony flopped on the bed, his back against the headboard. "Aw, don't sweat it, kid," he said. "Maybe I underestimated you. Maybe you're not ready for big time yet. You better stick with nickel and dime for a while."

Callahan was standing on the cheap carpet, hands in his pockets. "It was a mistake, Tony. I was — whatdyacallit — misinformed. How did I know the Kentucky was such a dump?"

Tony began to ignore the kid then. He drank from the bourbon but didn't offer it over. Tony was in his undershirt, sweating bullets in the close room. The whiskey made it even warmer.

"Air conditioning," he said out loud to no one. "That's what I need — air conditioning. And a television. I like to watch Lucy, and Topper too. God, I love that fucking ghost."

By the bureau Callahan stood unhappily. Wanting a drink. A look. Anything.

"You ever watch that Topper, Billy?"

"I never see television too much. What're we gonna do, Tony?"

"He's this fucking ghost, see."

"What're we gonna do, Tony?" And then he said it. "Boss?"

"How's that?"

"What're we gonna do, Boss?"

Tony smiled and sat up. "The Parrot," he said.

"You want me to take the Parrot?"

"Mel Dunston — who could be easier? Little bastard walks out of there every night with that leather bag under his arm. Won't let nobody but himself touch a nickel. The fucker's a holdup waiting to happen."

"Jesus, they know me in the Parrot, Tony."

Tony threw him a look from the bed. Sometimes Billy Callahan caught on faster than others.

"They know me at the Parrot, Boss."

"You wear a stocking, kid. Nobody knows nobody wearing a lady's nylon. Maybe I'll get you one of Lee Charles', how about that?"

But Callahan wasn't sure. When was he about anything?

Tony Broad drank and then waved his hand carelessly. "Hey — forget it, kid. I got a pal coming in from Cleveland. A pro. He'll take care of it."

"No." Callahan all but shouted the word. His face was flush. "I'll take care of it."

Tony looked at him doubtfully, not saying a word for maybe a full minute. And Callahan was left dancing like a monkey on a string, waiting — like he'd waited all his life. Then Tony capped the pint and tossed it over.

"Okay," was all he said.

TWENTY-TWO

Tommy ran in a pair of faded army pants and a t-shirt and a pair of old BlackHawk runners he'd had for ten years. He jogged along Front Street to River and then north on River Street and down into the Don Valley. T-Bone ran with him, breathing easily, breaking into song now and then. The arrowhead bounced against T-Bone's chest as he ran, reminding him it was there, buoying him up. Luck was in the flint, he knew.

After two miles, Tommy was winded badly and they slowed to a walk before climbing out of the valley again. They stayed by the bank of the Don, heading south now, hearing the noise of the traffic on the viaduct overhead.

"Shoulda brung our fishing poles, Thomas."

"Can't train for a fight sitting on a river bank, Bones."

"That's a fact." T-Bone stepped up and over a log along the way. "But there's somethin' to be said 'bout sittin' by a river with a piece of bamboo in your hand."

"Wait'll we get to the farm, Bones. There's a stream that runs down from a spring in Jake Bergsma's place, it pools up above some rocks in the bush. There's trout there, fat as hogs. All you need is a hook and a piece of bread."

"More partial to catfish myself."

Tommy looked over. "You spent too many years on that Mississip, that's your problem."

"That old muddy give T-Bone a good many dinners, Thomas. More than he remember."

T-Bone turned then and began to jog backwards in front of Tommy, throwing open hands in the air, bobbing his head with the punches.

"We got lots to do, Thomas."

"Yeah."

"Have to look for the timin'. You be all rusted up after this time away. You can catch him inside, this Wilson, he mighty 'ceptible to a uppercut." T-bone fired a punch to illustrate. "But you got to move to your right, all the time, to your right, stay away from his Sunday punch. He got some kick in his right hand."

"I've been hit before, Bones."

"I had the clap once too, Thomas. Don't mean I'm wantin' it again."

Tommy kicked into a slow jog then, looking ahead to the incline. His legs were cramping some and he hoped he could run it off.

"My wind is in the outhouse, Bones," he said. "I have to get in some kind of shape, good enough for five anyway."

"You figure on finishin' in five?"

"I have to go after him. No way I can go the distance. I'm not kidding myself, not with a week's running. I have to get inside and get him early. Remember, he's as dumb as a stump fence."

"He like to talk in the ring," T-Bone said. "And he rattle easy, lose his head."

"That's good."

"Sure enough, Thomas." T-Bone turned around now to run beside Tommy again. He pointed ahead to the hill. "You figure them old legs get you up this hill?"

"I can climb it," Tommy said. "Better than an old darky anyway."

"Put your feet where your mouth is, Mr. Cochrane."

Back in the city they ran directly to the gym. Mac Brady had done his part, provided gloves and equipment for them. Nicky Wilson was not around. There were a handful of writers milling about, but Tommy passed them and their questions without a word. Bert Tigers came into the dressing room as Tommy and T-Bone were changing.

"Couple reporters want to talk to you, Tommy."

"Tell 'em to talk to Wilson. He's good at it."

"You gotta talk to the press, Tommy. It's part of the game, you know that."

"I got nothin' to say, Bert. And when I got nothin' to say, I keep quiet. I'm not running for office here."

"Well, shit. Mac ain't gonna like it."

"Try to imagine how that upsets me, Bert."

Bert sat on the table and watched as Tommy pulled on the light gloves. T-Bone helped with the laces, head down, talking to himself beneath his breath.

"What about a corner man?" Bert asked. "I can set something up."

"I got a corner man right here," Tommy said.

"You got a cut man?"

Tommy stood up and pushed the gloves one into the palm of the other.

"Don't you be worrying your empty head about what I got, Bert," he said. "T-Bone is my corner man, he's my cut man, my trainer, my manager, and he's handling my stock portfolio too, if you want to know. So get your greedy eyes off my purse and worry about your own fighter. You hear me?"

"You saying I should be worrying about Nicky Wilson? You figure on taking him out?"

"What I figure is none of your damn business. Now get out of here, Bert. I don't want you in the building when I'm here."

Bert climbed stiff-legged down from the table. "I remember a time when a person could talk to you, Tommy. Way back when. I guess you're just a little bit better than everybody else these days. Well, we're gonna see about that. A week from now, it might be a different story. Maybe nobody'll want to talk to you a week from now."

"Suit me fine. Goodbye, Bert."

Tommy waited until Bert had left the building and then he went out and worked for the better part of an hour, hitting the speed bag and the heavy, skipping rope, doing sit-ups and push-ups, staying away from the weights, which would only slow him down. At the end he sparred with T-Bone for ten minutes, or rather Tommy sparred while T-Bone offered targets with his gloves, Tommy working the hook off the jab and combinating. Looking for timing.

The writers followed him around for a while, but when he wouldn't answer questions, one by one they gave up. They had all vanished by the time Tommy packed it in.

Except for the kid from the *Telly* who was waiting in the dressing room when Tommy went in to shower. The kid was after the grizzled sportsbeat look, cigar clenched beneath a peach-fuzz mustache, dark fedora and rumpled suit. Andy Hardy trying for Wallace Beery.

"So whatdya think, Champ?" he started.

"My name ain't Champ," Tommy said. "What do I think about what?"

Tommy began to strip the damp shirt away as the kid came closer. T-Bone walked in, carrying gloves and a towel.

"Excuse me," the snotty kid said to T-Bone. "Can you give me a minute with the Champ here? I'm trying to do an interview."

T-Bone glanced over at Tommy, who stood up and took the kid by the arm and shoved him into the shower. Tommy turned the cold water on and held the squirming kid there for half a minute, then hauled him to the dressing room door and pushed him outside. The nickel cigar was still wet in the kid's mouth.

"That some interview," T-Bone said.

Tommy went in to shower. When he came out he dressed and sat on a bench while he waited for T-Bone to finish in the shower. There was hot water today, and T-Bone stayed under the spray a while, soaking it in. Tommy could hear him singing in the stall. Presently he came out, towelled off and began to dress.

"How you feeling, Thomas?"

Tommy stood up. "Right now I feel good. Tomorrow morning I'll be stiff as a new hair brush."

"Right back at it, that's the thing."

"Yeah. But I don't think anybody's gonna say I overtrained for this one, Bones."

When they left the room, the kid was still there, sitting in a puddle on a bench outside the door. Beside him his notebook was running ink like blood from a wound.

"You feel like answering some questions now?" the kid asked.

"This youngster got some mule in him," T-Bone said.

Tommy reached down and picked the kid's fedora from the bench and held it by the brim as it drained water. Then he set it down again.

"One question," he said.

"All right," the kid said and he got to his feet. "You said you were through. Why are you fighting Nick Wilson?"

"Well," Tommy said slowly. "I'm a fighter. That's what I do."

"But why did you change your mind?"

"That's two questions," Tommy said and he went out the door.

The persistent kid would have followed him even then if not for the hand on his wet shoulder.

"Don't ask him nothin' else," T-Bone said softly. "Just let him be."

He caught up with Tommy down the block and they walked back to the hotel. Tommy had notions of going for a beer, but T-Bone nixed the idea.

"Got six days to do three months' work," he said. "That mean no beer and no Irish for you, Thomas. That old barleycorn a thief, be stealing what you get in the gym. You listen to me now, Thomas, I ain't foolin'."

"I hear you, mother."

Up in the room T-Bone lay on the bed while Tommy stood by the window, looking down to the street below. Lying there, T-Bone went over what he'd learned sparring with Wilson.

"Got no left hand to speak of," he said aloud. "Couldn't jab his way out of a church supper."

Tommy put his fingertips on his temples and imagined what it was like there, under the skin. From the outside everything was fine. Like a car engine about to throw a valve; everything ran along all right one moment and then the next . . .

"He fair to middlin' quick for a man his size," T-Bone was saying. "But clumsy like a day-old calf, and 'ceptible to the uppercut, mighty 'ceptible to that."

"Okay, Bones."

"And he foul you, if he get the chance. Like to hook low comin' off the break."

Tommy crossed over to sit on the other bed. "Let's just let it go for now."

T-Bone looked over as Tommy stretched out the length of the bed and looked at the ceiling.

"Tell about them trout again, Thomas. Reckon a body could get used to eating trout, if it had a chance."

"Another week or so and we'll be home, Bones. Then I'll take you out and show you."

"Yep," T-Bone said. "We damn near there already."

While Lee was setting her nerve to go see Mel Dunston, he sent a message through her landlady that he wanted to see *her*. Whether that was a good sign or bad she couldn't decide. She let him wait a couple hours and then walked down to the Parrot. Mel was sitting at his desk in his office, behind an adding machine from the last century and a framed picture of two dark-haired toddlers, a boy and a girl.

"I didn't know you had kids, Mel," Lee said.

"My cousin's children," Mel said.

They rent you the picture, Mel? Lee reined it in — no smart comments today — and moved to sit opposite Dunston. Mel smiled at her, the kind of smile people saved for bellhops and cabbies.

"Are you happy here, Lee?"

"Sure."

Mel moved a sheaf of papers from one side of the desk to the other.

"Well, we're happy to have you here."

Well, golly gee, she thought. But she kept quiet. Mel moved the same stack of papers back across the desk.

"I was wondering if you'd like to stay on," he said then.

"What happened to whatshername — Tempest Teapot?"

"Miss Torrence will be staying on the coast for a while. She got a job on a variety show. Singing and dancing, you know. A lucky break."

"Oh, yeah."

Mel smiled again. "So I am in the fortunate position to offer you a job here long term."

"Well," Lee said and she waited.

"Uh . . . how do you feel about that?"

"I'm honoured," Lee told him and she had to look away. "The money, though, Mel. I just can't make it on a hundred a week."

"I've thought about that," Mel said. "And I've decided to give you a raise. One hundred and ten dollars a week, Lee."

"Two hundred," she said, and Mel got so red she thought he'd suffered a heart attack. She hoped to hell he wouldn't need mouth-to-mouth; he'd have a tough time finding a volunteer in present company.

"That's impossible," he managed to say.

"Two hundred a week," she said again.

Mel made to move the papers again, then let it go. "This is ridiculous," he said. "Do you think I'm a wealthy man?"

"As a matter of fact I do," she said. "But I'll tell you what I'll do. I'll sign a year's contract for one-fifty a week, what about that?"

Mel's colour got better so quick she thought he'd been leeched. He even managed a smile. He'd expected a tougher negotiation from this woman. But not only had she dropped fifty dollars in thirty seconds, she'd offered to sign for a year. If he could get her down to one-twenty-five, he'd be dancing on the ceiling.

"But I need five thousand in advance," Lee threw in, and Mel got apoplectic again.

"What?" he shouted.

"I'm in a bind, I need some money," Lee told him. "What I'm offering you is a good deal. If you're an intelligent businessman, you'll take advantage of it."

"Five thousand," Mel said, like he never knew such a number existed.

"That's the deal."

"Get out of here, young lady."

"Better think about it, Mel. Get that adding machine to work."

"I want you out of here."

Lee got to her feet.

"You'll pay out more than that over the year anyway," she told him. "And you won't have Lee Charles. Recording Artist, the sign out front says. Now I'm not Greta Garbo, Mel, but we both know the reason your cash register is going ka-ching. You think people are packing this place every night just to get a glimpse of your sweaty face? Not fucking likely. You know why they're here, don't you, Mel? You can give me your answer tonight."

She left him there gasping like a fish on a river bank. Walking through the club she saw Tony Broad standing at the bar. He was becoming a permanent fixture there. Like a spittoon, Lee thought. He called to her, and she waved and went out the door.

She walked home, stopping at the Greek deli for a chicken sandwich and an RC cola. Elegant dinner for one. Two blocks from the rooming house, it began to rain and she ran the last distance, getting soaked anyway, hurrying drenched up the stairs and down the hall to her room, stepping inside to find the heavy-weight boxer Tommy Cochrane lying on her bed. The blinds were pulled, and he was lying there in the near dark, smiling at her, at her wet clothes and her crumbling bag of dinner and her earnest expression.

She set her package down and came over to sit on him, her skirt pulled up and her bare legs across his stomach.

"Hey, you're all wet."

"Never bothered you before," she said. "How'd you get in here?"

"I'm a shadow, I come and go as I please."

"Oh, yeah?"

Tommy smiled. "I stood at the corner and watched until your landlady went to the market."

"Some shadow," Lee said. He made an attempt to grab her, but she rolled off him, then feinted and tagged him lightly on the jaw with a small left hand.

"Breaking and entering," she said seriously. "Violating a lady's boudoir, you're in a lot of trouble, mick."

"I'm gonna throw myself on the mercy of the court."

She stood up and began to undress. "Well, you're lucky," she said. "The court is feeling very merciful today."

And they made love, remaining in bed for more than an hour, in a room so warm and humid from the storm outside that they soon were both as wet as Lee had been when she walked through the door. She was on top of him, her hands gripping the headboard, his on her waist, her ribcage, her breasts. Neither said a word — after Dunston, Lee was sick of talking anyway. When finally she came, she collapsed over him, falling against his chest, her hair covering him like water from a falls.

After a time Tommy rolled her gently to her side and kissed her on the forehead. Eyes closed, she smiled and put her hand to his cheek.

"You need a shave, mick," she said. "You always need a shave."

"Any bum can get a shave," he said. "What I need I got."

"What'd ya do today?"

"Worked out."

She opened her eyes and pulled back a little. "You're really going to fight."

"Yeah."

She pulled her hair back with one hand and turned onto her stomach. She propped her elbows beneath her. "I know about the aneurysm," she said.

Tommy looked at her in the faint light. "He shouldn't have told you."

"Maybe not. But he did. What're you fighting for — the money?"

"The farm. You know that."

"Is that the reason though? What about Wilson and Bones?"

"I never liked what he did to Bones," Tommy admitted. "But that part of Wilson will catch up to him sooner or later, it doesn't have to be me. I never set out to right all the wrongs in the world, Lee."

She glanced at him and then got out of bed to retrieve the sandwich and the cola from the dresser. They split the sandwich in bed and drank the warm pop.

"If you had the money," Lee said with her mouth full, "you wouldn't fight?"

"If I had wings, I'd fly to the moon."

"Listen to me," she demanded. "If I could give you the money, would you forget about fighting?"

"You don't have the money."

"If I did."

"You don't."

"Goddamn you!" she shouted and she spilled the cola on the sheets. "Three days ago you asked me to go to the farm with you. If I can get the money, will you say no to Mac Brady?"

Tommy could see she was scared. It didn't help much, on top of everything else.

"I don't want to fight, Lee. But there's no other way. Either I do this and get the farm or I hit the hobo road, end up in the old palooka's home, telling stories about things that never happened."

"Maybe there's another way," she said. "The only thing is — I wouldn't be able to come to the farm right off. I'd have to stay in the city awhile."

Tommy got out of bed and began to get dressed. "I got to get back to the Jasper. Mac's coming with the cash and the contract, today or tomorrow."

"Don't sign it, Tommy. Wait a day or two."

"You better get dressed, you'll be late for work."

"Jesus Christ," she said. "Aren't you scared?"

"I've been scared before," he said. "I always got over it."

He buttoned his shirt and, shoes in hand, he tiptoed out into the hall and down the back stairs.

TWENTY-THREE

Tony Broad stood stonily at the bar, sipping the same bourbon he'd acquired thirty minutes ago and keeping a dull eye on Mel Dunston, who was sitting at a table by the stage, worrying the pages of a ledger and biting his bottom lip like it was a piece of chewing gum. At Tony's elbow Billy Callahan was drinking rye and drumming his fingers on the bar top. Tony Broad was walking a wire with Callahan, buying him enough booze to keep his nerve going, but not so much that he would foul up.

Because tonight was the night.

Shortly Mel came to the bar and asked his bartender for a glass of buttermilk, a quart of which was kept in the cooler for the fickle nature of Mel's stomach.

"That's a hell of a drink," Tony said.

Mel didn't know Tony Broad from Adam. "For my stomach," he said vaguely.

"Having problems with the tummy, Mel?"

The older man shook his head darkly. "My problem," he said, "is with Lee Charles."

Tony played ignorant. "The singer?"

"Singer?" Mel snorted. "A robber is more like it." And he took his yellow milk into his office.

Tony called for another drink for himself and one for Callahan. "Now what the hell is that all about?"

"Who knows?" Callahan said. "Lee Charles is gonna be the least of his worries tonight."

"Keep your mouth to yourself," Tony told him.

When Mac Brady strode into the bar five minutes later, Tony waved him over and bought him a drink.

"You owe me that," Mac said. "I sprung for your steam the other day."

"I forgot to pay?" Tony asked. "Goddamn, I guess I did."

But Mac had no time for nickel and dime today. "You guys seen Bert Tigers around? I'm supposed to meet him here."

"The guy from the gym?" Tony asked. "Haven't seen him."

"Well, he's supposed to be running an errand for me." Mac took some papers from his pocket and put them on the bar. "I'm busier than a one-armed switchboard operator with the crabs. I got this contract for Tommy Cochrane and I got a meeting in half an hour at the Royal York."

"What kind of meeting?"

"I'm looking into this new show at the Belair Theatre. It's a hell of a thing. It's like Shakespeare, but with strippers, you know. I'm looking for backers, if you're interested."

"Maybe I'll sleep on it," Tony said.

The front door opened and Mac turned impatiently. Lee Charles walked in, looking cool and determined. She went past the bar and into Mel Dunston's office.

"Where in the hell is that Bert?" Mac wondered. Then he looked at Tony Broad. "I hear Miss Charles is not real happy about Tommy taking this fight. I think she'd queer the deal if she could."

"How could she do that?"

"She can't," Mac said. He took a short drink. "I got the contract and I got the cash. All I need is a signature, and Tommy's mine." He made to drink again, but didn't. "Where's that goddamn Bert?"

Tony glanced to Callahan, who was standing dumbly with his Canadian Club, mouth open and mind in neutral.

"You listening to this?"

"What?" Callahan asked.

Morons, Tony thought. The world is overrun with fucking morons.

When Bert Tigers finally showed, he was followed so closely by Herm Bell that Tony thought for a moment the two were together, an unlikely pair. But Herm, spotting the brain trust assembled at the bar, sat at a table across the room and ordered beer.

Bert took a tongue-lashing from Mac, then ordered a rum and coke. He sucked at the Bacardi like a man dying of thirst. A boozer for sure, Tony thought.

"I have to get to the Royal York," Mac told Bert. He pushed the papers on the bar over, then took a thick envelope from his pocket and tucked it forcefully into Bert's inside jacket pocket. "Tommy's at the Jasper. Get his goddamn signature on the contract before you give him the envelope."

Bert made to look in the envelope.

"Leave it," Mac said. "You just have to make the delivery. And get the signature. You follow?"

"Sure."

Then Mac was gone, off to do Shakespeare with strippers. Tony Broad couldn't believe what was happening. In a minute he was beside Bert Tigers, buying him another Bacardi. Bert folded the contract and put it in his pocket and took the free drink.

"What do you figure in the fight?" Tony was asking. Coming on dumb, like Bert Tigers was some expert.

"The kid kills him," Bert said. "Early."

"That's my thinking too," Tony said.

They had a couple more drinks and Tony Broad talked it up, about the fight and about what a wonderful trainer Bert was, and then Bert had to use the can. When he was gone, Tony turned and showed his teeth to Callahan.

"Forget Dunston," he said. "You know what we got here?"

Callahan had no idea what they had there.

"We got two birds. You ever kill two birds with one stone, Billy my boy?"

"I never killed any birds."

Tony laughed. "Well, tonight you're gonna learn how."

When Lee came out of Dunston's office, she avoided the sludge at the bar and, spotting Herm Bell, went over and sat down. She ordered gin and tonic. Her face was closed and angry.

"Nothing with Dunston?" Herm asked.

"Mel Dunston's a cheap, short-sighted, petty son of a bitch," Lee said. She glanced toward the office. "I'm gonna introduce him to my mother."

When her drink came Herm paid for it. Lee took a sip, then pushed it away. Liquor wasn't going to do it.

"You know any more good horses, Herm?"

"I wish I did."

"Me too."

The band straggled in as they sat there. Doc Thorne joined them for a quick whiskey, then went backstage. Lee said she should go as well, then called for another gin. She was strung out, Herm could see, her eyes darting, her hands restless on the cheap tablecloth.

Nowhere to turn.

"You know what I think?" Herm told her. "I think Tommy's gonna turn out Nick Wilson's lights in the first round. I think it's gonna be an easy night for him."

Lee was looking at her drink. "Well, we can bullshit all we want," she said. "But we both know the truth. You ever been to an Irish wake, kid?"

"No, and I don't figure to be going to one."

But she was looking away now. Her eyes were suddenly flat and cold — out of place in that face — and Herm realized that she was looking at Tony Broad. The kid Callahan was with Broad, like usual, and he was standing glassy-eyed mean at the bar. Lee downed her drink and got to her feet.

"Hey," Herm said.

"I'll talk to you later," she told him.

She walked across the room like she was walking to her fate, a woman of resolve in green velvet and high heels and seamed stockings. When Tony Broad asked if she wanted a drink, she said okay.

TWENTY-FOUR

A kid found the body the next morning around eight o'clock, in the alley behind the North Star Diner. The kid had three hundred handbills to deliver and after the first hundred he ducked behind the restaurant, intending to dump the rest in the trash there. Bert Tigers' body was jammed in among the cans, with his neck twisted upward, his rummy blue eyes wide open, and a bullet hole in his chest. The kid went inside and told the morning cook, who called the cops and went back to his grill.

The North Star was barely three blocks from the Jasper Hotel. By noon the cops were in Tommy's room, a uniform named Mostel and a middle-aged detective with a harelip. The detective's name was Randall. He showed Tommy the contract, which they'd found in the alley with Bert. The cop held the contract in a handkerchief, very professional.

"That all he had on him?" Tommy asked.

"That's about it."

"Then whoever killed him got five thousand dollars for their trouble." And he watched as the farm slipped away, this time for good.

"How do you know that?" the lip asked.

"Because it was my five grand," Tommy told him. "He was delivering it to me. Whose name is on the contract, Sherlock?"

The uniform was sniffing around the room. "You live here alone?"

"Like you didn't ask downstairs?" Tommy asked. "My friend lives here with me. Mr. Thibideau Pike."

"Coloured guy — right?"

"He's a colourful guy, yeah."

"I mean he's a Negro," the uniform said.

"You know, I believe he is a Negro. Should we get some rope and string him up?"

"You're a funny man," the lip said.

"Yeah, well I just got some bad news."

"That so?" the lip said. "Tell me, what do you know about Albert Tigers?"

"I know he was a nasty two-faced little prick. I can't figure how he lived as long as he did."

The lip looked at the uniform, then nodded. "We're going to have to search this room, Mr. Cochrane. Now we can have a warrant down here in ten minutes."

"Never mind the warrant," Tommy said. "Help yourself. You think you're gonna find five thousand dollars here? You think I went down the street and killed a man for five grand when all I had to do is wait here for two minutes and have him walk in and put it in my hand? What am I — an idiot?"

The uniform regarded Tommy narrowly for a moment. "Do you own a gun, Mr. Cochrane?" the uniform asked.

Tommy shook his head at the ignorance. "No, I don't."

"Does Mr. Pike own a gun?"

"No, Mr. Pike does not."

"Where is he?"

"Walking. He likes to walk in the morning."

The uniform walked around the room and then turned back to Tommy quickly, pure drama.

"Who do you know who has a gun?"

BRAD SMITH

Tommy pointed at the man's belt. "You do."

The search turned up nothing. The lip said he would have more questions for Tommy later. Said that he wanted to talk to T-Bone Pike as well. He told Tommy not to leave the city without informing the police first.

"I got no place to go," Tommy told him and it was true.

The two cops walked out into the hallway.

"If you haven't talked to Mac Brady yet — you'd better," Tommy advised them. "He's going to want to know about this."

"Why?"

"Because it was his five grand."

"I thought you said it was yours," the lip said.

"It almost was," Tommy said and he closed the door.

When they had gone, Tommy pulled a chair to the window and sat there, watching down into the street. In a minute he saw the lip and his partner making their way down Shuter, heading back to the diner, where they would be asking if anybody saw an Irish heavyweight and a coloured hanging around last night.

After a while he saw T-Bone strolling back to the hotel, walking long-legged and loose on the concrete, eating a fat red apple he'd cadged somewhere. Tommy always swore that T-Bone could eat on a dollar a week.

When he came into the room T-Bone pulled a second apple from his pocket and tossed it over. "This for after," he said. "Right now we goin' running. Get your BlackHawks on, Thomas."

"You can forget about that, Bones," Tommy said and he told him.

"Sweet Jesus," T-Bone said and he sat on his bed. "That Mr. Bert not such a bad man, I expect, once you get to know him."

"Bones, you'd give small change to the devil if you had it."

"Who do you think do somethin' like this, Thomas?"

Tommy shrugged. "Bert was a drunk. Maybe he got loaded and was flashing the wad around the diner. People'll kill you for a lot less than five grand these days."

232

"You think it finished, Thomas? Or you think that maybe Mac Brady come up with another five thousand?"

"I don't think so. I doubt the well's that deep. When Bert Tigers took that bullet last night, he bought the farm, and that's no joke."

"No sir," T-Bone said. "It ain't."

And Tommy continued to sit and look out the window, thinking about what might have been because it was easier than thinking about what was.

Tony Broad spent the morning on the phone long-distance, charging calls to a number of companies he found in the yellow pages. He had arrangements to make and damned little time to make them.

Billy Callahan was with him and the kid was jackrabbit nervous; he'd killed his first man and he'd been up all night — laughing, worrying, bragging. And talking. Around dawn Tony had given him a part bottle of Kentucky bourbon and after a few shots, Callahan had actually slept awhile. But now he was awake again, pacing and talking, and he was getting on Tony's nerves.

When Tony got off the phone this time, he jotted a time down on the phone book cover and then tore it off and handed it over to Callahan.

"I got a job for you, kid," he said. "I want you to meet a guy for me. Four-fifteen, at Union Station. Name of Bobby Dean, he's coming in from Detroit. He's our actor."

"How'm I gonna know him?"

"You saw him in the movie the other night. Remember — the guy with the horse cock?"

"I think so."

"Pick him up and bring him here. And keep the son of a bitch sober if you can. Let him drink a little beer, if he has to, but nothing else."

Callahan began to pace again. Then he realized that Tony was watching him.

"You want me to go now?" he asked. "It's four hours away."

"Go for a walk or something," Tony said irritably. "I got work to do and you're bothering me. We got one day to do this and one day only. And give me the goddamn gun — we don't need you getting picked up carrying an iron."

"I keep my gun."

"Give it to me, for fuck's sakes. Who's calling the shots here? You want Lee Charles or not?"

Callahan handed over his weapon and Tony put it on the night table. He indicated that Callahan should go now.

"You really gonna give five grand to Lee Charles?"

"Let me worry about what I'm going to give Lee Charles. Make sure Bobby Dean gets here, that's all you got to do. You're gonna have a night you'll never forget, kid."

So Callahan left the hotel and walked down Jarvis Street, his chest pounding, his heart in his throat. He'd set something off these past hours and now it seemed like he couldn't think, like his brain was doing somersaults.

He had forty dollars in his pocket, money he'd taken from Tigers' wallet. Tony didn't know about the forty or he'd have taken it away. Callahan decided he needed a drink. He went into Bryan's, on Jarvis, for a rye and water. After a while Danny Bonner came in and, while he was hardly Callahan's best friend, he was somebody to talk to, and Callahan needed to talk today. And Bonner would listen, as long as Callahan stood for the drinks. Besides, there were four hours to kill, and four hours was a long time to be alone with the kind of thoughts that Billy Callahan had in his head.

After the fight she'd had with Dunston, any excuse would be lame, so she waited until the last minute, then called and told Lucky Ned she wouldn't be in to work tonight. Ned didn't ask why and she didn't say. The band could play without her, instrumental, and Doc Thorne could handle a few vocals if he wanted. The world would keep on turning even without Lee Charles, saloon singer, for one evening.

On edge, she couldn't remain in her room, so she went out and took a walk around the city. She had a thought to go visit Tommy — he'd be in the gym — but she realized at once that he would know the minute he saw her, it would be splashed across her face like a sign on a movie marquee.

She called Patty Simmons from a pay phone on Spadina and asked her to meet her at the Rooster.

She was two gins up when Patty showed. Patty was late because she'd been to the doctor.

"I'm pregnant," she grinned broadly.

"Good for you," Lee said. "Let's drink to it."

"Sure, why not? I'll quit tomorrow. It's early, right?"

Patty was full of her news and Lee was glad for it. She kept her secret hidden away, a thing of shame.

"Here's to you and motherhood." Lee raised her glass.

"Righto," Patty said. "And here's to dirty diapers and puke on my blouse, all those things a woman yearns for."

"Did you tell Robert?"

"I called him from the doctor's. Get this — he's stopping at the library on the way home to pick up a book of names for the baby. I said, hey, we got eight months."

"Well, men are like that," Lee said. "They get a little nuts when it comes to kids. Probably because they spend so much time acting like kids themselves. Ties that bind."

"What about you? You ever think about it?"

"Sometimes I do."

"With Tommy."

"Sometimes."

Lee's glass was empty and she waved to the bartender. Getting drunk was probably not a terrific idea, but it sure beat the hell out of the notion of going in sober.

"Hey, aren't you working tonight?" Patty asked.

"Am I ever."

"You better take it easy on the Beefeater," Patty said lightly. "I got a feeling straight-arrow Dunston takes a dim view of boozy dames, especially if they happen to be in his employ. How long you sticking at the Parrot anyway?"

Lee looked across the table. "I've about run my string there. I may be leaving the city soon." She laughed without happiness. "Maybe on the noon stage, pardner."

"What about Tommy?"

"Maybe we'll leave together. Don't you believe in happy endings?"

"Yeah, but I didn't know you did. You going back to California then?"

"Fuck California," Lee said. "I've spent most of my life being in places I didn't want to be. All because I thought something good would come of it in the end. Well, that never panned out, so this time I'm going to shoot for something simple."

"And what's that?"

"I'm gonna become a farmer."

Patty laughed and took a drink.

"I'm serious," Lee told her. "Tommy's got a place, or he can get it if we can raise the money."

"I hear he's fighting this weekend."

"Maybe not. If I can get my hands on the cash, I can talk him out of it. I don't want him to fight."

"It never bothered you before."

"Things change, kiddo. Every day you get older, don't matter how fast you run from it."

Lee glanced at her watch and then took down the rest of her gin. She was aware of Patty's eyes on her.

"How are you going to raise the money?" Patty asked.

And Lee grinned through the booze, a false political smile that never quite made it to her eyes. "Remember what I said about being in places I didn't want to be. Well, this is it. But in spades this time. If there's a God in heaven, I hope he's in a forgiving mood these days."

She stood up to go. Patty didn't like the smile or the resignation behind it and she tried to grab Lee's arm.

"Wait. Where are you going?"

"Straight to hell," Lee told her and she left.

Herm Bell ran into Danny Bonner on Front Street, near Jarvis. Herm had just skinned a college boy for nearly thirty bucks playing shuffleboard in the Duke Hotel and he was feeling pretty good. The college boy had been with his snotty friends, and he was pretty fair with the rocks, but not in Herm's league. Herm had played him like a violin, lost three games for a dollar, then won four in a row at a fin a piece, then played the last game for a saw and closed the kid out in five ends. He left the cheeky kid in a pout, his allowance for the week shot. Herm knew he'd have to explain to daddy why he was broke and Herm laughed just thinking about it.

Danny was strolling along, hands in his pockets, tie loosened. At first Herm didn't notice his condition.

"Herman, Herman," Danny called. "What'd ya say?"

"How you doing, Danny?" Herm said. "You going to Ollie's tonight?"

"Ollie's tonight?" Danny repeated. "It ain't Wednesday already?"

"Jesus, you're polluted," Herm said. "Where the hell you been?"

"Just blowing the foam off a few, that's all." Danny made to do a soft shoe on the concrete and almost went down. "Me and Billy Callahan."

"Since when is Callahan your pal?"

Danny laughed. "Since he bought the drinks all afternoon. He's all right, that Callahan. But he's weird, you know? He was talkin' about stuff I couldn't even understand."

"He's a punk."

"God, I got to sit down," Danny said and he flopped onto the curb. "I'm drunk as a lord, Herm, and I'm man enough to admit it. Five in the afternoon and I'm stewed like a bowl of prunes."

"You'd better head it home," Herm said. "Sleep it off and you'll be up for the game tonight. Did you hear about Bert Tigers?"

"No."

"He's dead. Somebody shot him last night over on Shuter."

"No shit? Who's Bert Tigers?"

"Nick Wilson's trainer, you know that. He was carrying five thousand dollars over to Tommy Cochrane when he bought it. Now the money's gone and the fight's off, I hear."

"Son of a bitch. What was this fellow's name?"

"Bert Tigers."

"Ain't that a son of a bitch," Danny said again. "I always liked him."

"You never knew him."

"You're right, I didn't, I musta been thinking 'bout somebody else." Danny shook his head to clear his thoughts. "I tell you about Lee Charles?"

"What about her?"

"Billy Callahan says he's gonna fuck her tonight."

"He's full of shit."

"Could be. He's drunker than I am. But he says he's fucking her tonight, him and that Tony Broad and I don't know who else. Some hotel on Isabella. Says they're makin' a movie. Sounded pretty sure of himself, too."

"Consider the source, Danny," Herm said. "Callahan and Tony Broad are both a load of shit. Why don't you head it for home and grab some sleep. Come on, I'll get you to the streetcar."

Herm went home himself after that. But sitting there listening to the radio, he ran things over in his head and he kept coming up with the same scene. Early in the evening he phoned the Blue Parrot and asked for Lee Charles. Lucky Ned told him she wasn't singing tonight. Herm hung up and took a cab to the Jasper Hotel. But neither Tommy nor T-Bone were at the Jasper.

Herm hit the street then, heading south. A feeling of foreboding began to grip him; he walked quickly, even though he had no idea where he was going.

When he passed Sully's, he spotted T-Bone Pike through the plate glass; T-Bone was leaning on a pool cue and talking to Sully.

Herm went in and took T-Bone aside and asked where Tommy was.

"Out having a drink, I expect," T-Bone said. "That man Mr. Bert got himself killed last night and the money took, so the fight called off. So I figure Tommy gone off to have a drink, or maybe he with Miss Lee."

"I don't think he's with Lee," Herm said. "I think maybe Lee's got herself some trouble."

T-Bone put the cue away. Herm told him what he knew about Tony Broad and his business, about Callahan's boast, and about Lee not being at the Parrot. For a moment he thought T-Bone would actually hit him.

"You watch your mouth, Mr. Bell," T-Bone demanded. "You my friend, but I don't want to hear you talkin' on Lee Charles like that. She would never do a thing like that."

"Just think about it, T-Bone," Herm said. "Would she do it to save Tommy's life? What about you, T-Bone — what would you do to save his life?"

T-Bone looked at the floor. "She don't need to. The fight called off."

"Does Lee know that?"

T-Bone looked out at the street. "Maybe she don't at that. Where is this place you say, this hotel?"

"Right around the corner here. Big brick dump in the middle of the block."

They walked outside then and Herm pointed the place out. T-Bone looked out over the city. There was no way to figure where Thomas Cochrane might be. Or what shape he'd be in.

"Another thing," Herm said. "This Callahan carries a gun."

"Maybe the same kind of gun that shot Mr. Bert?"

Herm hesitated. "Now that's one angle I didn't figure."

T-Bone turned. "Can you let me have twenty dollars, Mr. Bell?" he asked.

Herm took out his wallet and handed over a pair of tens.

"This city is yours," T-Bone said then. "See if you can find Thomas. Maybe he at the Bamboo, maybe somewhere else. I figure you know better than me. But look 'til you find him and then we meet back at the Jasper. That all right?"

"Sure."

"I take care of the rest. Just find Thomas and bring him here, don't tell him nothing, just bring him."

After Herm left, T-Bone walked down the block to the pawn shop he'd passed every morning on his way to the gym. The guns were there in the window, beside the tennis racquets and the trout creel and the lamp with the three monkeys on it. An old Lee Enfield with a bolt, a single shot .22 and a double-barrel twelve gauge.

T-Bone went in and asked about the shotgun.

"Twenty-five dollars," the little man behind the counter said. "That's a Stevens, that double barrel, a good gun."

"Only got twenty dollars, sir."

"Then you're five dollars short. What do you want with this gun anyway, fella?"

"Gonna do some duck hunting with that gun, sir."

"Well, duck season doesn't open 'til fall. Come back when you got the money."

"But I need that gun today, sir. Be headin' out of the city, going up to the north country. Can't you take twenty dollars?"

The little man was interested in closing for the night. And he was suspicious of this coloured. "This ain't much of a duck gun," he said.

"I ain't much of a duck hunter."

"What've you got around your neck, fella? What's that stone?"

T-Bone looked down. "This a genuine Indian arrowhead. Given me by my good friend Thomas — well, it just an arrowhead, that's all, sir."

"I'll take the stone and twenty for the gun."

It nearly broke T-Bone's heart to part with that flint. But he took it off and handed it over, along with the twenty dollars. Then he asked the man for shells.

"Just a couple, sir, to try her out."

"You got a lot of gall," the man said. He reached into a box and handed over two shells. "All I got is number twos — you shoot a duck with one of these and there won't be enough bird left to stuff a pillow. But then maybe it ain't ducks you're after."

T-Bone just smiled and let it pass. "You got some sacking or somesuch to wrap that gun in?" he asked. "Some folks don't care to see a coloured man walking about with a scattergun. Makes folks nervous, I guess."

"I guess it does."

When the gun was wrapped in burlap T-Bone left the shop and walked directly to the Jasper. There would be a maintenance room in the basement, he knew, and he found it easily. The lock was cheap and he was inside in a minute. There were tools there, on shelves and in red boxes and hanging from pegs above the workbench there. T-Bone got down to work.

When he was a kid his father had a Cooey twenty gauge that he used for squirrel and rabbit and the like. And he taught young Thibideau to use the gun, and when his father went away to work, which was often, it was up to Thibideau to put meat on the table.

But that was going back some. A lot of years had passed since he'd touched a gun. There had been a time though. T-Bone had grown up reading the Bible and learning the Christian way from his mother and grandmother and as such he never cared for the killing of God's animals. But he had brothers and sisters to think about, and he'd been told by his father that he had to provide. So he would take that old hammerlock Cooey out to the woods and he would kill when the need was there, but each time he did he said a silent prayer for the animals he'd taken, because T-Bone believed that when his time came he would go to heaven and he believed that in heaven there would be squirrels and rabbits and woodcock, too. And how else would they reach those gates if someone didn't say a prayer for their creature souls?

It had been a long journey from that Missouri farm to this city tonight. He'd left the farm early; with the Depression on he'd reasoned one less mouth to feed would be a blessing to his family. Worked at an automobile wheel factory in Joplin, fought bare-knuckles in a box-car in New Orleans, cut wood in Arkansas. Barnstormed with a thief named Jaystone, boxing exhibitions all over the south. Turned pro in Chicago but never climbed the ranks, never neared the dizzy heights scaled by his idol, Joe Louis. Ended up sparring with champs, contenders and bums. New Jersey, New York, Detroit. A few years in the Catskills. And Jacksonville.

Jacksonville. Where Thomas Cochrane had saved his life. And he hadn't done it for money, or to make himself look good to others or to feel good to himself. He'd done it because it was right. And if that seemed like the easiest thing in the world, it sometimes seemed to T-Bone that it was the rarest, too.

And now, ten years later in this Toronto, Thomas Cochrane had bad trouble and Thibideau Pike, the Missouri boy who believed that squirrels and rabbits and woodcocks went to heaven too, had it in his mind to do something about it.

In the workshop he cut down and filed the barrels and the stock of the shotgun and then slipped the shells into the breech. The gun was barely two feet long now. T-Bone tucked the weapon under his coat and went out of the shop. He was whistling tunelessly as he climbed the stairs.

TWENTY-FIVE

L ike T-Bone said, it was Herm's city, but that didn't mean he could find a needle in a haystack. He checked every place that was likely, and more than a few that weren't, but he found no trace of Tommy Cochrane. Finally, about nightfall, he went into the Bamboo Club for the third time, thinking that maybe Tommy would go back to his job, now that the fight was off.

Billy Callahan was leaving as Herm walked in. Callahan had somebody with him; from across the room the man looked handsome and well-dressed, but up close he was just another bum. Callahan tried to put his shoulder into Herm as he passed.

"Move, cocksucker," he said.

Herm had a notion to push Callahan's face in, then and there. Get it over with. But he realized that whatever was in the cards tonight over on Isabella would happen with or without the likes of Billy Callahan. When he saw that Tommy was not in the Bamboo, he decided to follow the two jokers just leaving.

On Isabella Street Tony Broad was set up and ready to go. All he could do now was drink Kentucky mash and wonder if his actors would show. His equipment had been in a locker at the bus station. Lights and camera only. This wasn't a talkie, this was an action film.

Now Tony stood watching out the window, to the darkened street below, wondering where pea-brained Billy Callahan was with his actor, and wondering if Lee Charles would show at all. Tony knew the fight was off — no way Mac Brady could raise that kind of jack again on the quick. What Tony didn't know was whether or not Lee was aware of the fact. He figured his chances were fifty-fifty at best on that count.

As he watched now, a cab pulled up out front and the great Bobby Dean stepped out onto the curb, followed by Billy Callahan, who tripped over the concrete and went down to one knee. From the window, Tony couldn't tell if Bobby Dean was drunk or not. As far as Callahan was concerned, Tony didn't care if the kid passed out for the evening. Be one less headache for Tony.

As he was turning from the window though, he saw another cab, stopping along the curb half a block away. Herm Bell, the kid with the mouth and the luck at cards, stepped out under the streetlight and then made his way along the street toward the hotel.

"Shit," Tony said.

He walked to the dresser and picked up the pistol. After thinking it over, though, he slid the gun into the drawer and took a Buck clasp knife from his pocket. He opened the knife and slid it into the inside of his boot.

He went to open the door for Callahan and Bobby Dean.

"You guys sit down," he said. When he shook hands with Bobby Dean, he smelled only beer on his breath, and Bobby's eyes were clear, at least for Bobby Dean. Callahan was a zombie, stumbling on the carpet and falling into a chair.

"I'll be right back," Tony told them and he went out into the hallway. He ran down the back stairs to the ground floor and then went into the storage room by the loading dock at the rear of the hotel. There was a broken-down freight elevator there; Tony stepped inside and waited. From where he stood he could see the main elevator and the back stairs. It'd take a couple minutes, he figured, for the kid to get the room number from the front desk and make his way up.

Tony was guessing that Bell would make for the stairs and he was right.

When Herm approached the stairs Tony jumped him from behind, socking him above the ear and knocking him to the floor. But Tony Broad was a slug, and Herm could handle himself; he came off the floor firing both hands at Tony's head. Tony got hit hard and went down; when he tried to stand Herm went after him again, throwing right hand after right hand, knocking Tony back onto the floor of the freight elevator. In desperation Tony flung himself forward, grabbed Herm around the legs and bulled him to the floor. Herm got to his knees at once, took hold of Tony's coat and hit him again and again.

When first jumped, Herm had been alarmed, not knowing who or how many he was up against. Now he saw it was only Tony Broad and he knew he was all right. Sure, his lucky streak was going to end sooner or later. He knew that. But not like this. Not in this place, in this company. Not on this dirty floor of this cut-rate hotel.

And certainly not at the hands of a cheap hustler like Tony Broad, a man who never played a straight game in his life.

Now he slammed Tony Broad into the corner, hooked him in the ribs hard enough to double him over. Tony's hand went for his boot as Herm clubbed him to the floor.

Tommy wasn't out drowning his sorrows, as everybody thought. He'd spent most of the day just walking, had even gone down to the old dairy where he'd worked as a kid, but there was nobody there he knew anymore. Tommy thought there would be — fifteen years wasn't such a hell of a long time, especially looking backward. Forward was another matter. Forward wasn't something he wanted to think about today.

When he walked into the Blue Parrot that night, the band was playing and Doc Thorne was singing Leadbelly. Lee was not in sight. Tommy went to the bar and got a drink from Lucky Ned.

"Guy in here looking for you," Ned said. "Name of Bell."

"Yeah? Where'd he go?"

"Dunno. Said he'd be back though."

The band came off then and Doc Thorne made for the bar where Tommy was standing. Tommy shook Doc's hand and called for another shot for the horn player.

"Where's Lee?"

"Not singing tonight," Doc said. "Figured you'd know. Must be ailing or something."

"Where is she?"

"Over home, I expect."

Tommy shook his head. "I was just over there. Landlady put the run on me. But Lee's not there."

Doc put his fingertips to his whiskered chin. "I got no idea then where she be."

"I do," Tommy said. "She was talking about touching her mother for a loan. Probably where she went."

"I heard the fight is off," Doc said.

"Yeah, it's off."

Tommy was bumped from behind then and he turned to the charming face of Nick Wilson.

"Give me some room, pops," Wilson said. "Whatcha doing — celebrating the fact that I'm not gonna rearrange your face?"

But Tommy just grinned at the kid, showed him his glass of whiskey and the big Irish smile that drove the kid nuts. Wilson looked at Doc Thorne.

"On top of everything else, Cochrane, it seems you just love the niggers."

"You can kiss my ass, you honky punk," Doc told him.

"Watch your mouth, coon," Wilson said. "I'll be giving you a white eye, old man."

For a second Tommy thought that Doc would take a poke at the kid. Tommy got between the two.

"Don't push it," he said to Wilson.

But Wilson was learning from Tommy. He laughed out loud and moved down the bar, where he ordered a beer and a shot. Tommy looked at Doc and shrugged.

"The kid's oatmeal from the eyes up," he said to the horn player. "Ain't no cure for that."

"I hear ya, Tommy. But that kind of stuff catch up to a man sooner or later. At least I hope that's the way it is." He patted Tommy's hand on the bar. "Gotta go blow a tune, Tommy. Catch you later."

Tommy kept his distance from Wilson, but what Doc said was on his mind. Maybe there was no such thing as justice in the world anymore. Maybe there never was. But maybe — like a lot of other things — it was whatever you made it to be.

He felt a presence beside him and he turned to see the large arrival of Mac Brady. Old home night at the Parrot tonight.

"Guess I got enough left to stand you to a drink, Tommy."

"Okay."

Mac saw Wilson then, the kid was talking to a waitress at the end of the bar. Mac shook his head. "I see my fighter's still in training."

Lucky Ned brought shots for the two of them. Mac paid from a small roll.

"Any chance of you taking my note, Tommy?"

"Come on, Mac."

Mac nodded resignation into his drink. "I had to ask," he said.

"I know, Mac."

Mac tested the scotch gently with his tongue. "Ah, well, we almost had a fight," he said. "And you know, I think it would have been a good one. Tickets were selling like hotcakes. And now I have to give all that money back. Damn, I hate handing out refunds."

"Lay your hands on five grand and you've still got a fight," Tommy told him. "You know where I stand. When Bert went down in the alley, my farm went with him. You're still my only chance, Mac."

"I can raise it, but not in two days," Mac said. "I had to scramble to get it together the first time." He gave Tommy a classic Mac Brady look. "Now if you were willing to drop your price down, to say — two thousand?"

Tommy looked at the big man and laughed in spite of himself.

"You know what I like about you, Mac?" he said. "Some people get nervous around you because they're suspicious of your motives. I've never had that problem because I always know exactly what you're up to. You're always looking out for the fat guy in the three-piece suit."

Mac was offended. "You don't like my suit, Tommy?"

"Just paying you a compliment, Mac. Believe me."

"Believing you is something I've never had a problem with, Tommy." He pointed a thumb down the bar to Nick Wilson, still making time with the waitress. "How'd I get stuck with that dumb son of a bitch?"

"He's your boy," Tommy said.

"He's got talent, Tommy, that's the truth. He can hit like a sledge hammer and he's fast for a big man. Too bad he's such a peckerhead."

"Being a peckerhead doesn't mean he can't go places," Tommy said.

"That's true."

"It just means that nobody's gonna like him when he gets there."

Mac laughed and called for Lucky Ned. "Give us two more here," he instructed. "I'll tell you though, Tommy, this kid could do it. To be honest, I really don't think you could have handled him this weekend."

"Maybe not, but you'd have gotten your money's worth," Tommy said. "I mean, I wasn't going to stiff you on that. After all, the money was all I cared about anyway and I would've earned it. I

wouldn't have been interested except I was trying to get something
for after, you know. I never put anything away, was never any damn
good at handling my money. Now I'm done and I got nothing. This
fight was my one chance to have something."

"You mean the farm."

"If you've got land, you're in pretty good shape, Mac. Because
land is always there — you don't have to worry about it getting old
and rusty, it doesn't fall apart on you or up and leave you." Tommy
laughed. "Like legs, like reflexes."

He paused to take a drink of the fresh Jameson's.

"And I wanted it for Lee. You know, I never really gave her anything."

"Lee Charles is a straight-ahead woman," Mac said. "I think
she's got what she wants."

He was interrupted by Nick Wilson again. Wilson pushed his
way between them and stood facing Mac.

"I'm kinda short tonight, Mac," he said. "Give me twenty, will
ya? I got a thing with this waitress, you know how these girls at the
Parrot like to fuck."

Mac gave him twenty to get rid of him. "We're having a conversation here," Mac told the kid.

Wilson turned to Tommy, like he hadn't noticed him. "Hey,
where's Lee tonight? She's not singing with the band."

"Can't put nothing past you," Tommy said.

"We're having a conversation," Mac told Wilson again.

"Did Lee tell you about me and her?" Wilson asked Tommy.

"Go back to your waitress," Tommy said.

Hands held out, Wilson began to back away from them. "Hey,
I know how it is," he said. "Guys don't like to have their women
fucked by their betters."

And Tommy decided then. Mac had his hand on his arm, but
Tommy had decided and he just smiled. He was in no particular
hurry.

"Let's have another," Mac was saying.

"Sure, Mac."

"What can I say?" Mac asked. "The kid's a peckerhead."

In his room at the Jasper, T-Bone Pike sat in a chair by the open window and tried to read the Bible so kindly left for him by the Gideons. He couldn't concentrate though. His mind kept going to Lee Charles. He wished that Tommy would show, he wished that Herm Bell would show. He wished he knew what was going on.

During anxious moments in the past he'd managed to calm himself by reading favourite passages from the good book. Even that wouldn't work tonight. Finally, he decided to walk over to the hotel on Isabella, just to have a look around. He took one last glance at the open Bible as he laid it on the chair.

— *blessed are the meek, for they shall inherit the earth* —

"Could be they got their work cut out tonight," T-Bone said and he left the room.

When he reached the hotel, he could see the night clerk inside, seated at the front desk, reading a newspaper. T-Bone kept walking. He went into the alley past the hotel and walked around to the back. He climbed onto a loading dock there. The back door was open and he stepped into a cluttered storage room. There were stairs to the left, an aged elevator to the right. A single dim bulb overhead.

T-Bone stepped forward and slipped on the floor, almost fell. He saw that the planking was covered with blood and that it came from the elevator.

Herm Bell was inside, his back propped against the wall, his eyes half open, his right hand clutching his stomach.

"Mr. Bell!" T-Bone said. "Oh lawdy, oh lawdy. . . ."

He rushed into the elevator, skidding wildly on the bloody floor; T-Bone had never seen so much blood. Not even in the ring. Not even in Jacksonville.

"Oh, Mr. Bell. What they do to you?"

Herm's eyes flickered. "Hey, T-Bone. Hey."

His voice was cracked. He grimaced when he spoke and T-Bone saw at once that his gums were white. T-Bone put any thought of running for a doctor out of his mind. He knelt on the floor beside Herm, put his arm on Herm's shoulder.

"Hey T-Bone, you're here."

"Take it easy, Mr. Bell."

"Had a little . . . run in with Tony Broad. I duked him, T-Bone."

"Easy now."

"He got me with a blade, I think. Ain't nothing. We gotta . . . take care those creeps, T-Bone. Lee's got trouble. Room 403. She's gonna need us."

Herm closed his eyes against the pain.

"Okay, now."

Herm's ragged breath filled the elevator. He opened his eyes again, looked past T-Bone.

"Damn, lookit all the blood," he said. "I got him good, T-Bone. Didn't I get him?"

"You got him."

"Tell Tommy I got him good."

"I do that. Take it easy now."

T-Bone looked at Herm's right hand, clutched over the wound in his stomach. The knuckles were torn open from the punches he'd landed.

"Okay," Herm breathed then. "We gotta . . . take care of this."

"Easy now."

"We . . . take care of this," Herm said and he smiled. "Then we're going to . . . Sully's. Gonna give you a snooker lesson."

"Yup."

"Aren't you gonna . . . say it?" Herm said then. "Tell me . . . tell me where you're from."

T-Bone swallowed, tasted the salt from the tears running down his cheeks. "I from Missouri."

Herm nodded, closed his eyes a moment against the pain. "The show-me state."

"That's it."

"Okay then . . . we got a game at Sully's."

"Yes sir, Mr. Bell. We got a game."

"Penny a point."

"Yes sir. Penny a point."

"God, I'm tired, T-Bone," Herm said then. "Took a lot outta me, I guess. More than I figured . . . I just need . . . a minute to rest. Then we'll go get those creeps. Me and you, T-Bone. Me and you. Just let me . . . close my eyes a minute."

He slipped to the side then and would have fallen over except for the strong arms of T-Bone Pike. His breath became shallow, and T-Bone held him and then Herm Bell closed his eyes and he rested.

TWENTY-SIX

She was over an hour late when she finally reached the hotel. She'd stopped twice for drinks on the way, but no amount of liquor could make her numb tonight. She took the elevator in dread fixation. She'd been trying to concentrate her mind's eye upon some point down the road; she couldn't say the experiment was going well. She dared not think of Tommy at all; she forced him from her mind, dropped him from all thought and memory.

In the room Tony Broad was beginning to think she wouldn't show. He'd managed to keep Bobby Dean sober; he was lying on the bed, fully dressed except for his shoes, waiting to go to work. A handsome man whose looks were going fast, a never-was actor who'd fallen to whiskey and his own lack of intelligence and imagination, a lifetime loser whose only claim to fame these days was an over-sized cock.

Callahan was the loose cannon on deck, still boozing, still high from the killing the night before. If Tony Broad had a conscience he'd be worried about turning the addled kid loose on Lee Charles. But by that time the shooting would be finished and Tony wouldn't care what happened to the smart-mouthed bitch. Still, Tony was on edge. Herm Bell's arrival had made him nervous. Who else could he expect?

When he heard the small rap on the door, he knew he had his movie. He attempted to greet his actress with a kiss but she turned her head and all he got was ear.

Lee came into the room like Daniel checking into the lion's den. When she pushed Tony away she felt the hard steel beneath his jacket. Sure, she thought, why not guns? She was convinced that whatever could go wrong tonight would go wrong, and in a big way.

After a moment she took her coat off, and Tony placed it on a chair. Lee stood there quietly, trying to avoid eye contact with the clumsy camera and the other creeps in the room. The Callahan kid was standing, wild-eyed and hungry, by the door. There was a rummy-eyed man of about forty on the bed; he was wearing a tuxedo and Lee decided that the outfit was part and parcel of what was about to happen. Tony Broad asked if she wanted a drink, and she turned him down.

"I plan to be out of here quick as I can," she said. "Where's the money?"

Tony reached into his coat and pulled out a wad of bills wrapped in a rubber band. "Twenty-five hundred," he said. "You get the other half when the job is done."

"Let me see it."

Tony smiled and shook his head, then showed her the rest of the cash. He tossed it carelessly on the bureau. Lee counted the first roll then put it in her pocket.

"And I will collect the rest," she told him. "You'd better know that."

Tony showed his revolting smile again and then took a shimmering white evening dress from the bed. He indicated the bathroom.

"I want you to put this on," he said. "The two of you are dressed for an evening out, you know what I mean? Oh yeah, this is Bobby Dean."

The shadow on the bed looked at Lee without a flicker of expression, like she wasn't there at all. She welcomed the detachment, preferred it over the condescending Tony Broad and the leering punk

Callahan across the room. She took the dress from Tony Broad and turned away.

"And Lee," Tony said to her. "You don't wear anything under the dress. It gets too complicated, you understand?"

She went into the bathroom and closed the door. She laid the dress across a chair there, then stepped out of her pants and her blouse and her underthings. Then she sat on the edge of the tub and cried.

So much for the tough dame. So much for the broad with the smart answers.

She sat naked on the cool porcelain and for the first time in memory she cried for herself. She cried out of self-pity and disgust and she cried for what she would lose tonight and never find again. And when that gave way she cried out in hatred — for Tony Broad and his ilk and for the wheels that had turned to deliver her here tonight. Hatred for Mac Brady and Nick Wilson for what they'd brought Tommy to do. For Dunston, that tight-fisted bastard, and for her mother, sitting in Rosedale with her money and her inbred cat.

And for the memory she'd carry from now on.

But crying wouldn't do it, she knew. She stood and looked at the dress she was to wear. A sleazy piece of imitation silk, cut low in front and slit up the thigh. Tony Broad's idea of class. She laid the rag aside and looked at herself in the mirror, at the body that had gotten her into this mess.

Traitor.

Sure, it was simple for you, standing there in the mirror. You ought to try it out here sometime. It's not that easy. Sometimes the things that everyone thinks are so fucking wonderful are nothing but a curse. Look at that face, look at those breasts — how'd you like people to admire you for your tits? Do you have any idea how that feels?

No way. You stand in that looking glass, lady, and you got no idea. Out here men slaver over your body like it was a goddamn shrine; sometimes you wish you could leave it behind for a time, just step outside of yourself a while, go for a walk, get a drink maybe. Leave the half-wits to worship away in peace, they never gave a shit about *you* anyway.

In the refuge of the mirror, it was a snap. You're all flash in there, you're all style; you look great, but you only got two dimensions. It's the third one that kills you, don't you know?

The only man who ever made the connection between her body and her mind — herself — was Tommy Cochrane. Oh sure, he liked the body, but with Tommy it was different. He liked the whole package — elbows, knees, ears, teeth. *Her.* He knew that her smart mouth was nothing more than defence, like a fighter slipping a punch.

He knew *her*. In the end, it was that simple. Not only did he know her but he was the only one who ever had. And the only one she'd ever wanted to.

That alone made him worth saving. That alone justified being here. Because that *is* why we're here, right? You in the mirror, you listening? We're here to save him. Remember that.

But who says we have to do this? We got each other — who says we get to have the farm too? Each other, hell, that was more than most people ever end up with. More than we ever figured on. Who says we have to be tough and go for everything?

Being tough wasn't that easy, wasn't all it was cracked up to be. Besides, all the tough broads lived in the mirror anyway.

In the looking glass, where the living was easy.

There was a knock on the door, and she heard Tony Broad's insistent voice. Lee looked to the door, then back to the mirror, to the hard-eyed woman standing there.

On the other side of the door Tony Broad was getting antsy. He had the principals in place and he was hot to get on with it, to get the fucking thing shot and done with. Tonight was Tony's last night in the city. Billy Callahan didn't know it, but Tony was leaving on the one o'clock train and he was leaving his young gunsel friend behind.

Now he knocked impatiently on the bathroom door again.

"Yeah, get the tail out here," Callahan grinned from across the room.

On the bed Bobby Dean was staring at the wall, wishing he had a drink. What was going to happen in the next half hour meant nothing to him. He only wished to get it going because he knew he could have a drink when it was done. He'd fuck anything that moved, any way he was told; it meant nothing more to him than pissing against a wall. He'd seen that Lee Charles was a looker — couldn't miss that — but that didn't mean a hell of a lot to him either. Bobby didn't care much for women and he didn't care for men either. There were days when the only reason he didn't kill himself was that he didn't know if there was whiskey in the hereafter.

"Keep it on a leash 'til we're done shooting," Tony Broad was telling young Callahan.

"Sure thing, Boss," Callahan smiled.

And he was still smiling as the door crashed open, hinges ripping screws from the woodwork, and Thibideau Pike — from the great state of Missouri by way of the Catskill mountains — stepped into the room, holding a sawed-off double barrel in both hands. T-Bone was trembling with rage, his eyes were wild, his teeth bared; beside him Callahan looked like a girl scout.

"What the fuck — !" Tony Broad was shouting.

Bobby Dean made an effort to rise from the bed. Like in Cleveland, he was looking for a window to go out.

"You don't move, mister," T-Bone said coldly. "I come for Lee Charles."

In the bathroom Lee had thrown the gaudy dress into the tub and she was dressed in her own clothes again. She was through crying and she was through bargaining with the woman in the mirror. She didn't have to do this, and Tommy didn't have to fight, either.

Just as she didn't need this night to be on her mind and on her conscience now and forever.

"I'm leaving," she said to the mirror. "You do what you want."

She was ready to walk out on Tony Broad when she heard T-Bone Pike's noisy arrival. She saw the woman in the mirror smile — happy for the rescue, for what was going to happen and for what wasn't going to happen.

She opened the bathroom door and stepped out into the room. She gasped when she saw T-Bone. He was holding a gun and his shirt was covered with blood, but it was his eyes that took her aback. They were filled with hatred, with cold vengeance, with a malevolence she could not begin to associate with the man behind them.

T-Bone turned to Lee as she appeared and then suddenly Billy Callahan made his move, charging at T-Bone from the side. T-Bone swung the butt of the shotgun around and clubbed the punk in the face. He hit him again and then a third time, smashing bone there, collapsing the young hood's features into mush.

Then Lee remembered the steel beneath Tony's jacket. When she turned Tony was already reaching for the pistol.

"T-Bone!" she screamed.

She punched Tony Broad with all her might, landing the blow high on the cheek bone. He backhanded her viciously to the floor, then began to back away like a stone crab, his right hand still clawing beneath his coat. T-Bone spun away from Callahan as Tony showed the Colt and T-Bone shot Tony Broad full in the chest with a load of number-two twelve gauge, sending the cut-rate DeMille crashing backward through the bathroom doorway. He lay dead as a mackerel there, Hollywood heaven on a cold tile floor.

Lee got to her feet, looked at Tony Broad. T-Bone turned and put the other load on Bobby Dean, who was crying like a newborn on the bed. Callahan was unconscious on the floor; his face resembled fresh hamburger.

"Not me," Bobby managed to say.

T-Bone looked around the room. "Where the money, Miss Lee?"

"We can't do that, T-Bone."

"Yes, we can. They kill Mr. Bell. These bastards kill Mr. Bell."

Lee walked to the bureau, where Tony Broad had tossed the roll. She hesitated and looked back at T-Bone. Then she picked the money up.

"That for the farm," T-Bone said. "Now go on out of here, police be here."

His eyes softened and she could see it was T-Bone once again.

Bobby Dean, with a rummy's nerve, dared to move from the bed. He stood with his arms straight out, like Christ on the cross, and looked at T-Bone.

"Let me walk out of here, man," he pleaded. "I don't give a rat's ass about these cats. I got a train ticket for Detroit, on the dresser there, Tony bought it."

T-Bone nodded to Lee, beside the bureau. There were two tickets there. The other, Lee said, was in Tony Broad's name.

"You git on out now, Lee," T-Bone said and he took the tickets from her. "Trouble coming for sure."

She had her hand on his arm and she didn't want to leave him. "What're you going to do?"

"Me and this man goin' to Detroit, I reckon," T-Bone looked at Bobby Dean. "You and me and this scattergun goin' to Detroit and you gonna stick closer to me than a tick on a hound, you follow that?"

"I got you, man. Let's just get the hell out of here."

T-Bone backed him off with the shotgun, then he took Lee by the hand and made her walk to the door.

"Go on now," he said. "We all got to get a move on, leave this behind."

"Oh, Thibideau."

"Don't be startin' that stuff," T-Bone told her. "That ain't like you, Lee Charles. You got the farm sittin' in your pocket there, now you and Tommy go on." There were tears in his eyes. "Take care of that huckleberry for me, Miss Lee, take care of each other."

She kissed him and then he pushed her away, urging her to go. He pulled open the broken door.

"Sometime if a old nigger come to call," he told her, "let him set down to supper. Will you do that?"

"He'd better come to call."

"When you least expect it, Miss Lee. When you not even thinking about it, he be there."

And then he made her leave. T-Bone turned back to Bobby Dean, who was jumping like a frog on a hot plate. He'd been a drunk all his adult life and he'd never needed a drink so bad as this minute. T-Bone grabbed him by the shoulder and pushed him into the bathroom. He showed him the mess that had until recently been Tony Broad.

"See that?"

Bobby's stomach came up and he wretched into the bathtub.

"That there be you come morning 'less you mind what I say," T-Bone told him.

Bobby nodded. "Yes, sir."

T-Bone returned the nod. No one had ever called him sir before. He pushed Bobby toward the door.

"Come on," he said. "Detroit's waitin'."

Tommy had himself another Irish, then he bought Mac Brady a drink. The band was playing a few numbers, going through the motions. Doc Thorne sang a little Satchmo, but to the young studs around the bar, he was no Lee Charles.

Tommy stood and drank and waited. He was happy now that he'd decided and he didn't mind the waiting. The good things in life were worth waiting for. Besides, Mac Brady could never stand in one place too long and Tommy knew he'd get his chance, sooner than later.

"Too bad you couldn't just give me the ranking for old times' sake, Tommy," Mac said.

"Mac, we never had any old times."

"Ah, what the hell." Mac called for Lucky Ned to bring him some nickels for the telephone. "I'm a businessman. I still got my theatre interests," he told Tommy and he went off to phone.

Tommy watched him go and then picked up his Jameson's and moved down the bar to stand beside Nick Wilson.

"You want something, pops?" Wilson asked.

"Thought we could make peace."

"Go away. Your face bothers me."

"Hey," Tommy said. "There's no reason for you and me to be like this. We're not in the same boat anymore. I'm washed up and you're on your way. You're going places, kid. Believe it or not, I'm pulling for you."

"That what happens when you lose your nerve?"

Tommy showed a sheepish grin. "Let's just say I've been around long enough to read the writing on the wall. I've seen you spar, kid. There's no way I could've stayed with you, I'll admit that now. And maybe you're ready for the big time, but there's a couple things —" Tommy stopped and threw an annoyed look at the band. "Damn it, that music's loud," he said. He turned back to Wilson. "Maybe you're ready for the big boys and maybe you're not. There's a couple tricks I could show you though."

Wilson laughed in his face. "You're going to tell me how to fight?"

"Well, I've been around," Tommy said lamely.

"Yeah, too long," Wilson said. "What kind of tricks you talking about?"

"What?" Tommy cupped his ear and leaned in, then looked darkly at the band again. "I can't hear a damn thing over this racket. Been hit in the head too many times, I guess."

Wilson stood smirking, like Tommy was some punch-drunk palooka looking for attention.

"Let's go back here," Tommy suggested, indicating the back door. "We can hear ourselves think."

Wilson's waitress was working now. He looked at her, across the room, and then shrugged, holding the grin.

Tommy led the way. If he'd glanced up as he passed the stage he'd have seen Doc Thorne's smooth brown face break into a smile around his saxophone.

Wilson carried his glass of beer with him, out the back door and into the alley. Doc Thorne's Packard was parked there, like most nights, and Tommy noticed that Doc had put brand-new tires on the old sedan. Doc had gone for the wide whitewalls.

Wilson was holding his glass between his thumb and forefinger and he was still smiling; it seemed to Tommy that the kid was born with that insolent look.

"You know what you got going for you, kid?" Tommy began. "You're a mean son of a bitch. And that's what you need if you want to go anywhere. You want to be champ, you have to be mean."

"How would you know?"

"Because I've seen it," Tommy said. "Maybe that was my problem, who knows? Maybe I wasn't mean enough, maybe I wasn't willing to hurt people."

"I am."

"Oh, I know," Tommy agreed. "Like when you were sparring that day with Pike, the nigger. When you had him down, you finished him."

And Wilson was shaking his head in wonderment. "I thought he was your pal."

"I keep him around for laughs," Tommy said. "Nice to have a nigger around, you know what I mean?"

"Yeah."

"But when I heard that — I knew you were mean enough. You put him down, and then you finished him off. A kick in the mug, that's the way to finish a guy."

"To finish a nigger anyway."

"Right."

Now Tommy's pulse was pounding and he was trying to keep it in check. He wanted to do this right. He shook his head in mock admiration.

"That is mean, no doubt about it," he said. "You've got it, kid. It's a goddamn shame you'll never get to use it."

Now Tommy looked the kid straight in the eye and in that split second the kid knew. Tommy kicked with his right leg and the heavy brogue caught Wilson squarely in the balls and then Tommy was on the kid at once, clubbing with short right hands to the face. Wilson never had a chance; his beer glass fell and shattered as he went down on the concrete, and Tommy stayed right with him, throwing punches with both hands now — but not wildly, not like the kid he was hitting. He took his time with the punches, landed every one.

Wilson went out and Tommy continued to hit him, spreading his nose across his cheekbone and deliberately breaking the jawbone with a right cross.

When Tommy got to his feet the kid rolled over onto his back, his arms spread wide, the classic knockout pose. Tommy straightened his coat and walked to the door of the Parrot. Then he stopped and looked back at the man on the cement.

"What the hell," he said and he went back to stomp on Wilson's right hand. He could feel the bones breaking under his shoe and he knew that Nicky Wilson would never have to worry about being ranked again.

Inside, Mac Brady returned to the bar as the band was beginning its break. Mac's heart sank when he saw that Tommy and the kid were gone from the bar. Right away he headed for the back door but he was stopped by Doc Thorne, who threw an arm over Mac's shoulder and offered to stand him to a drink. Mac tried to beg off, but horn players are stronger than hucksters and he had no chance. He accepted the drink and waited, hoping he was wrong.

Maybe half a minute later Tommy Cochrane wandered back into the room and Doc released Mac. Tommy had his right hand in his pocket like he was hiding something there.

"Buy you a drink, Tommy C?" Doc asked.

"I'll buy you one, Doc."

"What'd you do to your hand?"

"Oh, maybe bruised a knuckle."

"Is it all right?"

"It's all right, Doc."

What was left of the heavyweight Nicky Wilson was coming around when Mac reached him. The kid was on his knees and he was holding his right hand before him in shock. Mac pulled up short and looked at the kid a moment, his mind already clicking, then he peeled a hundred from the roll in his pocket and dropped it on the concrete where Wilson knelt.

"This'll get you home, kid," he said and he walked away.

In the doorway he had to stop for a last look. The kid was probably the best prospect he would ever have.

"You know, you could have beaten him in the ring," Mac said. "But not out here — never in a million years. You can think about that when you're looking at nothing but wheat fields and dreaming about the big time in New York."

The kid looked up, his eyes swollen, his nose damn near in another county.

"You gotta help me, Mac."

In the doorway, Mac pulled his vest down. "Can't do it, kid. I'm a businessman."

She didn't do much the next couple of hours, just wandered around the city a little — the city she'd be leaving soon, maybe this time for good — with her collar turned up against the cool night air and her thoughts turned into herself. The leaving part didn't bother her — everything had a beginning and an end, even her.

It seemed that she knew that better with every day that passed.

There was no commotion at all when she left the hotel, no sign that anything out of the ordinary had occurred. Maybe a single gunshot in that neck of the woods wasn't a big deal. To Lee, it meant that T-Bone would get out safely and that was all she cared about.

Then it was past one in the morning, and she was sitting on the front step of the Jasper Hotel. In the shadows there, with her mussed auburn hair and her man's leather jacket and shapeless pants, no one could know of her great beauty, and no one could know that she held in her pocket five thousand dollars — the fate of more than a few this past week.

When Tommy walked into view he had his head down and his hands in his pockets and from the step she couldn't tell if he was happy or sad or somewhere in between. She stood up, and he saw her, and she came down the steps into his arms.

"I was getting worried about you," he said. "Where you been?"

"With your friend," she said and she began to cry. "Your great and true friend."

He had never seen her cry.

"What's going on? Where's T-Bone?"

"He's gone," she said. "He had to leave the city."

"What do you mean, he had to leave?"

"There was some trouble, and he had to get out of the city. He took a train to Detroit."

For some reason she turned when she said it and pointed in the direction of the train station, a city mile away. As if she could see the terminal and the westbound train, Thibideau Pike's smiling face.

Brown hand waving goodbye.

"He left something for you," she said to Tommy.

"What did he leave?"

She took his arm and kissed him, then held him there a long time.

"A place to put your feet up," she said.